DEFINING MOMENTS

DEFINING MOMENTS

JACQUELIN THOMAS

 NEW AMERICAN LIBRARY

New American Library
Published by New American Library, a division of
Penguin Group (USA) Inc., 375 Hudson Street,
New York, New York 10014, USA
Penguin Group (Canada), 90 Eglinton Avenue East, Suite 700, Toronto,
Ontario M4P 2Y3, Canada (a division of Pearson Penguin Canada Inc.)
Penguin Books Ltd., 80 Strand, London WC2R 0RL, England
Penguin Ireland, 25 St. Stephen's Green, Dublin 2,
Ireland (a division of Penguin Books Ltd.)
Penguin Group (Australia), 250 Camberwell Road, Camberwell, Victoria 3124,
Australia (a division of Pearson Australia Group Pty. Ltd.)
Penguin Books India Pvt. Ltd., 11 Community Centre, Panchsheel Park,
New Delhi—110 017, India
Penguin Group (NZ), cnr Airborne and Rosedale Roads, Albany,
Auckland 1310, New Zealand (a division of Pearson New Zealand Ltd.)
Penguin Books (South Africa) (Pty.) Ltd., 24 Sturdee Avenue,
Rosebank, Johannesburg 2196, South Africa

Penguin Books Ltd., Registered Offices:
80 Strand, London WC2R 0RL, England

First published by New American Library,
a division of Penguin Group (USA) Inc.

First Printing, April 2006
10 9 8 7 6 5 4 3 2 1

Copyright © Jacquelin Thomas, 2006
Readers Guide copyright © Penguin Group (USA) Inc., 2006
All rights reserved

 REGISTERED TRADEMARK—MARCA REGISTRADA

LIBRARY OF CONGRESS CATALOGING-IN-PUBLICATION DATA:

Thomas, Jacquelin.
    Defining moments / Jacquelin Thomas.
        p.   cm.
    ISBN 0-451-21775-6
    1. African Americans—Fiction.   2. South Carolina—Fiction.   I. Title.

PS3570.H5637D44   2006
813'.54—dc22   2005028511

Set in Centaur
Designed by Ginger Legato

Printed in the United States of America

ACKNOWLEDGMENTS

While the characters and events in *Defining Moments* are fictional, multiple sclerosis is not. It is usually considered a disease that adults get, but it is occasionally diagnosed in children. MS is a real disease, one that affects over two million people, one of whom was my oldest sister, Beverly.

I would like to thank the National Multiple Sclerosis Society for all the information they generously provided. For more information on this devastating disease, please visit their Web site at www.nationalmssociety.org.

God was trying to get my attention but I wasn't listening. It took Him allowing me to have MS to get my attention.

—LOLA FALANA

CHAPTER ONE

T he first day of spring delivered devastating news to Sheila Moore, leaving her with a wretchedness of mind she'd never known before. "Miss Moore, you have multiple sclerosis..." The neurologist's words played over and over in Sheila's head.

Before her diagnosis four days ago, she was a woman going forward with her life while nursing a broken heart.

Now she was nothing more than a broken woman.

When her neck ached and she couldn't raise her right arm higher than midway, she went to see her chiropractor. The numbness and tingling sensations were all attributed to the constant spurts of fatigue Sheila had been experiencing for the past three or four months. She'd just assumed this was all part of perimenopause, just like the hot flashes and night sweats she suffered from time to time.

She didn't consider seeing a doctor until her coordination was off and she began experiencing problems with her vision.

Now, after a battery of uncomfortable tests Sheila had been forced to endure, Dr. Hill confirmed the reason.

Multiple sclerosis.

She swallowed hard, fighting back tears. Throwing a tantrum wouldn't help her now.

Sheila had heard of the disease, but didn't actually know anyone who had it.

Until now.

Sheila glanced down at her body. She thought back to the days when all everyone did was tease her. Back to when her hair was short and nappy and she wore thick bottle-cap glasses. Back to when nearly every penny she earned went to laser and cosmetic surgery, not to mention the expensive dental work and thousand-dollar hair weaves.

I've worked too hard to look like this.

Sheila gulped hard, hot salty tears slipping down her cheeks. Life had never been fair to her. All she wanted was a little piece of happiness. From the moment she was born, Sheila had been searching . . . searching for love and acceptance.

Sheila swiped at a tear falling from her eye. If she couldn't be happy in life—why couldn't she at least have her health?

She was only forty-two years old. Why did her body have to fail her now?

"Jake . . ." Tori held the phone in her outstretched hand. "It's Sheila," she announced dryly.

Jake's soft brown eyes clung to hers, studying his wife's reaction. He could tell by the coolness in her tone that Tori wasn't pleased that the caller was Sheila.

After everything he'd gone through with her, Jake decided that Sheila could only call his home in the event of an emergency. "Something must've happened," he offered as an excuse.

A shadow of annoyance crossed Tori's face. Covering the phone with her left hand, she whispered, "With Sheila, you never know. That woman's always got something up her sleeve."

Frowning, Jake took the receiver from her and placed it to his ear. "Hey, Sheila."

"I need to take a leave of absence from Madison-Moore," she blurted without preamble. "So we're going to need someone to manage the office here in New York."

He was momentarily speechless in his surprise. He'd never expected to hear those words coming from Sheila's lips. The design firm they'd started together was her baby.

Recovering from the shock of her words, Jake inquired, "Is something wrong?"

"Nothing you need to know about," Sheila sniped. "My leave is for personal reasons."

"I see." Jake glanced over his shoulder, stealing a peek at his wife.

Tori moved around the kitchen, seemingly engrossed in cooking, but he had a strong suspicion that most of her attention was centered on his telephone conversation.

"Well, do you have any idea how long you'll be gone?" Jake asked.

"No, I don't. I just wanted you to know that I'd be taking some time off. If someone comes to mind to replace me, just give me a call at the office."

Jake pushed for more answers. "Wait a minute, Sheila. When are you planning to leave?"

Out of the corner of his eye, he glimpsed Tori standing a few feet away. She had stopped cooking and was now watching him and listening.

"We'll need time to train someone, and there's the upcoming campaign for Orion Entertainment—"

"You don't have to worry," Sheila interjected. "I've taken care of everything. It's done. The new campaign for Knight Electronics is ready as well. I wouldn't even consider leaving here without closing out my projects, Jake. Trust—"

Her words and tone contained a suggestion of reproach, causing him to respond, "Sheila, I wasn't implying that."

"Right."

Jake was completely baffled. He didn't know what to make of this new turn of events. Sheila was a bit of a control freak and very dedicated to Madison-Moore. She wasn't the type of person to just walk away from her work.

What's going on with her? he wondered.

Sheila continued talking, her mellow alto edged with control. "I plan to start my leave thirty days from today. That should be enough time to train the person who'll be taking my place. I was actually thinking about Randy Copeland. Do you think he'd be interested in relocating?"

"I'm pretty sure he'd be interested," Jake responded. "He loves traveling up there to work with you. Always the first to volunteer. I'll speak to him about it tomorrow."

"Great. I really like him and he's a good worker—very dedicated."

"If he doesn't want to go, what about Marla?" Jake tossed out. "She actually has seniority."

"Do you think she's up to the demanding hours? She just had a baby a few months ago."

"I'll talk to her about it first. I know she and her husband have been thinking about moving back to New York so this may be right up her alley. If she turns down the position, then I'll ask Randy."

"Maybe we should consider having them both transfer up here," Sheila suggested after a moment.

They talked a few minutes more about Marla and Randy. When the conversation came to a close, Jake felt the need to add, "Sheila, please let me know if there is anything I can do."

"There isn't."

Her voice sounded bitter, and Jake knew his words had hit a tender spot, an old wound that had not completely healed even four years after it had first opened.

"I'll call you in the office if something else comes up."

"Sheila . . ."

"What?"

Her clipped tone made him lapse into silence.

"Well, what is it, Jake?" Sheila prompted. "What were you going to say?"

"It's nothing," he replied. "Just keep me posted. I really hope everything is okay with you."

"Thankfully, you don't have to worry about it. I'll let you get back to your family."

Before Jake could utter another word, Sheila had hung up.

He turned around to face his wife, who stood there studying him with intense curiosity.

"Did I hear you correctly? Sheila's leaving?" Tori questioned.

She'd tried to concentrate on cooking, but couldn't because she was too distracted by Sheila's phone call. Maybe God had finally answered her prayer.

"No."

His answer disappointed her. "Then what's going on?" she asked as she retrieved a stack of plates from a nearby cabinet.

Shrugging in resignation, Jake answered, "All I know is that Sheila's suddenly decided to take a leave of absence."

"She didn't say why?" Tori asked, relishing the rough feel of the etched floral border around the plate.

"For personal reasons. That's all she said."

Tori laid the plate down on the counter with the others and turned her attention back to him.

Jake stood with his back pressed against the wall. "She was so hostile that I didn't want to press her for more information."

"Sheila probably just wants you to think something's wrong so you'll go chasing after her." Tori leaned over to steal a peek into her oven. "Maybe she thinks you've forgotten everything she did to us."

Jake reached for Tori, pulling her into his arms. He stared down at her, his gaze filled with longing. "Honey, if Sheila wants to take a leave— then I say goodbye."

Tori took a step away from him. "I'm with you. The last thing we need is to let Sheila back into our lives. She put us through so much. It's been four years in reality, but emotionally, it still feels just like yesterday to me."

Jake pulled her back into his arms, kissing her. "I want you to know that I'm so sorry for what I put you through. I—"

Tori placed a finger to his lips. "You don't have to apologize, Jake. I forgave you a long time ago."

"But you can't forgive Sheila?"

"Have you forgiven her?" she countered. "Not too long ago, you were very angry with Sheila—you wouldn't even talk to that woman for almost a year after she moved to New York."

Nodding, Jake responded, "I forgave her. To be honest, I really can't shift all the blame to her. I had a part in it—no matter how reluctant. I'm still guilty."

"It's not so much that I don't forgive Sheila," Tori said. "I just haven't let go all of my anger toward her. She never admitted that she was trying to destroy our marriage or even apologized to me—just kept trying to blame you. We even caught her in the act of attempting to become pregnant with your child, but still she kept on denying everything."

"Then you haven't completely forgiven her," Jake pointed out. "You know what the Bible says. Pastor Allen preached on forgiveness just last Sunday."

Tori considered Jake's words. "I guess I haven't then. She needs to be a woman and come to me face-to-face with the truth. I just want to hear her say it. She owes me that much."

Jake cocked his head to the side, listening.

"Are the kids up from their nap?" Tori asked before turning off the oven. "Can you hear them?"

"I think so." He took Tori by the hand and led her up the back stairs. "I promised JJ that I'd take him kite flying after dinner."

"What about Brittany? She's gonna want to go with y'all."

"I know, but she's only two years old—I don't think she's old enough to fly kites. I do have an idea though. Why don't you take our daughter out for ice cream?"

Tori considered Jake's suggestion. "I think I will. We can spend a little mother-daughter time before she has her bath and bedtime."

Tori leaned into Jake as she wrapped her arms around him. "I miss our Tiffany. I keep thinking that it's going to get easier, but losing her still hurts. . . . If she were here, she'd be in first grade right now."

A little boy ran out of a nearby bedroom when they reached the second level. "Daddy," he called in excitement as he ran up to Jake. "Can we go now?"

They heard a younger voice calling out, "Da-yee, Da-yeee . . ."

"I'll get her," Tori said. She paused long enough to run her fingers through her son's curly hair. "Hey, you."

He grinned. "Mommie . . ."

"I'm going to get your sister, sweetie. I'll be right back."

Tori strode into a bedroom, returning a few minutes later carrying a little girl.

Jake picked up his son. "Little man, you're getting heavy," he teased. "Pretty soon you're gonna have to carry me."

This sent the toddler into giggles. "Daddy, I'm only three. I can't carry you. You're too big."

"I don't know. If you get any bigger I'm not gonna be able to do this . . ." Jake tickled his son.

Watching them, Tori burst into laughter.

Jake leaned over and planted a kiss on his daughter's forehead. "Hey, Princess Brittany."

"Da-yee," Brittany cooed as she placed her tiny hand to her father's lips.

Tori shifted her daughter to her other side before following Jake and JJ back into the little boy's racing car–themed bedroom.

She loved her family more than her own life. She sat Brittany down, then picked up a discarded blanket left on the floor.

Tori held the blanket close to her heart, lifted her eyes toward the ceiling and sent up a silent prayer of thanks.

Hearing laughter, Tori turned around. Jake was down on the floor crawling around with their children. Both of them shared Jake's soft brown eyes, full lips and sun-tinted golden brown complexion. She stood there admiring her husband's handsome features as he played with JJ and Brittany.

"JJ, you're gonna have to put on your shoes if you're going outside with Daddy after dinner."

"Wanna go out . . . side," Brittany said. "Me go, too."

"We're gonna do something special together, sugar." Tori picked up her daughter. "Just you and me."

Jake stood up.

"Honey, can you get JJ's jacket and shoes for me?" Tori asked.

"Sure." Jake paused. "Tori . . ."

Jake looked at her as if he were photographing her with his eyes. A grin spread across her face. "Yeah?"

"I love you."

She murmured in response, "I know. I love you, too."

"I wuv you, too," Brittany sang.

Tori felt blissfully happy, and she gloried in the blessing that there were no more shadows across her heart where her marriage was concerned.

Jake opened the doors to JJ's closet and stepped inside. He came out with a pair of sneakers and a lightweight jacket.

"Is this okay?" he asked his wife.

She nodded.

His gaze roved and lazily appraised Tori as she instructed JJ on tying his shoes. She was the more patient parent when it came to things like this.

Jake enjoyed spending time with his wife and children. He valued the time they shared and cherished the memories they created.

Past mistakes had almost cost him his marriage, but moving forward, Jake vowed to be the kind of husband and father his family deserved.

Holding his son's hand, Jake followed Tori and Brittany downstairs.

They sat down to feast on meat loaf, mashed potatoes, mixed vegetables and homemade biscuits.

"We'll be back in a couple of hours," Jake said when they were finished.

"Have fun," Tori called out from the table. "Bye, JJ."

"Bye, JJ," Brittany echoed from her high chair. "Bye, Da-yee."

Jake bent down to plant kisses on Tori's lips and Brittany's cheek.

"I get ice cream."

"You gonna bring me some back?"

Laughing, Brittany shook her head no. "I gon' eat ice cream. I eat it all."

Jake pretended to be sad.

This sent the toddler into more laughter.

"That's okay, Princess Brittany. Mommie will bring me a treat. Won't you, honey?"

"Only if you're good," Tori responded.

"I want a treat, too," JJ said. "Please."

"I'll bring you one, baby," she promised.

Jake planted another kiss on his wife's lips before taking JJ outside.

A few minutes later, Tori and Brittany walked out of the two-story Colonial Jake had built as a gift to his wife.

After waving goodbye to Tori and Brittany, Jake and his son spent the next hour outside flying kites on the four acres of land clustered on Edisto Island, a true jewel of the South Carolina coastline.

Father and son ran through healthy-looking green grass, laughing as their kites took off in the gentle breeze.

"Stay away from the pond," he cautioned.

Jake rushed to JJ's side when the child tripped and fell down. He knelt and began brushing the leaves and dirt off JJ. "You're okay, son."

JJ nodded and firmly held on to the string attached to his kite. "It's flying high in the sky, Daddy."

Shortly after Tori and Brittany returned home, Jake and JJ put their kites away and went inside to join them.

They gathered once more around the dinner table, laughing and talking while enjoying their ice cream.

It was times like this Jake enjoyed the most. But the phone call from Sheila was still fresh on his mind, disturbing him.

What was so important that it could draw Sheila from the one thing she truly loved? Madison-Moore Creative Visual Solutions Inc. was her heart and soul.

CHAPTER TWO

Sheila's brief telephone conversation with Jake kept running through her mind, fueling the anger that smoldered within.

That no-good dog had actually pretended to be concerned about her, but Sheila wasn't fooled by his words. Jake didn't care about her—he never had.

He'd used her and he'd been rewarded with a loving family, while she'd been publicly humiliated and forced to leave Charleston. Now she had multiple sclerosis.

But Jake wasn't suffering. She might have manipulated him into a sexual relationship, but she certainly didn't force him into bed with her—he had been a more than willing participant.

Life sucked, she decided bitterly.

It wasn't like Sheila's life had suddenly taken a turn for the worse either. Things had always been this way for her, from the moment she departed her mother's womb inside that four-room shanty in Frogmore.

Rejection became her constant companion the day her father, whom she'd adored, left them and never looked back. When he abandoned them, her mother turned to pills and alcohol, leaving Sheila to take care of them both.

She matured quickly. Sheila also realized early on in life that she didn't want to travel the same path as her mother. She would be in charge of her own destiny.

She had not been born with beauty, so Sheila did the next best thing—she spent thousands of dollars altering her physical appearance.

Sheila had not been born into a wealthy family, so she studied hard and worked two jobs to get into a prestigious university. She was determined to have the life she'd always dreamed of—no matter the cost.

In college, Sheila met Jake Madison, the two of them becoming study partners and even best friends.

Back then, Sheila knew all about his relationship with Tori, but didn't consider her a real threat. She figured Jake would one day open his eyes and see the woman standing in front of him.

But then Jake announced that he and Tori were getting married.

Sheila had been in love with Jake for years—did everything she could to win his affection, including the creation of Madison-Moore—but despite her best efforts, the fool still chose Tori.

Sheila was galled to her very soul that everyone had been right in their predictions that Jake would never love her. She'd been so sure he would eventually return her affection.

The sting of his rejection had dissipated a while ago, leaving in its place anger and bitterness. Apart from her father, Jake was the only man she'd ever loved.

And they'd both rejected her. She would never forgive either of them.

It was best if Jake didn't know about her condition, Sheila decided. Eventually he would find out, but for now—her secret was safe.

He was tall and well-built, muscles bulging from sleeves that gripped his arms like a jealous lover. His skin was the color of soft butter and his hair an ebony mass of curls. His facial features she could no longer remember clearly, but she would never forget the way he'd turned and walked away.

A little dark-skinned girl called out for him. "Daddy, when you comin' back? Kin Uh go wit' you?"

The man never answered, just kept walking with his back straight and head held high.

For the next three days, the girl stayed at the window, looking for signs of her father's return. Her tears ran down her face until no more would come.

"D-Daddy . . . ," Sheila murmured in her sleep. The pain in her heart still burned, bringing sobs to her throat.

She tossed and turned, seeking a place to die. Death could bring about a peace that life could never offer. Sheila's heart still ached from the hurt of her father's leaving.

In childlike innocence, she'd only known the goodness of her father, so Sheila had blamed her mother for his leaving—until one day when that illusion was shattered.

There had been days when Sheila survived on cereal, bread and whatever a five-year-old could manage. Her mother took pills to sleep, and then needed pills to make it through the day. She drank a lot in between.

Their neighbor, Miss Minnie, often came over to check on Sheila and her mother. She made them dinner, made sure Sheila brushed her teeth, took baths and made it to school.

Miss Minnie taught Sheila how to care for her mother. While most children were playing around outside and running from house to house, Sheila made sure her mother put food in her stomach; she made sure her mother bathed and she made sure the house was clean.

A tear slipped from Sheila's closed lids at the memory. She clutched the coverlet in her fist, holding it close to her heart as if doing so could make her feel more secure.

Sheila rolled over to her left side, moaning softly, her tears staining the hand-embroidered pillowcase. She opened her eyes.

She reached over and retrieved a tissue to wipe her face.

After a moment, Sheila sat up in bed, her knees folded to her chest, staring in the darkness of her bedroom.

She'd had another dream about her father. Sheila didn't like to think about the past. She hated reliving the agony of her childhood.

If only she could escape her memories.

The heels of Sheila's shoes tapped a steady rhythm as she moved through rows and rows of books. The series of clicks reverberated through the store, slicing through the silence.

When Sheila found the section she was looking for, she paused, browsing through the offerings. She planned to read up on the effects of primary progressive multiple sclerosis so that she could get an idea of what to expect as her condition advanced.

Sheila was amazed to find there were so many books written on the subject. She picked up book after book, scanning the contents.

A short time later, Sheila decided on four books and made her way toward the front of the bookstore to pay for her selections.

She slowed her pace, sniffing. Following the slightly musky scent of a French cologne, Sheila turned around, searching. There was only one man she knew who wore that particular scent.

A few yards away, a tall, well-dressed man with closely cropped hair, skin the color of golden honey, and gray eyes stood talking to one of the store employees.

His eyes met hers in recognition, and he grinned, then waved.

Nicholas Washington.

He excused himself from the employee and walked toward her.

Smiling, Sheila met him halfway. He looked good.

The words "What are you doing here?" popped out of her mouth almost immediately.

"I have a new book out. I came here to do a book signing."

"I don't know why I asked such a stupid question. I should have realized as much." Sheila's eyes darted around the store, noting the poster-sized flyers announcing his signing. She had been so focused on her situation that she hadn't noticed them until now. "I completely missed the flyers."

His eyes traveled the length of her body. "You must have a lot on your mind."

"I do." She placed a hand over her books. She wasn't ready to reveal her secret to anyone. "A lot has been going on with me."

Nicholas nodded in understanding.

"How have *you* been?" Sheila inquired, attempting to take the attention off her for the moment.

"Fine," he responded. "And you? You like living up here?"

"I actually prefer Charleston," Sheila confessed. "I'm not crazy about the New York winters."

Nicholas's eyes met her gaze. "I'd like to talk to you more. Are you planning to stick around?"

Sheila felt an electrifying jolt of shock run through her and took a quick breath of utter astonishment. "Did I just hear you correctly? You want *me* to stay?"

Nicholas nodded. "We can have dinner afterward."

Her body stiffening, Sheila regarded him with a speculative gaze. "Why?"

"Why not?" he responded.

"You're not exactly a fan of mine, for one thing." Sheila took in his powerful presence and drank in the sensuality of his physique. The man was *fine*. And those sexy gray eyes of his . . . they could make a woman melt just from the heat of his gaze.

Since he and Tori grew up together, Nicholas couldn't be more than thirty-three or thirty-four years old. *He's almost ten years younger than me,* Sheila noted in silence.

His words cut off her thoughts.

"Sheila, I have nothing against you."

She didn't believe him for one minute. Nicholas knew all about her and Jake. He knew how hard she'd worked to break up Tori and Jake's marriage. There had been a moment when she'd even tried to draw him into her schemes. "Uh-huh."

Nicholas checked his watch. "They're going to get started soon. So, I'll see you after the signing, right?"

Sheila shifted the stack of books in her arms from one side to the other. "Sure. I'd like to hear more about this new book, anyway. I love mysteries."

Sheila almost added that she especially loved his books and had read all of them, but doubted that Nicholas would believe her. Besides, she didn't want to come off as some pitiful excuse for a groupie.

"It's good to see you again, Sheila."

A new and unexpected warmth surged through her, emanating from the way he was looking at her.

When Nicholas disappeared around a corner, Sheila wondered, *What am I doing? This is the last person I should be having dinner with. I must be desperate for male companionship or something.*

Sheila wanted to forget about Jake and especially Tori. It had been a hard task for her to swallow the truth that she and Jake had no future together. He loved Tori and they were now the proud parents of two beautiful children. They were happy together and moving forward with their lives.

She had to do the same—and Sheila had been trying to do just that. It wasn't easy though. At least, not for her.

Sheila constantly struggled with trying to find a way to stop the pain and heartache, but nothing worked.

And now this recent news of her condition. The time had come for her to pay for her sins.

CHAPTER THREE

Throughout the question and answer segment of his book signing, Nicholas's eyes kept straying over to Sheila, observing her. She sat among the other women, slender, dark and fiery, with eyes that pierced the distance between them.

Nicholas hadn't considered he'd be seeing Sheila again after all these years, but it was always nice to see a familiar face in the crowd.

A young lady stood up to speak, drawing Nicholas's attention from Sheila to her.

"I love all your books, Mr. Washington—"

He interrupted her by saying, "Please, just call me Nicholas."

She blushed, putting her hand up to her mouth. Gathering herself, she managed, "Okay. Nicholas. I just love your books—you're one of my favorite authors and I just have one question. Are you gonna write more books with your character, Magda? I really like her a lot."

Others in the audience murmured their agreement.

"I really like Magda myself," Nicholas responded. "She's a great character to write. You'll see her pop up in one or two more novels."

"I know she isn't a real nice person but with each book, you give us more insight into her character."

"Deep down, Magda isn't as complicated as she seems," Nicholas explained. "She's just a woman who's been through a lot—mostly of her own doing—but all she really wants is for everything to go her way for once."

"Magda wants to be loved, I think," someone from the audience interjected.

"I agree," Nicholas replied. "Magda is definitely looking for love. She never experienced the love of a mother or a father. And she believes she'll find that love in a husband and a family of her own."

Sheila raised her hand.

Smiling, Nicholas asked, "You have a question?"

"Yes. I'd like to know how you come up with your characters. Are they drawn from real people—people you know or have met?"

"My characters are not modeled after people I know personally. I study character behaviors in movies, and I'm a people watcher. And I must confess that there's a little bit of me in all of my characters."

Another person in the audience raised her hand. Nicholas gave Sheila a quick smile, then moved his attention to the other woman. He could feel the weight of Sheila's eyes still observing him.

Nicholas answered a couple more questions before the bookseller announced that it was time for the autographing.

From time to time, Nicholas's eyes sought out Sheila. She was still seated and appeared to be reading one of the books she'd purchased on multiple sclerosis.

Maybe she's been diagnosed recently, he guessed.

Nicholas tried to keep his attention on his readers, but couldn't resist checking on Sheila every now and then.

After all this time, what was drawing him to her?

The question remained on Nicholas's heart for the rest of the evening.

Even in a crowd, his presence was compelling.

Sheila settled back in her chair, eyeing the numerous women in the audience vying for Nicholas's attention. Some of them were practically throwing themselves at him while he was signing books.

I can't believe the gall of these women, she thought smugly. *I never acted so cheaply, or so obviously. Boy, I could definitely teach them a thing or two.*

Her gaze strayed back to Nicholas. *I know he thinks I'm no better than these pathetic lonely women, especially after the way I went after Jake . . . but I'm nothing like them.*

Sheila allowed her eyes to linger, appreciating the strong lines of his well-formed cheek and jaw. But it was those gray eyes of his that arrested her—intelligent eyes that seemed to peer through to her very soul.

She surveyed him with an artist's sensitivity, taking in the arched brows, faint lines above his forehead and the full upturned edges of his mouth. He was wearing expensive silk trousers in a khaki color, a cream-colored, long-sleeved shirt and European loafers.

He's charming and highly skilled at dodging queries about his personal life, she silently acknowledged.

"Aren't you gonna get your book signed by the author?"

Sheila glanced up at the person asking the question. "Actually, no—at least not right now."

The woman standing beside her chair glanced over her shoulder. "Yeah . . . it's a real long line. I was trying to wait till it got a little shorter, but it looks like there are more people coming, so I figured I'd better get in line now."

Sheila glanced over her shoulder. "You might want to hurry on over there—I see a couple of women heading this way carrying an armload of Nicholas's books."

She chuckled as the woman practically leapt over a chair to get in line.

Sheila stole a peek at Nicholas and found him watching her. She awarded him a tiny smile before dropping her eyes.

Why am I wasting my time playing coy? she wondered. *It's not like Nicholas is interested in me. I know he isn't. I don't even know why he wants me to hang out with him.*

Probably so he can report back to Tori. Little does she know that I don't want a thing to do with Jake. I've got too many things to worry about in my life right now.

It didn't matter, she decided. After tonight, she probably wouldn't see Nicholas again.

Tori put away her Bible and notes as Carla Webber began to speak.

Tonight was their weekly Bible study and they had arrived at the sharing portion of the evening.

"Some of you may already know about this, but for those of you who don't—Jeff and I are getting back together."

"Carla, that's wonderful," Tori exclaimed. "Praise God."

"I want to thank all of you for your prayers and your support. You ladies kept me together all these trying months. God heard my plea and I'm so thankful."

Tori felt extremely happy for Carla. She rejoiced each time she heard about the restoration of a marriage.

Thank You, Father God, for restoring the marriage of Jeff and Carla Webber. There is still much work to restore the faith and trust that those months of separation cost, but like all of us, Jeff and Carla are works in progress, Father. You are an awesome God and we just thank You for Your faithfulness and for working out their relationship in Your perfect time. In Jesus' name. Amen.

Tori thought of the way she used to cry out to the Lord, asking Him to bring Jake home. God had answered her prayers by bringing her prodigal husband home. He had restored and blessed her marriage to Jake. It was her ultimate joy when her husband gave his life to the Lord.

Tori felt a smile spread on her face. *God is so good.*

". . . Jeff has even agreed to go to counseling with me," Carla was saying. "He had me pray the sinner's prayer with him. My prayers for his salvation have finally been answered. Praise God."

Shouts of "Hallelujah" and "Praise the Lord" sounded around the room.

When Carla finished talking, Tori passed out brochures to everyone. "This is the information for the upcoming Marriage Encounter weekend. We're going to Tybee Island, Georgia. We'll be at the Ocean Plaza Beach Resort. It's the largest hotel on the island and *very* nice. The dates for Marriage Encounter are April twenty-second to the twenty-fourth. If anybody has any questions, just see me before you leave."

Tori was excited about the weekend because she and Jake were one of the couples facilitating a seminar. They planned to speak on the topic "How a Relationship Can Turn Ugly."

On her way out, Tori stopped to speak with her pastor's wife.

"Sister Allen, Jake and I talked about the Retrouvaille program for the church. We think it's a wonderful idea and we'd love to be a part of it. We have no problem sharing our testimony of how God restored our marriage."

"I'm so glad to hear it. God laid it on my heart when you told me what you and Jake would be discussing at the Marriage Encounter weekend. The word *retrouvaille* means rediscovery. It's a program that gives couples the chance to explore and rediscover themselves all over again. I don't think we take time out of our busy lives to do this much. There are a lot of husbands and wives who need help in learning how to keep the love alive in their marriage."

"Now you know Jake and I don't consider ourselves counselors."

"The Retrouvaille program isn't counseling, Sister Tori. It focuses on couples learning how to communicate effectively with one another. You and Brother Jake have a wonderful testimony of how God restored your marriage. I just believe you two are a perfect fit with this program."

"We're definitely interested, Sister Allen. If we can help save a marriage by sharing our story of how God restored ours—we are more than happy to do so."

"God bless you, Sister Tori. You and your husband are truly a testimony to the covenant of marriage."

During Tori's short drive home, Sheila invaded her private thoughts. Her phone call three days ago still bothered Tori. It wasn't that she was upset with Sheila calling the house—she'd called Jake at home before.

Tori feared that Sheila was once again trying to snare Jake for herself. The woman just wouldn't give up. Tori wasn't worried about her husband leaving her—she just didn't relish revisiting all that drama.

Sheila's up to something, and I'm going to find out exactly what it is, Tori vowed. *She's not going to blindside us a second time. I refuse to let that happen.*

Even after Sheila moved to New York, Tori had thought about her. She dreamed about Sheila, and saw her in every woman she met. If she glimpsed a woman who bore the slightest resemblance to Sheila, Tori's stomach churned.

Four years had passed, but that one phone call had once again fueled the feelings of jealousy, resentment and anger Tori had thought long dead.

Tori had forgiven Jake, but not Sheila. He was just as guilty as Sheila, so why was it hard to forgive her?

She knew the answer.

Pastor Allen once told them during one of their counseling sessions that nothing heals the hurt in a marriage like prayer.

Through constant prayer, Tori was able to trust God and hold on to her faith that He would turn her troubled marriage into something beautiful once again.

With Sheila, it was different.

Back then, Tori couldn't bring herself to pray for the disturbed woman—she didn't *want* to pray for Sheila.

A voice within gently inquired, *Are you ready to let go of this now?*

Tori's skin prickled from the cold rushing through her body. She began to shake.

"Sheila tried to tear my family apart. She didn't care who she hurt . . ." Tears fell from her eyes. "I just can't forgive her.

Tori pulled into the driveway leading to her house. She wiped away her tears and touched up her makeup. She didn't want Jake to know she'd been crying, or that her stubborn feelings of unforgiveness were threatening to destroy her.

CHAPTER FOUR

A fter the book signing, Nicholas and Sheila shared a late meal at a nearby restaurant.

"This place is a favorite of mine," Sheila told him. "I eat here at least once a week."

"This is a nice place." Nicholas dove into his honey barbecue chicken. "The food is really good."

He wiped his fingers on a napkin before reaching for his water glass.

Nicholas took a long drink. "Hey, thanks for waiting. I thought you were going to give up on me when the manager brought out that extra box of books for me to sign."

Sheila couldn't help returning his smile. "It must be a wonderful feeling to have all those people lined up waiting for you to autograph your books for them. And the way those women are all over you—I'm sure you must be in heaven. You can have any woman you want."

Nicholas shrugged. "I appreciate the readers coming out to support me. I'm grateful they read and enjoy my books."

Sheila wasn't easily swayed. "You look like you're enjoying the attention from the women, too."

"It's nice," Nicholas admitted. "But I don't come to book signings looking for women. This is my business."

Sheila leaned back in her chair, admiring the way Nicholas's navy blazer fit his muscular build. "So you want me to believe that you've never picked up a girl at one of your signings? Not even once?"

"Not even once," Nicholas repeated.

Wiping her mouth with the corner of her napkin, Sheila inquired, "Have you been to New York in the last four years?"

Nicholas nodded. "I'm up here probably three or four times a year. Why?"

Sheila's eyes strayed to his. "It's just very clear to me that if I hadn't run into you earlier—I wouldn't be having dinner with you now."

"You're probably right," Nicholas admitted after a moment. "But maybe not."

Sheila let her fork drop from her fingers. "What do you mean by that?" Her voice rose in surprise.

"A couple of times I did consider contacting you," Nicholas confessed. "But I didn't."

"Why not?" Sheila asked as she reached for her water glass. She took one sip, then another. And another.

"I thought that you might need some time."

She knew Nicholas was referring to her feelings for Jake. Setting the glass back down on the table, Sheila said, "Today is April Fools' Day—a day celebrating people like me. I was a fool over Jake, as much as I hate to admit it."

"I wouldn't say that, Sheila," Nicholas countered. "You were a woman in love—it was just with the wrong man."

"Thank you," Sheila murmured after a moment. Instead of meeting his gaze, she pushed her broccoli from one side to the other with her fork.

"For what?"

"For not saying I told you so. I really appreciate it. I've certainly heard enough *I told you so*'s already. Nobody seemed to understand..." Sheila raised her eyes to his. "I was fighting for the love of my life. I just wasn't the love of *his* life."

"I'm not saying what you did was right, Sheila," Nicholas said. "But I don't think you should spend too much time dwelling on past mistakes. Life is way too short. Just chalk it up to experience and learn from it."

"Sometimes the past is all you have," she said. "Sometimes looking back at the past is much better than looking toward a bleak future."

"You're not eating," Nicholas observed. "Aren't you hungry?"

Shaking her head no, Sheila responded, "Not really. I have a lot on my mind."

"You want to talk about it?"

Guarded, her eyes drifted to his. "About what?"

"MS . . . multiple sclerosis."

"I . . . what are you talking about?"

Nicholas gestured to the shopping bag containing the books she purchased earlier. "I saw all the books on multiple sclerosis in your arms earlier."

"Oh . . ."

"Have you been recently diagnosed? Or someone close to you?"

Sheila felt a knot in her stomach and debated whether or not to tell Nicholas her secret.

"Me. A little over a week ago," she admitted after a short pause. "I'm still in shock over the news. There's a big part of me that can't accept this as reality."

The words continued to spill out of her mouth—words she'd yearned to share with someone. It was hard keeping something like this bottled inside.

"I went to my doctor when I started having some problems with my eyes and my coordination—I knew there was something going on when she ordered so many tests. She suspected MS but said she could be wrong. She then referred me to Dr. Hill. Turns out she was right after all.

I feel like it's happening to someone else. I keep telling myself that this can't be my life, because I've got too much living left to do." When she finished, Sheila felt like she'd purged herself.

"I can imagine."

Biting down on her lower lip, Sheila whispered, "I don't know what I've done to deserve this."

"You shouldn't look at this as a punishment, Sheila. You—"

She interrupted him by saying, "I don't know how to look at it any other way, Nicholas. This is one of the worst things that could have ever happened to me. There is no cure for MS. Who knows what I'm going to be like a year from now—a few months from now. I may not be able to walk or be able to control . . ." Sheila's voice died.

"What seems impossible to you is possible with God, Sheila."

Her eyes grew wet, annoying her at the transparency of her feelings. She blinked rapidly to keep her tears at bay.

"Have you told anyone—your family?"

Sheila shook her head no. "I thought about calling my mother, but I need some time to adjust to this myself. I don't really have anyone else."

"I understand." Nicholas reached out, lacing his fingers with her own. "Sheila, if you need a friend, I'm here. You don't have to go through this alone."

His hand was strong, firm and protective, but it was his words that completely surprised her.

"Now, why would you want to do this for me?" Sheila wanted to know. "I remember the time I wanted to . . . um . . . shall we say get to know you better, and you just blew me off. So why all the sudden interest in my well-being? Wait . . . hold up . . . this isn't pity, is it?"

Sheila pulled her hand away from his, her lips puckered in annoyance. "I don't need your pity, Nicholas."

"I don't pity you, Sheila. I just figured you might need a friend." Nicholas finished off the last of his chicken. Shrugging, he added, "I made the offer—it's up to you to accept."

They finished the rest of their meal in silence. Sheila managed to eat her vegetables, but she didn't touch her meat.

Nicholas signaled for the check. While they waited, he wrote his cellular phone number down on a napkin. "Call me anytime you feel like talking."

"I'm moving back to Charleston," Sheila blurted. "I took an extended leave of absence from Madison-Moore so that I could get a handle on my MS. Besides, I think I'd feel better knowing my mother is nearby."

"I live in Charleston now," Nicholas told her. "I moved there almost two years ago."

"I didn't know that."

"So you see, I'll also be close by if you need me." Nicholas finished off his drink.

"I'm still having a hard time believing you want to do something like this for me. We're not exactly close friends, Nicholas. In fact, we're not friends at all."

"We can change that, Sheila."

She gave him a tiny smile.

"Have you told Jake about the MS?"

Folding her arms across her chest, Sheila shook her head. "No, and I don't intend to—not for the time being. I don't want him involved in such a personal part of my life. Our relationship is strictly about business. Nothing more."

Sheila was a broken woman.

Nicholas hadn't missed the pain and fear that shined bright in her eyes. Sheila was terrified of what she was facing and his heart felt for her.

It was true that she'd often crossed his mind during each trip to New York, but Nicholas refused to act on his thoughts.

Sheila Moore was trouble.

But seeing her tonight, however, Nicholas wasn't so sure anymore. Four years had passed—surely Sheila knew Jake and Tori were happy and fully committed not only to each other, but also to God.

Sheila was a survivor—he'd known that about her from the first time he met her. She'd managed to move on with her life, and Nicholas had no doubt in his mind that she would find a way to conquer multiple sclerosis.

Nicholas stepped onto the elevator and pressed his floor number. His mind was still on Sheila when he reached the tenth floor.

Just as he got off, his cell phone began to ring. Nicholas answered it. "Hello."

"I can't go through this alone. I need you."

Sheila's words brought a smile to his lips.

"I have to ask that you do this one thing for me, though."

"Sheila, what is it?"

"You have to promise me that you won't tell Jake or Tori about my condition. Nicholas, I have to be able to trust you."

"You have my word. I won't tell a soul."

Sheila's sigh of relief was audible. "I have another doctor's appointment on Monday morning. I know we don't know each other that well, but I'm deathly afraid of going alone. Could you please go with me?"

Nicholas didn't hesitate in his response. "I was flying out tomorrow, but I can change it. My next signing is Tuesday night. I'll be here to go with you. Just give me all the information."

Sheila was silent for a moment before saying, "Thank you, Nicholas. I really appreciate this."

"No problem. I don't mind hanging out in New York for the weekend."

"If you like, we can do something tomorrow. I'm the keynote speaker at a dinner tomorrow night and I'd love to have you escort me. Denzel Washington is performing in *Julius Caesar* on Sunday, if you're into Broadway plays. It'll be my treat."

"Sounds like we have a full weekend."

"I'll see you tomorrow then."

"Good night, Sheila."

Nicholas hung up the phone wondering what type of damage befriending Sheila would do to his longtime friendship with Tori.

He would be foolish to dismiss the way Sheila had treated Tori four years ago, how she'd schemed to destroy her marriage.

But people changed. Maybe with Sheila having to contend with MS, she would reconsider her actions.

Nicholas felt in his spirit that he should pray for her, so he immediately dropped to his knees beside the king-sized bed.

His head bowed and hands clasped together, Nicholas spoke from his heart. "Heavenly Father, I come to You on behalf of Sheila Moore, a young woman who truly needs You. The Scripture says that by His stripes we are healed, and that whosoever believes in Him shall not perish but have everlasting life. Father God, the Bible also says that You will strengthen the person who looks upon You on their bed of affliction.

"Lord Jesus, when You lived on this earth, You went about doing good and healing all kinds of sickness and all kinds of disease among the people. You died and rose from the dead for our sins so that we may have eternal life. I believe with all my heart that You are present even today with all that miracle-working power. Lord, please have mercy upon Your child, Sheila, and help her to overcome this disease, if it is Your will. Let it be done for the glory of Your name. It is in Jesus' name I pray. Amen."

Sheila slowly turned the doorknob and opened her door, widening the entrance. She stepped into the bedroom. At the far end of the room, a floor-to-ceiling window gifted Sheila with a looking glass to Manhattan.

She crossed the varnished hardwood floor in bare feet toward the rich mahogany bed that framed a suede vanilla-colored comforter and several pillows.

Sheila sat down on her bed and leaned back against the stack of pillows adorning the king-sized headboard. She was relieved that Nicholas would be going with her to her doctor's appointment.

The truth of the matter was that she had another motive for getting closer to him. She intended to use Nicholas as a way of getting back at Tori.

Saint Tori would surely lose it if Sheila and Nicholas became close. Just the mere thought of driving Tori crazy delighted her.

Restless, Sheila climbed off her bed and strode over to the bay window in her bedroom. She let her gaze drift over the moonlit sky, trying to recall memories of better days gone by. They were so few and far between. Sheila couldn't remember a single moment she'd ever experienced any true happiness—she felt so alone.

What's wrong with me?

She'd asked that question many times over the years. Sheila dropped a string of curses from her lips as she blamed Jake and Tori for everything bad in her life.

"Why do I always have to be the one to suffer?" she complained. "I'm so tired of it."

Sheila continued her rant. "Everybody else can have the life they want . . . they don't have to worry about pain, loss of bladder control or wheelchairs. This is just *not fair*."

Hot tears rolled down her cheeks. "All I w-want is to be h-happy and have someone love me for *me*. Nobody's going to want me like this!" she cried out. "I don't w-want to end up in a wheelchair."

She fell into a downward spiral of self-pity. "Nobody wants me now and for all they know, nothing's wrong with me." She burst into another bout of tears. "I'm t-tired . . . I'm just s-so tired . . . tired of being alone. I'm tired of everything."

After composing herself, Sheila smoothed a lock of hair into place and wiped her face with her hands. She continued standing there at the window, listening to the steady rhythm of New York nightlife below.

The spring weather still held a trace of brisk air, prompting Sheila to rub her arms to ward off the chill.

Nicholas popped back into her mind. Why *was* he being so nice to her? What did he want? He couldn't be interested in her. Sheila wasn't really interested in him either; however, she couldn't deny the man was gorgeous, with those gray eyes that reminded her of silver lightning.

Sheila didn't really care what his motives were at the moment. She just couldn't bear to go back to the neurologist alone. Making friends was never a priority for Sheila, so she didn't have any.

"Please let him tell me that it was a mistake," she prayed. "Please let Dr. Hill be wrong."

Sheila stood rooted in place for nearly twenty minutes. She glanced down at her body, struggling to feel something other than despair. "Please let my doctor be wrong."

Sheila strode to the opposite side of the room where her large walk-in closet was located. Packing boxes lined the bottom, but the rest of the closet was filled with designer fashions and accessories. The smaller closet held her shoes and purses.

She pulled out a robe and slipped it on.

Sheila ventured into her living room and sat down, exhausted but too nervous to sleep.

She sat there in the dark contemplating her future.

CHAPTER FIVE

※

Despite what she was dealing with, Sheila managed to make the weekend enjoyable for Nicholas. They spent most of Saturday shopping and sightseeing until it was time for them to get ready for an evening fund-raiser where Sheila would give the keynote address.

Sheila stood up on the dais, looking as if she owned the world in a hand-embroidered silk jacket and matching pants. She delivered an incredible speech and received a standing ovation in return.

No one in attendance had a clue that beneath all Sheila's outward poise and beauty, deep down, devastation dwelled in the caves of her lonely soul.

On Sunday, Sheila and Nicholas watched Denzel tackle the classic role of Marcus Brutus in *Julius Caesar*. Afterward, they enjoyed a late dinner before parting ways for the night.

Nicholas had really enjoyed spending the day with Sheila. He'd observed that although she appeared to be having a good time, she wasn't fully relaxed around him. She'd never seemed to really let her hair down the few times he'd seen her in the past, either.

That night while lying in bed, Nicholas tried to recall if he'd ever seen her look like she was truly happy.

He couldn't.

Nicholas woke up early the next morning, read his Bible and said another prayer for Sheila. Only the good Lord above could give her the strength she needed to keep going.

He met her ten minutes after nine outside the medical building where Dr. Hill's office was located. His fingers took her arm with gentle authority. "Let's go inside."

There was a pensive shimmer in the shadow of Sheila's eyes as they stood in the reception area, prompting him to ask, "You alright?"

She shrugged and nodded. "As well as I can be, I guess." She felt a hot flash coming on—the second one this morning. She used her hand to fan back and forth.

He reached for the elevator and held it open. "After you."

Sheila switched her Louis Vuitton purse from one side to the other before saying, "Just give me a few minutes. Okay?"

A few minutes lapsed into waiting for the next elevator to arrive.

"Would you rather reschedule your appointment?"

Shaking her head no, Sheila's voice drifted into a hushed whisper. "I need to get this over with."

When the elevator arrived and the doors opened, Nicholas urged Sheila to step inside.

She lingered there for a moment more, took a deep cleansing breath, then said, "C'mon . . . let's go on up before I change my mind."

They rode to the fourth floor and got off. Nicholas followed her through the doors of the doctor's office. They found two empty seats and sat down.

Sheila sat with her back straight, her legs crossed and her hands clasped together tightly in her lap. Her thick hair hung in long graceful curves over her shoulders, moving every couple of minutes when she glanced back to see if anyone was coming to the reception area.

Despite her outward calm, Nicholas had a strong feeling that deep down, Sheila was a ball of nerves inside.

His suspicions proved correct when she nearly jumped out of her chair at the sound of the nurse calling her name.

Her face became clouded with uneasiness, pushing Nicholas to reach over and take her hand once more. His fingers were warm and strong as he held hers.

"Let's see what the doctor has to say," he urged.

"I'm r-ready," she stammered.

Nicholas tried to encourage her. "It's going to be fine."

Biting her lip, Sheila looked away.

"Let's go."

Sheila held on to Nicholas's hand as if it were a lifeline. She didn't release her grip on him until they were sitting in Dr. Hill's office.

Sheila didn't waste any time. "Dr. Hill, I still have some questions. You may have told me a lot of this during my last appointment," she murmured. "But I was so stunned by the diagnosis that I don't remember everything you said, so I apologize if I'm being redundant."

Dr. Hill gave her a reassuring smile. "I'm sure being told you have MS comes as quite a shock, Ms. Moore."

"What exactly happens in progressive MS?" Nicholas inquired. "I'm not really familiar with this disease."

"Progressive MS can manifest itself differently in each individual; in most cases the damage occurs within the central nervous system. And with each attack, the areas of damage increase."

Sheila's fingers drummed distractedly on her crossed knee. "Does this mean that I'm looking at some sort of severe disability in a relatively short time?"

"The disease could worsen rapidly or slowly over the years, Ms. Moore."

Sheila's expression was tight with strain. "Do you think that stress can trigger a flare-up?"

"In my personal opinion, possibly. Ms. Moore, there is a chance that the disease will hit a plateau and maintain its current level of severity."

Nicholas stood behind Sheila, placing his hands on her shoulders in a possessive gesture. "So if I'm understanding all this—Sheila's condition will eventually move on to a steady progression. Is there no chance of a cure?"

"MS can't be cured, but it can be slowed down through the use of disease-modifying drugs."

Sheila went over her notes. "I've done some research on those drugs. Can someone with progressive MS take Avonex, Copaxone or Rebif? I read some articles on the Internet that said they were due to be approved in the United States soon."

"They're available," Dr. Hill confirmed.

"If I could, I'd like to try Copaxone."

Dr. Hill agreed. "Copaxone significantly slows down the progression even though it's not a cure. It's usually very well tolerated, but there are some side effects."

Sheila's eyes narrowed. "What are they?"

"Injection-site reactions. For example, there could be some swelling and tenderness in areas. Some people have experienced tremors, a runny nose and fatigue. Others complained of sudden weight gain and itchiness around the injection site."

"None of them sound particularly inviting as far as I'm concerned," Sheila said. "But I'm still interested in trying the Copaxone. I like what I've read on the drug."

Dr. Hill nodded in agreement. "The nurse will show you how to prepare and inject your first dose. It's also available in a prefilled syringe, but you'll need to purchase an autoject2 device."

"I'll get whatever I need. I'd rather not have to worry about measuring and mixing."

"A few people have experienced temporary reactions after injecting Copaxone," Dr. Hill explained. "You may feel as if you're having an anxiety attack. Your chest may tighten or you might feel as if you can't breathe. Just try to remain calm and it will soon pass. This doesn't happen often."

Sheila closed her eyes to keep her unshed tears from escaping. A part of her just wanted to go home and end her life. This was a horrible way to have to live out the rest of her days.

Nicholas reached over, touching her elbow lightly, urging yet protective.

She turned her gaze to him.

"It's going to be okay. You can get through this," he assured her. "You don't have to do it alone, because I'll be right by your side."

Sheila gave a slight nod. Those simple words spoken by Nicholas held such promise, motivating her, urging her not to abandon the fight.

"Are there any therapies available to help her if she starts to have problems with her hands or walking?" Nicholas inquired.

"Physical therapy, occupational therapy . . . there's cognitive rehabilitation—"

"What is that?" Sheila cut in.

"Specialists find ways to help patients improve or compensate for mental functioning problems."

"Like memory loss?"

Dr. Hill nodded. "Yes, Ms. Moore. They help in areas of attention deficit and information processing. There's also psychological counseling available, and sex therapy."

Sheila stole a peek at Nicholas.

"Do you have any other questions for me?"

"One more," Sheila responded. "How am I supposed to cope with having MS?" She held up a hand. "Actually, don't bother. I know you can't really give me an answer to that question."

She folded her arms across her chest, took a deep breath and said, "I'm ready to do battle against this disease, Doctor, so what's our next move?"

Nicholas smiled, glad to see Sheila still had some fight left in her.

Sheila pressed the elevator button. They had left the doctor's office an hour ago and were now in the building where her apartment was located.

"Why are you looking at me like that?"

Nicholas gave her an innocent smile. "Like how?"

"I don't know. You just keep watching me. Are you waiting for me to fall apart after everything the doctor just told us?"

"Sheila, I'm not expecting anything. You don't have to react a certain way or try to be a pillar of strength for me. Just be you."

"That's all I know how to be." Sheila pulled out a set of keys from her purse. "I can't be anybody else."

Nicholas reached over and took her hand. "Don't forget that you're not alone."

"I won't." Sheila found herself getting lost in his gaze and looked away hastily. Getting emotionally attached to Nicholas was totally out of the question. She'd been down that road before.

Sheila began to pace back and forth.

The elevator arrived.

Nicholas was a perfect gentleman. He waited until Sheila stepped inside before joining her.

Between the third and second floors, she turned to him, asking, "Do you really have to leave tonight?"

Nicholas nodded. "Yeah, I do. I have the book signing in Washington, D.C., tomorrow night and another one in Richmond, Virginia, on Thursday."

"When will your tour end?" Sheila asked.

"Right after Richmond. I go home after that, and I'll be so glad. I really need to get back to working on my new book. My deadline is coming up quick."

"How soon?"

"Less than two months. June first."

Awkwardly, she cleared her throat. "Nicholas, are you sure you can take time out of your busy schedule to deal with me and my issues? I don't want to burden you."

"I meant what I said, Sheila," he assured her. "I'll be here for you whenever you need me. You have my word."

"Thank you, Nicholas."

"Now, I want you to remember what the doctor said. Dr. Hill wants you to take several naps throughout the week. You need to make sure you follow his directions to the letter. He also said that you need to keep your stress level low and learn to accept the help of friends and family. I hope you were listening."

"I heard him," Sheila confirmed. "Right now I usually take naps during the weekends—it seems to be working okay for me. I'm going to eat right and do what Dr. Hill suggested, including reducing my stress. That's why I went on and took a leave of absence. I didn't want to worry about Jake finding out."

"Dr. Hill said you didn't have to take naps every day, but that you need to do it on a regular basis. Especially when you feel really tired."

"I will," Sheila promised. "With the weather getting warmer, I'm sure I'll get tired more."

In the apartment, she strode straight to the kitchen and retrieved a pitcher of lemonade from her fridge. She poured the liquid into two glasses she'd filled with ice and then handed one to Nicholas.

"I'm glad Dr. Hill said I could continue to exercise. The last thing I need is to get fat on top of everything else."

Nicholas's eyes traveled from Sheila's face and down her slender but shapely figure. "I don't think you have to worry about that."

She awarded him another smile. "You're so sweet for saying that." She pulled at the band of her pants. "I've lost weight—about ten . . . fifteen pounds, I think."

"Have you lost your appetite? I noticed that you don't eat much."

"I haven't really felt like eating lately," Sheila admitted. "I have days when I just don't feel good and I'm not hungry."

"What about now? Do you think you can stomach a light lunch?"

Sheila finished off the last of her lemonade. "Maybe a sandwich, I guess. You want to eat here or go over to the deli across the street? I have some ham, I think."

"I'm open," Nicholas murmured. "Whatever you like."

"Let's go to the deli. I'm kind of in the mood for pastrami."

Sheila paused for a moment. "There's something I'd like to ask you," she began. "The annual charity ball for the Make A Dream Come True Foundation is coming up on the thirtieth of this month. I'm planning on attending, but I didn't want to go alone."

She forced a demure smile. "Would you please escort me?"

"Sure . . . if you'd like me to."

"Thanks," Sheila responded with a grin.

Nicholas looked as if he was studying her, trying to discern if she was resorting back to her manipulative ways. Sheila kept her expression blank.

"I usually attend, but I haven't seen you at the last three or four," he said. "Why this one?"

"I wasn't ready before, but I am now. Besides, it's a charity I'm very passionate about. Children who are terminally ill should be able to enjoy something special. Jake's mother worked hard to get the monies needed to grant wishes."

Nicholas folded his arms across his chest and asked, "You can handle seeing Jake and Tori together?"

Sheila gave a short laugh. "Of course. Nicholas, I was serious when I told you that I'm completely over Jake. My attending the ball has nothing to do with him or Tori. There will be about two or three hundred other people I can talk to."

Sheila took Nicholas by the hand and led him to the door. "C'mon. You're going to love this deli. They have some of the best sandwiches in New York as far as I'm concerned."

Nicholas enjoyed seeing her so animated. He'd been worried after they left the doctor's office, but Sheila seemed to be dealing with her diagnosis. And she actually appeared to be moving on without Jake. However, Nicholas vowed to keep an eye on her, just to be sure. He would not allow Sheila to make Tori's life miserable.

He would become her distraction.

"The contracts are here, Mr. Madison," Selma announced as she entered Jake's office. "Miss Moore just faxed them over."

He accepted the documents she handed him. "Great. I've been waiting on these."

"I heard that Miss Moore was leaving the company. I can't believe it."

"She's not leaving the company," Jake corrected. "Just taking a leave of absence."

"Oh. Well, I'm glad to hear that." Selma smiled. "I know how much she loves Madison-Moore. She probably just needs a break. Miss Moore works so hard."

"Yeah, she does," Jake agreed. "She has worked real hard to build this company. We wouldn't be a success if it weren't for her diligence."

"And yours," Selma contributed. "You and Miss Moore make a great team."

When Selma left his office, Jake read over the contracts.

Everything looked perfect. Sheila had secured the Maxwell Fashions account, and Jake would be designing their new Web site.

He was glad they'd made the decision to promote Marla to vice president of sales and Randy to vice president, marketing. Marla and Randy worked well together and would be an asset to the New York office.

Their combined responsibilities would include creating new sales revenues and divisional growth, and developing innovative solutions for companies on the Internet.

Sheila was at the top of her game when it came to identity design, media presentations and Web applications, and no one person could fully replace her.

Jake couldn't deny that Selma was right. He and Sheila made a great team, but he felt she was truly the genius behind Madison-Moore. When they first started the company, he'd merely gone along for the ride. He'd been too distracted by the problems in his marriage back then. That's how Sheila was able to cause havoc between him and Tori.

After he found out about his partner's scheming ways, Jake had been so angry with her that he'd seriously considered terminating his partnership with Sheila. It was an answer to a prayer when she suggested opening the office in Manhattan. And a profitable one as well.

Jake picked up the telephone to call Sheila but changed his mind.

There was no telling what mood he would find her in—Sheila changed like the weather. Most days she was distant but professional. Lately, though, she'd been almost rude.

Sheila blamed him for leading her on—something he wasn't guilty of, in his opinion. He shouldn't have been involved with her intimately in the first place, Jake acknowledged. But he'd never given her the idea that he wanted more than her friendship.

I should be the one with the attitude, he thought. *Sheila tried to trick me into getting her pregnant. If Tori hadn't found that condom . . .*

Jake didn't want to think about what could've happened. "Thank You, Father," he murmured. "Thank You for protecting me from that woman."

CHAPTER SIX

~~~

A fter a restless night, Sheila decided to sleep in until nine a.m. and work from home. She spent most of her morning in her loft on a conference call with a prospective client, then stumbled into her bathroom for a long, hot shower. Exhilarated from soothing water that woke up her senses, Sheila wrapped her body in a burgundy-colored silk robe and returned to the loft to work.

Around one thirty, Sheila decided to call it a day. She was too distracted by the thought of relocating to Charleston. She was excited about moving back home, but with so much to do within a short period of time, she felt a bit overwhelmed.

She spent the rest of her afternoon looking at houses in South Carolina via the Internet. She would be leaving New York on the fourteenth of May and she wanted to be in her new house no later than the twentieth. She didn't relish living out of her suitcase any longer than necessary.

Sheila scrolled down the computer monitor, looking at house after house after house, searching for a place to live when she returned to Charleston. She still owned her condo there along with three other properties, but they were all rented.

"Mmmm . . . this one is nice," she murmured. She made a note of the MLS number.

Having lived in South Carolina all of her life, Sheila knew exactly where she wanted to live—Mount Pleasant. It was just across the bridge from Charleston near the waterfront and the beach. She loved the ocean and often fantasized about living in one of the mansions that bordered the coast up and down the Carolinas.

She also preferred finding a one-story house. Because she didn't know what to expect with her condition, she decided to forego multilevel homes.

"Five bedrooms ... two-car garage ... swimming pool ..." she mur-mured as she read the list of features slowly, not wanting to miss any-thing. This house was perfect for her.

"Fireplace in the bedroom ... hmmm, sounds romantic. Four thousand square feet ... located in gated community. Okay, I really like this one."

She reached for the telephone and dialed.

"Hi," she greeted when someone answered. "I'm calling to set up an appointment to see a house. I'm flying down this weekend and would like to see the house on Woodlake Drive. I have the multiple listing number, if you want it."

"One twenty-one Woodlake Drive?"

"Yes," Sheila confirmed. "It hasn't sold yet, has it?" She crossed her fingers as she awaited a response.

"No, ma'am."

"I like what I've seen so far on the virtual tour located on your Web site. I'm very interested in this particular house. Please call me if some-one makes an offer before I have a chance to get there on Friday."

"Are you working with a real estate agent?"

"No. I don't feel I need one; I still hold my real estate license in South Carolina. I'm interested in another listing as well. The MLS number is 2438743 ..."

They talked for a few minutes more before Sheila hung up.

She pushed away from her desk and descended the stairs carefully, her metallic silver slippers balanced on each step. Her body trembled in weariness by the time she stepped down into the den, so she lay down on the burgundy leather sofa, silently assessing her life.

She lived in a beautiful condo on the Upper East Side just steps away from Carl Schulz Park and the East River. She had already amassed nearly a million dollars in real estate and she was a partner in a very successful business. She had money, power and beauty. But for what?

To be the pathetic, lonely and brokenhearted creature that she was today?

She fanned back and forth with her hand, hoping to recover from her hot flash.

Sheila missed Nicholas already. He'd only been gone for one day and here she was, acting like some little schoolgirl with a crush. She was desperate for companionship.

I can't do this to myself. Nicholas is no more interested in me than I am in him. He's just nursing his broken heart over Tori, like I am over Jake.

Forcing Jake from her mind, Sheila shifted her position on the sofa, trying to get comfortable. "I need to start packing up the apartment," she muttered to herself. "I'll get Elsie to do it."

Sheila made a mental note to call her housekeeper. She would need Elsie to work at least three days this week to help her with everything.

She reached for the pad and pen on the coffee table.

Sitting up, Sheila made a list of everything she needed to do before leaving New York. She worked on her checklist until she could no longer keep her eyes open.

Nicholas, what are you doing? he thought silently. *You know the kind of woman Sheila is, so why are you even bothering with her?*

She was a woman scared and alone.

It's not like I'm trying to have a relationship with the woman—I'm just trying to be something she needs. A real friend.

Nicholas knew all about Sheila's scheming ways. She'd even tried to pull him into her plans to break up Jake and Tori.

But it hadn't worked. Tori and her husband were happier than ever. Their marriage had survived Sheila and all her antics.

"I'm just being a friend," he whispered. "The poor woman is scared to death of what's happening with this disease and she needs support."

Sheila knows that I won't allow her to manipulate me, and that we will never be anything more than friends.

He had to consider that Sheila might still be up to her old tricks. She might try to use their friendship as a way to get to Jake, his heart cautioned.

I'll see through Sheila's ploy, Nicholas decided. He wasn't a stupid man. He'd know if she was playing him.

Nicholas felt sure Sheila's battle with MS would be prominent in her mind, keeping her too busy to focus on Jake.

After changing into a pair of sweats, Nicholas sat down at the desk in his hotel room in Richmond, Virginia, and opened his laptop. He tried to force Sheila from his mind as he turned on the computer to work on his latest project.

Nicholas gave up after ten minutes because he couldn't stop thinking about her.

The beautiful woman was diagnosed with multiple sclerosis. On the outside Sheila appeared controlled, but he figured she had to be all over the place emotionally.

All Nicholas could do was listen to her whenever she needed to talk or a shoulder to cry on. He'd already promised that he would be there for her.

The other thing he could do was to educate himself on the disease, but most importantly, Nicholas knew he could continue to pray for her.

He spent the rest of the evening surfing the Internet for information on MS.

Sheila walked out of the Sasha Tricoci Hair Salon and Day Spa on East Fifty-seventh Street. She'd just gotten her weave redone, had a pick-me-up facial, and a manicure and pedicure with reflexology. After spending most of her afternoon in pampered luxury, she looked and felt like a million dollars.

Men were eyeing her from head to toe, smiling and trying to win her complete attention. She wasn't interested, though. Right now a man was the last thing she needed—besides, life had taught her that men couldn't be trusted. They would use her, then toss her to the wayside.

I'll never let another man do that to me. Not ever. I refuse to let another man get close to my heart.

Sheila hailed a taxi.

She climbed inside and settled back, weariness clouding her emotions. She hated feeling so tired all the time. As soon as she got settled in Charleston, she had to find a neurologist.

Dr. Hill had given her the name of one. Sheila made a mental note to give the doctor's office a call.

She hated this disease.

Every morning before she climbed out of bed, Sheila went through a mental checklist to see if her body worked normally.

Dr. Hill told her that her condition occurred in only ten percent of patients diagnosed with multiple sclerosis—people like her, in their forties and fifties.

Lucky her . . .

Dr. Hill also warned her that she could experience a slowly worsening spinal cord syndrome. Sheila forgot what it was called exactly. However, she remembered that it meant she would experience a gradual decline in her ability to walk over the next few months, or if she was truly lucky, a year or so.

She didn't want to end up in a wheelchair—just the very thought devastated her. Sheila couldn't bear anyone seeing her like that.

Her worst fear was that Jake would push her out of the company once he found out about her condition. He would take Madison-Moore from her and she would be powerless to stop him.

Her other fear was that she would end up living in Frogmore with her mother.

She could only imagine what her life would be like if she had to go back. For Sheila, it was almost a death sentence.

CHAPTER SEVEN

~~~

Tori stood up, waving to get Nicholas's attention. She'd arrived first at the restaurant and had been seated already.

Smiling, Nicholas strolled over, nodding at a few people he knew as he moved toward the table.

He bent down and planted a platonic kiss on her cheek. "You're sure looking good, Mrs. Madison."

She sat down. "You're not looking too bad yourself, Mr. Best-selling Author. I see your book is number one hundred twenty in *USA Today*. Congratulations."

Nicholas broke into a big grin as he dropped down into the seat across from Tori. "Finally . . . man, I've been waiting a long time for this day. Now if I can make it to the *New York Times* . . ."

"*Point of Deception* is a great book," Tori exclaimed. "I read it in two days. I just couldn't put the book down."

Nicholas laughed. "Yeah, right. You say that all the time."

"I'm not just saying that because you're my friend. I really mean it."

The waiter arrived to take their drink order.

"I'll have sweet tea, please," Tori stated with a smile.

"I'll have the same and a glass of ice water."

"So how did your signing go in Richmond?" she asked when the

47

waiter left. "My cousin Kelly called me last night and said she met you at the signing."

"Yeah, I met her. She's a sweetheart. I think the signing went well. Lots of people—more than I've had before. Standing room only. I'm not complaining though, because this is a writer's dream."

"Your books are wonderful, Nicholas," Tori told him. "I can't keep any of them in the store."

"It's not hard to sell two copies," Nicholas responded with a laugh.

A flash of humor flickering in her eyes, Tori folded her arms across her chest. "Now you know I ordered more than two copies of your book."

The waiter returned with their drinks. After setting the iced teas on the table, he pulled out pen and pad to write down their food orders.

When he disappeared around the corner, Tori took a sip of her tea before saying, "Nicholas, you won't believe who called the house not too long ago." Tori paused. "*Sheila.*"

Nicholas's left eyebrow rose a fraction. "Really?"

"Yeah. She normally doesn't call the house, but she did this time."

"You're not still concerned about—"

"No," Tori quickly interjected. "Not at all."

"It's been four years since she left South Carolina. Do you really believe she still wants Jake?"

Tori stiffened. "I don't know, but if she does, she won't get him."

"I doubt she'd set herself up like that again. She's a smart woman, Tori. Sheila knows that she doesn't have a chance with Jake."

Tori's lips puckered in annoyance. "I just want her out of my life once and for all. I wish she'd sell her share of Madison-Moore to Jake."

"I really think you need to let this go, Tori," Nicholas advised. "You and Jake have been back on track for quite a while. You don't have a thing to worry about."

"I'm not worried," Tori responded a little too quickly. "Why would you think that I'd be worried?"

"Well, for one thing—you're acting pretty defensive."

The waiter chose that moment to appear with their food, cutting off further conversation.

"You're right," Tori admitted when they were alone. "I *am* being defensive and there's no reason why I should be. I know Jake loves me."

"Sheila has enough on her plate right now. She doesn't have time to worry about Jake." Nicholas sliced off a piece of fish and put it in his mouth.

Tori studied his face. "You sound as if you've talked to her. Have you?"

Swallowing his food, Nicholas nodded. "I saw Sheila when I was in New York. I ran into her at the bookstore."

"Ran into her? Nicholas, you're much smarter than that. Sheila knew you were signing there. I'm sure they advertised the event. C'mon now."

"I saw her face, Tori. She didn't know I was going to be there." Nicholas hoped Tori would drop the subject.

It became clear that wasn't going to happen. "There were no signs anywhere? No flyers? Remember, I own a bookstore and your publicist always sends me promo stuff for your signings."

"Believe me, Tori. Sheila had no idea I was signing there."

Tori shook her head in disbelief. "I don't buy it, Nicholas. If it were anyone but Sheila . . ."

"I believe it," Nicholas insisted.

"Well, what's going on with her that makes you say all this? There must be a reason."

"There is, but I can't tell you, Tori."

Her brows drew together in an angry frown. "Why not?"

"It's not your business."

The corner of her mouth twisted with exasperation. "I see."

"Tori . . . I might as well tell you that I'm escorting Sheila to the charity ball."

She leaned back in her chair, her eyes slightly narrowed. "*Please* tell me that this is your version of a joke. Nicholas, you can't be serious."

"We're attending the fund-raiser together," he confirmed.

"Her idea or yours?" When Nicholas didn't answer, she shook her head. "You've lost your mind, messing around with that woman," she huffed.

They stared at each other across a sudden ringing silence.

When she couldn't stand the heavy air of tension between them any longer, Tori said, "Nicholas, I'm sorry. I shouldn't have said that."

"You have nothing to apologize for—it's alright."

"It's just that you're my friend."

"I *am* your friend, Tori," Nicholas said with quiet emphasis. "And I'm a good friend." He'd expected Tori to be upset, but he hadn't thought she'd react so strongly.

"I know that." Tori stared down at the plate of food in front of her.

"Then you should know that you have nothing to worry about. I can handle Sheila, if it comes to that."

"You're right." She sighed with resignation. "I don't want Sheila hurting you. Can't you understand that?"

"I appreciate your caring about me."

Her mouth was tight and grim. "But you just want me to mind my own business?"

"Let's get back to you telling me what a great writer I am."

Seeing the amusement in his eyes, the beginning of a smile tipped the corners of Tori's mouth. "I think your head is big enough."

"How is your crazy cousin?"

"Charlene is doing great. Better than great, actually. She and Shepard are expecting a baby."

Nicholas's eyes widened in surprise. "Really?"

"Yeah. She's due in August. She was really worried that she'd never be able to conceive, but here she is—almost four months pregnant. She didn't want anyone to know until after her first three months."

"I'm very happy for them. They'll make great parents."

Tori agreed. "I'll tell Charlene you said that. She's so afraid that she won't be a good mother."

"If I know you, you're going to spoil your little niece or nephew to death."

"I can't wait to be an auntie." She made a face. "I'm going to be an aunt, right? I guess I'll also be a cousin, too. Poor baby—he or she is gonna be so confused." A grin spread across Tori's face. "I'm so looking forward to seeing that little one. I just love babies," she gushed.

"I bet you've already bought out the baby stores. I remember when you were pregnant with Brittany, you tried to drag me around to every baby store in Charleston when you found out you were having a little girl."

"I'm dying to go baby shopping, but Charlene wants to hold off."

"Has she had any problems?"

"No, she's just being cautious, I think." Tori reached for her drink and took a sip.

"Since you love babies so much, why don't you and Jake have a few more?"

Tori laughed. "Jake would probably faint if I told him I wanted to have another baby."

"Do you want another child?"

"Yeah, I do."

"Then you should discuss it with him," Nicholas suggested. "He needs to know how you're feeling."

She dabbed at her mouth with her napkin. "What about you? Do you want to have any children?"

Nicholas nodded. "I do. I'd like to have at least two—a little girl and a boy."

A mischievous look came into Tori's eyes. "Does Sheila want children?

"I don't know. It's not something we've ever discussed."

"Sorry about that. I just couldn't resist. But I'm surprised she doesn't want children. She was trying to get pregnant for Jake. I told you about the condom I found that time."

Nicholas cracked up with laughter. "You can't help yourself."

Tori rolled her eyes at him. "Ha ha. You're so funny."

After lunch, Nicholas walked Tori to her car. "Tell that husband of yours I said hello."

"I will."

"And kiss the babies for me," Nicholas instructed. "Speaking of babies . . . have that talk with Jake."

Tori broke into a big grin. "I will. The more I think about it, the more I really want to have another baby. I think Jake's a wonderful father."

Nicholas glanced up. "It's starting to rain," he noted. "Drive carefully."

"You too," Tori responded. "The way those clouds are looking, I think it's gonna come down hard. I hope I make it back to the store before it does. I didn't bring my umbrella with me this morning."

They said their goodbyes. Nicholas waited until Tori drove away before he left.

Considering the angst she felt where Sheila was concerned, in the end Tori had reacted better than he'd anticipated. Nicholas knew she would be a little put out, but for the most part, Tori respected his feelings and his decisions.

The first thing Nicholas did when he walked into his house was settle down in his office. He picked up the telephone and dialed.

"Hey, Sheila. It's me, Nicholas."

"I spoke with Jake this morning," Marla announced. "The Vectors Record Company launch party will be May twenty-eighth. He wants to know if you'll be able to make the event."

"Let me think about it," Sheila answered. "I'll let him know as soon as I decide."

The telephone rang, interrupting their conversation.

"Why don't you get some lunch," Sheila suggested. "We'll finish up this afternoon."

Marla asked, "Would you like me to bring you something back?"

Shaking her head no, Sheila picked up her phone on the fourth ring. "Thanks," she mouthed before saying, "Sheila Moore speaking."

Hearing Nicholas's voice on the other end of the phone brought a smile to Sheila's lips.

"I was just thinking about you, Nicholas." She dropped down in the chair at her desk.

"So how're you doing?" he asked.

"It's been a pretty good day. I've been training my replacements. I'm so glad it's going well."

"Good. The last thing you need is to worry about your company."

"Jake and I hired the best," Sheila responded. "We have very talented and dedicated employees."

They talked for a few minutes before Sheila had to take another call.

"Give me a call later, Nicholas. That's if you're not too busy."

"Sheila, I'm never too busy for you. Don't forget that."

"I won't. Talk to you later."

She hung up and accepted the call on her other line. "This is Sheila Moore . . ."

Why am I so drawn to Sheila?

The question stayed on his mind, and Nicholas felt no closer to the answer. Maybe it was because he knew how much she'd loved Jake—she was like a woman obsessed.

He had loved Tori with almost the same passion, but deep down, he'd always known to whom her heart belonged.

It appeared that Sheila had finally come to the same realization.

Jake and Tori belonged together.

He admired the fight in Sheila. She wasn't a quitter; instead she was always girded for battle.

She was such a beautiful woman—but she hid it beneath fake hair, tons of makeup, designer clothes and jewelry.

He was thankful that they weren't involved. Nicholas doubted he could afford Sheila—she was definitely high maintenance.

The more they talked, the more they found in common. He and Sheila shared a love of reading thrillers and mysteries, they loved jazz and old-school music; they both loved being near the water and beaches; they even both enjoyed tennis.

He'd been more than a little surprised to discover that Sheila had played basketball in high school.

Smiling, Nicholas strode into his office and sat down to work on his book.

For the next four hours, he was enveloped in his characters and their issues. Although he had never really noticed it before, Magda did remind him of Sheila.

He heard the children playing in the yard next door. Their laughter brought a smile to Nicholas's lips. He loved children and looked forward to being a father one day.

Nicholas was ready to settle down—it was finding the right woman that was the real challenge. He wasn't worried though.

He trusted God to lead him to the one woman destined to become his wife.

CHAPTER EIGHT

———

Rain poured down, creating puddles all over the parking lot of TC's Books and Gifts. Tori used an old newspaper to shield her short hair, and stepped away from the water gathered on the corrugated burgundy rubber mat just outside the door.

Running her fingers through rain-damp hair, Tori gazed upon row after row of bookshelves—pale oak that gleamed under the fluorescent lighting of the store. A handful of browsers walked around, a couple of them holding books and other gift items.

Tori spied Charlene standing behind the counter talking to one of their customers. She waved to her cousin on her way to the office located in the rear of the bookstore.

She quickly brushed her teeth and touched up her makeup, then spent a few minutes trying to salvage her hair before walking back to the front of the store.

When the store emptied a short while later, Tori and Charlene split up to do some light housekeeping. Tori straightened and rearranged the children's area, while her cousin worked on one of the fiction aisles.

"Girl, what's on your mind? You look a million miles away," Charlene said.

"I was just thinking about Sheila."

Charlene's mouth twisted into a frown. "Why in the world you thinking about her?"

"I told you that she called Jake a few weeks back saying she was taking a leave of absence, right? Well, Nicholas told me that he saw her when he was in New York." Tori placed her hands on her hips. "Can you believe that he's bringing her to the charity ball?"

Charlene's mouth dropped open in surprise. "What?"

"You heard me, cuz."

Folding her arms across her chest, Charlene said, "I sure hope Nicholas isn't crazy enough to get involved with that snake."

"He isn't. He's just being his usual sweet and caring self. Sheila probably gave him a sob story. He's just trying to be a friend, but you know Sheila—she'll take it too far."

"Isn't he still seeing Irene Chandler?"

"Not anymore," Tori answered. "They broke up about three months ago."

Charlene gasped. "I didn't know that. Where have I been?"

"He didn't really broadcast the breakup. Irene told me. But that's because she wanted me to help them get back together."

"What happened between them?"

"I really don't know. Nicholas only told me that they weren't a good match. But I'm sure it's because Irene's so jealous."

"I can believe that. She did get a bit clingy whenever other women were around Nicholas."

Tori released a sudden burst of laughter. "Girl, you one to talk. Remember how you used to act whenever Shepard was talking to another girl?"

Charlene laughed. "That was in my young immature days. And before I found Jesus."

"I was a bit insecure myself," Tori admitted. "It bothered me living in Brunswick while Jake was in Charleston. I couldn't wait until the summer."

"Humph. I used to think you were coming up here to see me, but I soon found out—Jake was all you had on your mind."

"Like Shepard wasn't on yours," Tori shot back.

A customer burst through the front door, pausing briefly to shake the rain from her raincoat. After propping her umbrella in a corner, she moved to peruse the bargain table.

Charlene strolled to the front to greet the woman, Tori following behind her.

"Hello, ladies. The store is really nice. I'm so excited about the café you're opening soon."

"Thank you," Tori and Charlene responded in unison.

"What can we get for you, Misty?" Tori picked up a book from the rack and said, "We have the new series from Carol Taylor-Grimes."

"Ooh, I love Carol. You know I want that."

Tori made a few more suggestions while Charlene went to assist another customer who'd just entered the store.

After their customers left, Charlene turned to Tori saying, "We are so blessed. We have two of the most wonderful men in the world as husbands."

"I know that, and I'm so thankful," Tori replied.

"I just hope that if Sheila is up to her old tricks, you'll beat her down this time around."

Tori cracked up with laughter. "Now, you know that isn't the Christian thing to do."

"No, it's not," Charlene agreed. "But it would sure feel good, don't you think?"

"Yeah, it would. Sometimes when I think about the past—I regret not laying Sheila out at least once." Tori curled her fist. "I really wanted to choke the life out of that witch."

Charlene burst into laughter.

"Boy . . . that felt so good." Tori put her hands up to her face, laughing. "I've been wanting to confess that for four years now."

"Girl, that's the Tori I know."

Sobering up, Tori said, "Charlene, I don't really have regrets at all in the way I handled Sheila. I had to do it the way God wanted—I know a lot of folks thought I was a fool to take Jake back, but I don't give a flip." She gave a short laugh. "I have to answer to the good Lord above—not these folks around here or anywhere else.

When Jesus was up on that cross, He could've gotten down anytime

He wanted. But He didn't, Charlene. Because He made a commitment. In spite of our sins—Jesus died for us. Well, when I married Jake—I made a commitment. For better or worse."

"Girl, you don't have to explain that to me. I understand."

"Don't get me wrong. Not all marriages are worth saving, but that's because the couples are unequally yoked. Sometimes we get impatient and we don't wait on the Lord to send us our mates—that's when we get into trouble and marry the men we want."

Charlene agreed. "Yeah, girl . . . you right about that. I tell the young women at church that they don't have to go looking for a man. If they just put their trust in God, He will bring them their Mr. Right."

"It's about being patient," Tori said. "Being patient *is* hard. Like waiting on the contractor and his people to finish up the café." She pointed to the area that had been secured by yellow safety tape. "We're scheduled to have the café open on June second."

"Stop worrying, Tori. It's gonna open on time. Tom gave me his word. There's not much more to be done."

Tori released a sigh of relief. "Thank you, Jesus."

When their part-time employee arrived, Tori walked over to the counter and picked up the telephone to call Jake.

"Hey, honey . . . I'm leaving in about ten minutes. Just wanted to make sure your plans to come home early hadn't changed, because I'm making your favorite tonight. When you get this message, call me on my cell. Bye."

"You and Jake got special plans tonight?" Charlene asked.

"Not really. I just want to set the mood for a serious conversation we need to have. I want to have another baby, and I need to find out if Jake feels the same way."

Charlene embraced Tori. "I'm so happy for you."

Tori held up her hand. "Whoa . . . I have to find out if Jake even wants to try again. He may not, so don't say anything to Shepard yet."

"I won't. Now you gotta think positive, girl . . ."

Tori headed to the office to get her purse and keys. When she came out, she said, "See you later, cousin. Don't work too hard."

Jake pulled into their three-car garage just minutes behind Tori.

He greeted her with a kiss, then led her up the wooden steps to the house. "I called you earlier at the store but Charlene said you were at lunch with Nicholas."

"Yeah, I was. He told me that he saw Sheila when he was in New York for a signing."

Jake was surprised. "Really?"

"He says they *accidentally* ran into each other, but I really believe Sheila manipulated that meeting. She had to know Nicholas would be signing there."

"What would be the reason?"

Shrugging, Tori responded, "I don't know. Nicholas made it clear that whatever's going on between them isn't my business."

Unlocking the front door, Jake burst into laughter.

"What's so funny?"

He stepped aside to let Tori enter. "Honey, he's right. We wanted Sheila out of our lives. Let's not bring her back in."

Tori laid her purse on the hall table and checked her watch. "We need to pick up the children around four. Aunt Kate has Bible study tonight."

"Okay." Jake pulled Tori into his arms. His eyes traveled her face, giving her a tender look. "Sheila can try to come between us, but it won't work. Tori, we're so much stronger now—we're together in every way. Am I wrong about this?"

"No, you're right. I'm sorry, Jake. I guess Sheila still makes me a little paranoid."

"Let's not go back down that road again. You have no reason to be insecure."

Tori backed out from her husband's embrace. "Jake, I know this. I really do. I think not knowing what Sheila's up to is what really bothers me. And I hate that she's involving herself with Nicholas. I don't want to see him hurt."

"He's a big boy," Jake reminded her. "If anybody can handle Sheila— Nicholas gets my vote."

"I hope you're right, Jake." Tori reached over and wrapped her arms around him. "Honey, I need to talk to you about something."

"What is it?"

Tori led him over to a nearby chair. "Let's sit down," she murmured.

"Hmmmm . . . this sounds pretty serious."

"It is . . . not in a bad way though." Tori broke into a smile. "You can relax." Jake smiled back, the warmth in his eyes giving her the courage to go on.

"When Nicholas and I were having lunch, we got to talking about Charlene and the baby . . . and, well, I realized something."

"What?"

"I'd like to try and have another baby." She paused a moment before saying, "I need to know how you feel about this. Be honest . . ."

Jake grinned. "When do you want to start?"

"Are you serious?"

He nodded. "Honey, I love my children. I would love to have one more. This huge house could use another child."

Tori reached over and hugged Jake. "Ooh, you've made me so happy. I'm so excited."

"I love making you happy. Tori, you are the answer to a prayer for me. I just thank the good Lord above for all He's blessed me with—my family, the company and . . . I thank Him for everything. The good and the bad."

"Jake Madison, you are one of a kind."

He ran his fingers through her short curls. "Do you think you'll ever grow your hair out? I loved you with long hair."

"You don't like my hair this way?" Tori asked.

"You're beautiful with it short or long . . . but I prefer it long."

She shook her head, but she couldn't help smiling. "Okay. For you, Jake. But if it drives me crazy, I might cut it again."

"Fair enough," Jake agreed. He gave her a quick kiss. "Thank you."

She wrapped her arms around him a second time. Tori closed her eyes and sent up a short prayer of thanksgiving.

"You know, we have a few minutes before we have to pick up JJ and Brittany. We could start on our new addition," he hinted.

Grinning, Tori took him by the hand and led him up the stairs to their bedroom.

Sheila picked up the telephone, intent on calling her mother, but she was so tired, her nerves throbbed.

Talking to her mother while her whole body was engulfed in tides of weariness and despair wasn't a good idea, so she put the receiver down.

Although there were times Sheila missed her mother, she didn't miss anything about the tiny village located half a mile from Penn Center, the first school established in the South for freed slaves.

She was so sick and tired of everyone telling her that she should be proud of her heritage. To her, it wasn't anything to be proud of—Sheila wanted nothing to remind her of where she had come from.

It disgusted Sheila that her mother continued to live in the way of her ancestors, rejecting all the luxuries Sheila offered.

"The woman is crazy," Sheila muttered. "But I do love her."

An hour later, she picked up the phone and dialed, but after the eleventh ring, she gave up. "I wish that woman would use the answering machine I bought her," she complained. "It doesn't make any sense . . ."

I'll just drive out to see her when I fly down for the charity ball, she decided.

The thought of the Make A Dream Come True benefit brought a smile to her lips.

Sheila couldn't wait to see Tori's face when she strolled into the hotel on Nicholas's arm. She made a mental note to start her search for the perfect designer evening gown. Sheila planned on being the belle of the ball.

Her well-dressed appearance at the fund-raiser would also push aside any suspicions Jake might have had about her leave of absence.

Sheila made a move to rise, but suddenly fell back against the sofa. She'd experienced weakness in her legs before but not to this magnitude.

"NO!" she shouted in anger. "I'm not going to let this beat me."

Although she said the words, Sheila wasn't sure she actually believed them. Everybody talked about having a positive outlook in life, but no matter how upbeat she tried to be—it just felt like she'd been knocked on her behind once again.

Sheila sat there a moment before trying to stand a second time. She placed both hands over her eyes to ward off the pain. Even her teeth on the left side hurt.

Please don't let me have a sinus infection.

When Sheila felt like she could walk without falling, she got up and headed straight to her medicine cabinet to get Tylenol. The pain was getting worse.

Sheila lay down.

She didn't get up until two hours later when her pain finally subsided.

Sheila pulled out her journal to go over her notes from her last appointment with Dr. Hill. He'd warned her that there were some nerve pain symptoms associated with MS.

She hated being in any kind of pain. Tears sprang to her eyes as she worried that for the rest of her life, her body would be racked with pain.

Dr. Hill had also told her that he was reluctant to prescribe narcotic pain relievers if the pain was chronic or recurring.

If my pain gets worse—I'm going to need something stronger than Tylenol. This was something she would discuss with her new doctor.

Sheila made a notation in her journal, recording the location and duration of her recent pain. She wanted to be able to accurately recount everything that was happening to her.

The telephone rang. Sheila checked the caller ID and smiled.

It was Nicholas.

The deep voice on the other end of the telephone lulled her frazzled senses to a quiet calm.

"Are you injecting the Copaxone nightly? I hope you're doing everything the doctor advised . . ."

"I am, Nicholas," Sheila assured him. "I'm doing what I'm supposed to do. You really don't have to worry about me."

"Have you been experiencing any pain?"

"I had a lot of pain on the left side of my face earlier. My teeth were hurting, too."

"Did you take anything for the pain?"

"I took Extra Strength Tylenol and it helped this time, but I don't know if it will the next time."

Running her fingers through her hair, Sheila changed the subject. "So how did your signing go last night?"

"It was nice," Nicholas responded. "We had a great discussion about the book."

"And about Magda, too, I'm sure."

"Yeah. People either love her or they hate her. There's no in between."

"Magda reminds me a lot of myself."

"In what way, Sheila?"

"Well, she always seems to want what she can't have, for one. Then there's her attitude of self-importance. There's something I want to know—and be honest. Is she based on me, Nicholas? Or at least your perceptions of me?"

"No, she's not. Magda was in my head long before I ever met you. In fact, she's appeared in all of my books—not always as a major character, but she's there. That's why I started working on her story—she just wouldn't go away."

"That's right. She's been around from the beginning. I forgot about that."

"Sheila, is that how you really see yourself? Like Magda?"

"It's what everybody says—including my mother. I really don't care though."

"What *do* you care about?"

She gave a slight shrug, although he couldn't see her. "I care about Madison-Moore; my mother—I care about her. I care about me—I *have* to care about me. If I don't, nobody else will."

"Trust doesn't come easy for you. Why is that?"

Sheila pulled the phone from her ear and laughed. "I can't believe you asked me that," she responded. "The truth is that I've been hurt by a lot of people. A whole lot of people."

Sheila pushed to change the subject. "I don't want to talk about this anymore, or about me. Tell me about Nicholas Washington."

"There's not much to tell," he began. "I'm a regular man with simple needs. I don't want much."

"C'mon now . . . there's more to you than that, Nicholas. I know better."

"Really, there isn't. I write for a living; I'm working on my relationship with the Lord and I hope to one day get married to a wonderful woman and raise a family."

Sheila couldn't resist asking, "You want to get married?"

"You sound like you don't believe me."

"So, do you have anyone special in mind?"

"Not at the moment," Nicholas answered. "What about you, Sheila? You have any prospects for marriage?"

"No . . . not a one."

"Sometimes we need to take a break just to regroup."

Sheila chuckled. "You think I need to 'regroup,' as you put it?"

"It could only help."

"Tell me something, Nicholas. How did you do it?"

"Do what?"

"How did you just let Tori walk out of your life and into Jake's arms? How can you be friends with them?"

"Tori and I have been friends for a long time."

"You were in love with her," Sheila interjected. "Are you going to deny it?"

"No," he responded. "At one time, I thought about us as a couple. But Tori didn't feel the same way about me. She has loved Jake for most of her life and he loves her, too. I loved her enough to let her be happy."

Sheila didn't comment.

"Hey . . . you still there?" he asked.

"I'm here. I was just thinking about something."

"What?"

"It must be nice to have a cheering section. Everybody is *so* happy for Jake and Tori."

"Sheila, if you found your Mr. Right—I'd be just as happy for you."

"I believe you would, Nicholas," she said after a moment.

They talked a few more minutes, just the sound of Nicholas's voice bringing a smile to Sheila's lips.

"I put in my offer for that house I told you about," Sheila announced before they ended the conversation. "It was accepted and I'm in escrow. Did I tell you about this already?"

"I knew you'd put in your offer, but I think you said something about the owners being out of the country for five days or something."

"Okay . . . yeah. Nicholas, you know my mind works every other day, it seems." Sheila tried to make a joke out of her memory loss episodes. "It might be a good idea to leave notes for myself, or maybe even invest in a tattoo. I could have my name and address drawn on my arm."

Nicholas howled with laughter.

"It would have to be in fancy lettering, of course. To keep with my image. Also, I'll need a picture of you, so that I can write your name on the back in case I wake up one day and have no idea who you are."

"Sheila . . ." He was still laughing too hard to finish the sentence.

"Hey, I think it's a good idea."

"You're a funny woman."

"Nobody has ever accused me of being funny. I don't usually have a sense of humor. It must be the MS. You think?" Sheila ran her fingers through her curls. "Have I scared you yet?"

"No, sweetheart. It'll take more than humor to scare me."

She smiled. "Glad to hear it. Not many people know this about me, but I can be a little hard to take at times."

Sheila placed a hand to her cheek. "I think I need to take more Tylenol. The pain's coming back."

"I wish that I could do something for you."

"So do I," Sheila responded with a moan. "I hurt."

"Go get some rest. I'll check on you tomorrow."

Sheila got off the phone, then went in search of more medication to soothe her throbbing face. If she could, she would've gladly chopped off her face to stop the pain.

CHAPTER NINE

The day of the charity ball arrived with a full expectation that the evening would go exactly as she planned.

Sheila had flown in the night before and checked into the Charleston hotel where the fund-raiser was being held because she wanted to be well-rested for the event.

Nicholas met her for breakfast.

"Did you get enough rest?" he inquired. "You sounded exhausted last night when I spoke to you."

"I was, but I'm feeling much better this morning." Sheila reached for her glass of cranberry juice. "I'm looking forward to this evening."

Nicholas sampled his scrambled eggs. "I'm not crazy about wearing a tux. I'm real comfortable just wearing some jeans and a T-shirt."

Sheila leaned back in her chair, frowning. She wouldn't be caught dead in a pair of jeans. She'd worn her last pair of faded denims the day before she graduated from college and vowed she'd never put on another pair.

"Why?" she asked. "You look great in everything you wear. Why just throw on a faded pair of jeans when you can clothe yourself in some wonderful, men's couture collection? You could have been a male model, you know."

"Not me. I'm not the fashionable type."

"You could've fooled me." Sheila glanced around the restaurant. "I see a lot of people I recognize. I used to think Charleston was huge, but after living in New York, it doesn't seem big."

"It's bigger than Brunswick," Nicholas commented.

"I'd like to go down to Saint Simons Island one weekend. I want to see Jekyll Island, too."

"I'll take you down there when you're feeling up to it."

"That'll be nice," Sheila murmured.

They spent most of the day together until it was time to get ready for the fund-raiser.

Nicholas dropped Sheila off at the hotel, leaving her there to get dressed. He returned an hour and a half later.

"You look gorgeous," Nicholas complimented as his eyes traveled from her head to her feet, looking her over seductively.

Sheila was strangely flattered by his interest. It had been a while since any man had looked at her like this. "Mr. Washington, I must say that you look very handsome tonight. I don't know why you hate wearing tuxedos. You wear them so well."

His gaze fell to the smooth expanse of her neck. "That necklace must have set you back a pretty penny."

Sheila grinned. "Actually, I did some work for this jewelry company and they gave me the necklace as a gift."

"That's some gift."

Ten minutes later they took the elevator down to the lobby, walking toward the Crystal Ballroom.

Sheila could hardly contain her excitement. She didn't relish confrontations, but she knew one would be forthcoming. Tori was going to throw a fit the minute she saw her with Nicholas. She couldn't wait to see Saint Tori's expression. It would be priceless.

"You're moving pretty swift tonight," Nicholas observed. "I was a little worried about your wearing those shoes."

"They're not bothering me," Sheila said. "I feel great."

As soon as they entered the huge ballroom, Sheila's eyes bounced around, searching for the two people she hated the most.

Sheila's lips turned upward when she spotted them standing near the buffet table, appearing to be in deep conversation with the mayor.

She glanced up at Nicholas to see if he'd followed her gaze, but he was looking straight ahead.

"I think I should get something to eat," Sheila whispered. "I'm feeling hungry."

Nicholas gave her a look of concern.

"Don't look so worried. I just need to eat something."

He led her by the hand over to the buffet table.

When Sheila saw the muscles in his cheek tighten, she knew he'd seen Tori and Jake.

As they neared the table, Sheila pretended that she'd just spotted them as well. "Oh, dear. Maybe we should go say hello to Senator Latham," she suggested.

"I'm okay. What about you?"

Sheila gave Nicholas a big smile. "I've never felt better."

Seconds later, they stood face-to-face with Tori and Jake.

"Mr. and Mrs. Madison," Sheila began. "Hello." Deep down she savored Tori's blatant look of disapproval. She actually looked ready to pounce all over her. But who would she be defending?

Nicholas or Jake?

Sheila wasn't really worried—Saint Tori would never allow herself to be viewed in such a bad light. She thought too much of herself.

Jake glanced over at Tori, who struggled to keep her expression blank. She'd known Nicholas was escorting Sheila, but seeing them together like this . . .

"Hello, Nicholas. Sheila," Jake greeted.

Tori didn't offer a greeting. It was hard watching her best friend stand there with that snake. She didn't take her eyes off Sheila for a moment. She itched to wipe the smug look off her face, but Tori vowed she wouldn't let Sheila ruin this night for her.

Nicholas shook Jake's hand and then leaned forward to embrace Tori.

"Thank you both for supporting the Make A Dream Come True Foundation. I hope you'll enjoy the ball," Tori said with feigned sweetness. "Oh . . . make sure you two stay for the auction. We have a fabulous collection of items to bid on. Something for everyone."

Sheila held up the small evening bag she carried. "I brought my checkbook."

Tori was grateful when Nicholas had the good sense to escort Sheila away. Looking down at her, Jake asked, "You okay?"

"Uh-huh. I'm fine."

Shepard and Charlene walked over to where they were standing, followed by Kate.

"I can't believe Nicholas actually brought that tramp to the ball," Charlene muttered.

"What in the world is that boy thinking?" Kate wondered aloud. "He got to know Sheila ain't working with a full tank. She gon' mess him up for good, if you ask me."

Tori turned to her aunt and cousin. "C'mon, y'all. Let's just enjoy our evening. You know this fund-raiser was Mother Madison's baby. Shepard and I, along with our committee members, have worked hard on this event. We want to make enough money to keep fulfilling the dreams of terminally ill children. That's my focus tonight. I'm not gonna let Sheila spoil this night for me. I suggest y'all don't either."

Shepard agreed. "She's Nicholas's problem. Not ours."

Tori stole a peek over her shoulder to where Sheila stood holding court. She couldn't deny that Miss Moore looked exquisite in her teal-colored ball gown.

"I've never seen you look more beautiful than you do tonight," Jake whispered in her ear.

Her gaze met his. "You always know the right things to say."

Embracing her, Jake suggested, "Let's get something to eat. I'm starving."

Tori prayed Sheila would behave herself tonight. She knew that Jake was doing the same. He didn't want a scene.

"Don't look so worried, hon."

Jake gave Tori a sidelong glance. "I don't want her ruining this night for you or bringing back unpleasant memories," he explained.

Sheila's mere presence had done that, Tori thought to herself. "Are you referring to the night that you suddenly decided to return to our marriage?"

Jake seemed a little taken aback by her tone. "Yeah."

"If you want to know the truth—it was your surprise appearance that had everybody talking. It wasn't Sheila."

"Sorry I brought it up." Jake started to walk away.

Tori caught him by the hand. "I'm not trying to be mean—just honest."

"I shouldn't have embarrassed you and my mother like that. I wasn't really thinking back then."

"Jake, we were both very happy to see you. Anyway, it's in the past. Look at us now." Tori gestured toward a couple with her drink. "That's Maggie Brentwood. She and her husband donated a large sum of money to the foundation. I want you to meet them."

Tori felt the hair on the back of her neck stand up and glanced over her shoulder. Sheila was standing a few yards away, her lips turned upward. It really bothered her that Nicholas came with Sheila. She felt the bite of betrayal.

Turning her attention back to Jake, she murmured, "Let's grab Maggie while she has a free moment."

Sheila wiped the grin off her face. She couldn't let Nicholas see her gloating. Although Tori displayed an outward calm, Sheila was pretty sure that she was ready to strangle Nicholas.

He brushed a stray curl away from Sheila's face. "What are you thinking about?"

She glanced up at him. "Nothing important."

"Nervous about being here?"

Shaking her head, Sheila responded, "Not at all."

Out of the corners of her eyes, she could see Tori watching them. Sheila's skin prickled with excitement. She inhaled the sweet smell of victory.

Nicholas must have smelled it, too, because he said, "I have a strong feeling that you couldn't wait for Tori and Jake to see us together. Am I right?" His expression was impenetrable.

"I will admit that I was a little curious as to what their reaction would be," Sheila confessed, then quickly added, "But that isn't why I asked you to be my date."

Nicholas's mouth took on an unpleasant twist. "Sheila, let me be clear. I'm not going to be a pawn in your little game. Okay?"

She pretended to be offended. "I don't know what you're talking about. I wouldn't do that," she lied. "That was the old me."

Then she gave him a sexy grin. "C'mon, Nicholas," she pleaded. "Let's have a good time tonight. Okay?"

Nicholas clearly wasn't going to let the subject drop. "Sheila, I'm serious. If I find out that all this has been some kind of ploy, you're on your own."

He was getting on her nerves. Sheila didn't like being threatened. Instead of replying, she moved closer to the table, took a plate and began placing food on it. She helped herself to a cheese cube and put it in her mouth. Then she picked up another. She loved cheese.

A moment passed before Nicholas joined her. He stood beside her silently watching her, trying to assess her.

Sheila met his gaze. Smiling, she said, "You really should try the hors d'oeuvres. Delicious."

"Would you like something to drink?"

"Yes. Thank you," she responded. "A drink would be nice."

While Nicholas was off getting drinks for them, Sheila eyed the people in the ballroom. Her gaze landed on Tori, who was standing across the room talking to that big-mouthed cousin of hers.

"You may have Nicholas fooled, but ain't nobody else around here believing you've changed."

Wearing a thin-lipped smile, Sheila turned around to face Tori's aunt. "Hello to you, too, Miss Kate."

"Nicholas is like a son to me. Don't you think for one minute that I'ma let you run over him. He's too good a man for the likes of a tramp like you."

Kate's face was marked with loathing and her remarks stung Sheila, but she refused to let her wounds show. "Miss Kate, I'm not going to stand here and argue with you. I came tonight to support the foundation, so if you'll excuse me . . ."

She moved to walk around Kate, but the woman blocked her path.

"I'm watching you, girl."

"Move out of my way, old woman. You know . . . that dress you're wearing is much too beautiful for an old dried-up prune like you."

Kate inched closer to her filling Sheila's nostrils with the sickly sweet scent of cheap perfume. "I'll show yo—"

"What's going on here?" Tori demanded in a loud whisper. She and Charlene appeared out of nowhere.

"Ask your aunt," Sheila said.

"Aunt Kate, this is not the place—"

Charlene chimed in. "Mama, please don't embarrass Shepard and Tori. They worked really hard on this event—don't ruin it by fighting with Miss Thang over there. She's not worth it."

Sheila swallowed hard, trying not to reveal her anger. Both Charlene and Tori were looking at her as if she were at fault.

"Sheila, we'd like to enjoy the evening and raise money for a good cause. Why—"

"I'm here for the very same reason," she interjected in a harsh whisper. "I didn't do anything. Your aunt approached me. Maybe you should keep her on a leash."

Tori practically snarled. "Don't you ever say such a thing to me again. I should have you thrown out of here."

Sheila looked around for Nicholas and breathed out a soft sigh of relief when she spied him coming her way. "Have a good evening, ladies," she murmured before walking to meet him halfway.

"What just happened back there? Tori looks like she's about to kill somebody."

She didn't have to look back to know Tori, Charlene and Kate were fuming.

"Just a verbal attack from Miss Kate. For some reason, she felt the need to threaten me. Tori and Charlene thought it was all my doing, of course. I guess they're all pretty upset about my being here with you."

Nicholas's eyes strayed over to where Tori, Charlene and Kate were gathered, talking. "Maybe I should go over and say something. We don't want any confusion."

"No," Sheila interjected. "Just let it go. I have. We don't need to make a spectacle of ourselves. Been there, done that."

He laughed.

Sheila could feel their eyes watching her most of the evening and she loved it. She even glimpsed Jake watching her from time to time. For once, she'd come out the victor.

Sheila posed for a couple of press photos with the mayor, the senator and several other VIPs. She made the rounds smiling and laughing as if she didn't have a care in the world.

But walking around the room networking had begun to wear her out, so Nicholas led her back to their table to sit down.

After the auction, she decided to call it an evening. Nicholas walked her back to her room.

"Do you mind keeping my paintings until I relocate here?" she asked. "I don't see any point in bringing them back and forth."

"You decided when you're coming back?"

Sheila nodded. "I'm moving on May fourteenth. You never did tell me what you thought of the house I'm buying."

"It's nice. Real nice."

"I like the area you live in," Sheila began. "But I didn't want you to think I was trying to be all up in your space."

"I never would've thought like that."

"Uh-huh," she muttered. "You say that now."

Nicholas made sure Sheila had everything she needed before he left for home.

Right after her injection, Sheila packed her overnight bag and got ready for bed. Traveling seemed to tire her more, so she wanted to conserve her strength for her flight home to New York.

CHAPTER TEN

M onday morning, the first thing Sheila did was call her hairstylist to see if she had a cancellation.

Sasha had a three o'clock opening, so Sheila snatched it.
She needed a shampoo and set, a minifacial, spa manicure and pedicure.

Sheila was grateful to have gotten through the weekend without much
pain. At the charity ball, she had strutted around as if she didn't have a
care in the world, but Sunday morning, the bottom of her feet had felt
like they were on fire.

By the time she left for the airport, Sheila had felt like crying. But
when her plane took off, she was back to normal—free of pain.

Monday afternoon, Sheila sat in the chair admiring Sasha's handiwork.

"Thanks, Sasha. My hair looks gorgeous." Staring at her reflection
in the mirror, Sheila ran her fingers through her curls. "I love this
style."

"I can't believe you're leaving New York in thirteen days. I'm really
gonna miss you. You're one of my best clients."

"Don't worry, Sasha. I'll be flying up here to get my hair and spa treatments done. You are a miracle worker." Sheila continued to finger her
curls. "Nobody would ever believe that this hair isn't mine."

"So what you planning to do with your apartment? You selling or what?"

"I'm planning on leasing it. Why? You interested?" Sheila handed Sasha her credit card.

"Actually, one of my clients is looking for a place in your neighborhood."

Sheila pulled out a business card and handed it to her hairstylist. "Have her give me a call."

"Her name is Jasmine Larson. You've seen her a few times in the shop. She usually has the Friday appointment after you."

Sheila searched her memory. "I think I know who you're talking about. Just tell her to call me if she'd like to see the apartment. And thanks so much for squeezing me in today. It was raining so hard yesterday in Charleston, I looked like a wet rag. This morning I couldn't do a thing with all this hair."

She didn't mention that her fingers couldn't seem to grip the curling iron or the blow-dryer well.

"Okay, girl." Sasha picked up her appointment book. "Are you still coming on Friday? Or do you want me to cancel your wash and set?"

"No. I want to keep the appointment. I'll just have you style me, and I'll need my waxing." Frowning, Sheila added, "I really need it."

Laughing, Sasha opened the door to the private room where she serviced her hair-weaving clients. "Yeah. Have a good weekend, Sheila."

"You, too." She picked up the book she'd been reading and stuck it inside her tote bag.

Sheila slipped on a pair of dark sunglasses and navigated to the front of the salon, exiting through double doors.

She slowed her pace when she noticed the sound of her right foot slapping on the pavement as she walked. Sheila convinced herself that it was her imagination.

Just as she hailed a taxi, Sheila remembered she hadn't sent a report Jake had requested before leaving for her hair appointment.

She was usually good about sending any information Jake needed in a prompt manner.

He isn't my boss, so why am I so worried?

But she knew the answer. She didn't want to give him any ammunition to use against her when he found out about the MS. Sheila wanted to prove she was still very capable of doing her job. She would never allow Jake to force her out of Madison-Moore.

She suddenly felt uneasy about taking her leave. Maybe she was being too hasty.

The appearance of the yellow taxi brought Sheila out of her reverie. She climbed in and gave the driver the address of Madison-Moore's New York office.

Jake had already called twice and left a message for her to call him back.

Frustrated, Sheila walked straight to her desk and clicked on her computer monitor.

Since her assistant had limited access to her files, Sheila had to come back to handle the sensitive report herself.

I should have taken my laptop with me. I could've sent it from the hair salon.

Sheila printed the report. While she waited for it to finish, the phone rang. She glanced at the caller ID.

Jake's extension.

Only then did it occur to her that she could e-mail the report directly to him.

She muttered a curse.

The call had been transferred to voice mail. She quickly attached the file to an e-mail and sent it to Jake.

She didn't bother checking her voice mail. She grabbed her things and headed to the door.

Marla caught her near the elevators.

"Jake just called. He needs th—"

"I sent it to him via e-mail," Sheila cut in. "He should have it by now. Could you let him know?"

"Sure. I'll give him a call right now."

In the elevator, Sheila released a long sigh. Maybe she was about to suffer a stroke on top of everything else. First her leg, and now there was a slight tingling in her arm.

And what if she was experiencing memory loss? Sheila covered her mouth with trembling hands to keep from crying out.

When she reached the lobby area, Sheila rushed outside the building and hailed a taxi.

It wasn't until she reached her apartment that she released the deep sobs racking her insides.

She was afraid. Afraid of all that could happen to her.

Sheila eyed Jasmine as she sashayed out the front door of the apartment. "I don't like that woman," she muttered to herself. "But her references are impeccable."

She recalled seeing Jasmine from time to time at the hair salon. Sheila knew they were similar in that they both had very expensive tastes. Jasmine was often covered in designer originals from head to toe.

Sheila recognized that Jasmine was a bit flamboyant. She demanded the attention of everyone around her.

It was that very quality Sheila didn't care for. She had no desire to compete with women like Jasmine. With her looks and perfect body—it was a losing battle for Sheila and she'd had enough of those to last her a lifetime.

She went back through the tiny stack of applications, hoping to find someone other than Jasmine, but there wasn't anyone else that she really felt comfortable leasing out her apartment to.

Frowning, Sheila made her decision.

Jasmine Larson.

Sheila decided to wait until the next day to call her new tenant. She didn't want to give the impression that she was by any means desperate.

"Hello."

"Jasmine, this is Sheila. Sheila Moore. You were interested in a lease option on my apartment."

"Oh . . . hello."

"I wanted to let you know that the apartment is yours. Since you're planning to purchase it eventually, feel free to decorate it to suit your tastes."

If she was waiting for Jasmine to gush in gratitude, Sheila knew she would have a very long wait. Jasmine remained as cool as a cucumber. In fact, she didn't even respond right away.

"Hello?"

"I'm here," Jasmine said.

"Do you still want the apartment?" Sheila inquired.

Determined to stay in charge of the conversation, she went over the details and made payment arrangements. ". . . after the fifth, rent is considered late. The late fee is—"

Jasmine cut her off by saying, "I'm never late. In fact, I'll be buying the place within six months."

Her cool, aloof manner irked Sheila. *Who does this chick think she is?* she wondered. "Do you have any questions for me?"

"You *will* have the apartment cleaned after you move out?"

Sheila gave a short laugh to cover her annoyance. Her place was spotless. "Of course."

"When exactly will you be moving out? My decorator and I would like to be able to stop by and take measurements."

"I'm leaving on the fourteenth," Sheila announced. She really didn't like the superior tone in Jasmine's voice. It grated on her nerves.

"When can I pick up the keys?"

"I'll leave them with the concierge. I'll have the apartment cleaned the same day that I leave."

"Great. I'll make arrangements to move the following week. I don't want to have painters and my decorator running around while I'm trying to unpack my things."

Whatever, she wanted to mutter, but kept her tone professional. "Well, if there are no more questions, we're done."

She ended the conversation.

Seven days later, Sheila stood in the doorway of her apartment surrounded by luggage. She was leaving for the airport shortly.

"I'm leaving New York," she whispered. "It's time to go home."

It was true. She was thrilled to be going back home to Charleston. She was even looking forward to seeing her mother.

Marla's family had relocated to New York a week ago. She and Randy were more than capable to take up the reins of Madison-Moore's upscale Manhattan office.

Sheila had spoken to her earlier and felt assured she'd made the right decision in selecting Marla. Randy Copeland would also be moving to New York within the month to assist her.

Her eyes strayed to her watch, checking the time. The limo would be arriving soon.

Sheila looked up and around the apartment that had been her home for the last four years. She had a passion for rich colors, so the main wall in the living room was painted a sapphire blue, a vivid contrast to the other sand-colored walls and ivory furnishings.

"It's been fun," she whispered.

Sheila set the luggage outside her door, then closed it softly behind her. She stood there for a moment, taking slow breaths in and out.

Her self-imposed exile was over.

Sheila was surprised to find Nicholas standing near the exit doors located in the baggage claim area at the Charleston International Airport.

As she made her way to him, he whipped out a bouquet of yellow roses from behind his back.

Grinning, Sheila took the flowers. "Thank you for meeting me. I figured you'd just wait for me in the car."

"Me?" Nicholas shook his head. "You don't know me at all. I wouldn't do that, Sheila."

"I wouldn't have been offended."

"It's not the way I do things. I'm not going to leave you to retrieve your luggage. I plan to get it for you. And I drove my SUV because I wasn't sure how much luggage you'd be traveling with."

Sheila broke into a short laugh. "I've already shipped some things ahead to the hotel where I'll be staying until my house is ready."

"I meant what I told you. You are more than welcome to stay with me."

She shook her head. "I don't want to intrude, Nicholas. We're just getting to know each other. Besides, I'll be closing on the house Friday morning."

"Okay." Nicholas embraced her. "I'm glad you're here, Sheila. Now, let's get your luggage."

Sheila handed Nicholas her plane ticket. "The claim numbers are on here. The luggage is pretty easy to identify—it's all Louis Vuitton."

Her eyes searched his face, trying to reach into his thoughts.

They stood side by side at the baggage carousel.

Sheila pointed. "There's one of them."

Nicholas went to retrieve it. He stayed rooted to the spot by the conveyor belt until he had claimed them all.

"So how does it feel?" Nicholas inquired.

Sheila answered him with a question of her own. "How does *what* feel?"

"Being back here."

She looked around the baggage claim area. "Okay, I guess."

His eyes roamed over her figure. "It's good to see you, Sheila."

His words brought a smile to her lips. "Really?"

Nicholas nodded. "Yeah. I'm glad you're back here in this area so I can keep an eye on you."

"Hey, I'm not expecting you to babysit me. I'm a grown woman."

"You ready?" When she nodded, he continued, "Let's get out of here."

Sheila studied Nicholas as they walked to the car. He was a gorgeous man, but he seemed a little too good to be true.

"I can't believe this is all you have. Three pieces of luggage. Wow, I'm really impressed."

"Don't be." Sheila laughed. "You should see what all I shipped."

"You really don't have to stay in the hotel, Sheila. I have three guest bedrooms."

Sheila wasn't as trusting as she wanted Nicholas to believe. "You're sweet, but I think I'll just stay in the hotel. It won't be for very long."

"I went by the house and it's nice. Real nice, Sheila."

"I fell in love with it the very first time I saw it on the Internet, and when I actually walked through the house—I just knew it was the one."

Nicholas led Sheila to the car.

"Ooh. I'm so glad to be home," Sheila exclaimed. "New York is nice but it never felt like home. I didn't feel as if I really belonged— Charleston is different for me. I love living here."

"I really like it here myself," Nicholas said.

"I figured you moved here to be near Tori."

"No. Not really. Don't get me wrong. I enjoy being around my friend, but it was more than that. I really love the rich and diverse history of Charleston."

"I see your books are mostly set here in this area. At least the last three have been."

"You're going to see more books with settings in Charleston. This area really speaks to me."

"I know what you mean," Sheila responded. "I feel the same way."

While Nicholas drove along I-526 East, she stared out the car window, admiring the picturesque view of the Low Country.

Sheila preferred the quiet peacefulness of Charleston to the hustle and bustle of New York City. Her neck actually ached from turning it to see on every side. Charleston had changed some since her last visit, but not to the point that she wouldn't recognize the city.

The blending of the past and the present still existed in the mixture of stately antebellum houses and modern homes shouldering the narrow streets. Sheila loved the elegant architecture and the wrought-iron fixtures adorning them in intricate patterns. She longed to take a stroll along Rainbow Row on East Bay Street to view the vibrantly hued historic homes that represented the very heart and spirit of Charleston.

Sheila had always loved Charleston and was glad to be back in the place she affectionately called home.

She was so absorbed in the scenery that she almost didn't realize that Nicholas was talking to her. "I'm sorry. What did you say?"

"I asked how you were feeling."

"Okay," Sheila responded with a smile. "I'm just really glad to be home."

She settled back in the passenger seat, enjoying the ride and the attractive male company.

Her return to Charleston had been better than she ever anticipated.

CHAPTER ELEVEN

heila treated Nicholas to dinner downstairs in the hotel restaurant later that evening.

"This is my way of thanking you for all you've done for me, Nicholas," she told him after they were seated.

"You don't have to thank me, Sheila. This is what friends do."

Her guard was back up. "That's what I don't understand, Nicholas. Why? Why would you, of all people, want to befriend me?" *Nobody else puts forth this much effort to be my friend*, she almost added.

"Because I think you truly need one."

Rolling her eyes, Sheila laid her napkin across her lap. "Am I really that pathetic?"

"It's not like that, and you know it," Nicholas said with a defensive edge to his voice.

Sheila's mouth twisted wryly. "I'm not going after Jake anymore, so if you're keeping track of me for Tori, you really don't have to. I don't want her husband."

"Tori and Jake have nothing to do with our friendship. Alright?"

"If you say so," Sheila managed through stiff lips. She didn't believe him.

He leaned forward, saying, "I do."

His infectious grin set the tone. Sheila's mouth curved into an unconscious smile.

"I like seeing you smile. You should do it more often."

Sheila gave a half shrug of her shoulders. "It's not like I've had a lot to smile about, Nicholas. My life has never been easy."

"Neither has mine. Life isn't easy."

"It *is*, for some people," Sheila argued. "Some people have all the luck . . . they end up getting everything they want. Me . . . I get an incurable disease."

"Sheila, you have so much mo—"

"Don't, Nicholas," she interjected quickly with a slight wave of her hand. "I don't want to hear it. You can't possibly understand what I'm going through. You have your health. Jake and Tori—they're healthy, too. I'm sorry, but I just don't happen to think it's fair. I've been through enough in my life and now this . . ."

"I'm sure this isn't easy on you, Sheila. I can understand that much, but you can't let this disease beat you. Trust that God has your best interests at heart. If you ask Him—He'll keep you. That's all I'm trying to say."

"That's something I'd expect my mother to tell me."

"Speaking of your mother—have you called her yet?" Nicholas asked.

"For what?"

"To let her know you made it here safe."

"I tried a couple of times but didn't get an answer. I haven't called her back yet."

"Sheila, is there something going on between you two?"

"Not really. I'm just not ready to deal with her. I'm not thrilled with the way I had to grow up, and she's not real happy over the way I turned out." Sheila paused a moment before adding, "She's ashamed of me."

"I don't believe that."

"Well, it's true whether you believe it or not," Sheila retorted. "And since I'm being honest, I have to say I'm embarrassed by her. In this day and age, my mother still refuses to give up the old ways—she might as well have been a slave, too."

"Some people aren't comfortable with change."

"I have four houses in Charleston—really nice homes that I'm renting to complete strangers. I offered to buy her a house. Nothing extravagant, mind you. Just something nice and quaint." Sheila's mouth turned downward. "She didn't want it. Said she was happy living in that broken-down shack she calls a house."

"She loves her home. You can't blame her for that."

"How can you call something like that a home? Nicholas, you need to see that place. The paneling is about to fall off the wall and at night you can hear roaches and mice . . ." Sheila shuddered. "I can't live that way and I don't know how she can. I mean . . . the house isn't nasty. My mother keeps a very clean house. It's just old, and it smells old. I've tried to have it repaired but somehow the bugs and rats just keep getting inside."

"Was your mother born in the house?"

Nodding, Sheila muttered, "So was I."

"Have you considered having it restored and painted—maybe even updated with more modern appliances?"

"Not really. I think it should be burned down, to tell the truth."

"That house is part of her legacy, Sheila. Your mother loves that house—you shouldn't try to take it from under her."

"I don't know why anyone would want to live in a shack like that. I couldn't wait to get out of that old raggedy house. To this day, I won't live in a house over five years old."

"I understand what you're saying, Sheila. But you have to also understand that your mother doesn't share your feelings. Offer her a compromise—instead of wanting to buy her a new one, offer to just have the house completely restored. Your mother is obviously proud of her heritage, and that house is her link to the past. You shouldn't take that from her."

Sheila considered his words.

"Maybe you're right, Nicholas," she replied after a moment. "I'll try it. But I still think that house needs to be torn down."

"Is your mother in Charleston?"

Sheila shook her head no. "She's a hop, skip and jump from Charleston. She lives in a village called Frogmore."

"I went to Frogmore a couple of months ago."

"It's backward, I know . . ."

"I wouldn't say that," Nicholas countered. "The Gullah people can trace their roots all the way back to the villages of the Sierra Leone."

"I know that, Nicholas. I'm Gullah."

"You should be proud of your heritage."

"Why? Because we excel in music, basket-making—oh, and let's not forget growing rice and fishing." Sheila frowned. "My mother used to weave baskets so that she could buy fabric to make my school clothes. I looked a *mess* in those handmade dresses."

Nicholas downed the last of his water. "I heard that during the Second World War, the Japanese were able to break our codes until an African American who spoke Gullah began sending code in his language."

"I'd heard that, too, but I really doubt that it's true. It was the Navajo." Sheila picked up her glass of iced tea and took a sip.

"Things have changed," she continued. "Look at Daufuskie Island— white islanders outnumber the blacks now. Property taxes over there are so high that it drove the natives away, and for the few who are still living on the island, they have to share the palm shade with posh golf courses and great big mansions with high security gates." Shrugging in nonchalance, Sheila added, "If you can't beat 'em—join 'em."

"If Gullah dies, Sheila, so will the most significant and purest link to your past. I know you don't want that. Consider any children you may have. They won't know anything about the Gullah heritage other than what's written in the textbooks. It's cultural genocide."

Sheila shrugged again. "I don't ever plan to have children, so I don't have to worry about it."

Nicholas was surprised by her response. "I can't believe this doesn't bother you at all."

"It doesn't. You don't know how I felt when I heard someone say I was speaking bad English. I was so ashamed, Nicholas. I hated I was born Gullah."

"You have nothing to be ashamed of. The Gullah people have held on to their African heritage more so than any other African American group. I think that's something to be proud of."

"I tried to erase my history from the way I looked—especially from the way I talked—I am not that same person who was born in that shanty my mother refuses to leave."

"Sheila, all those things you tried to erase are what make you beautiful." Gesturing with his hands, Nicholas said, "It's not all this makeup, the nails, the hair . . . when are you going to learn the difference?"

She didn't respond. Sheila was too stunned by his words.

Sheila's second morning in Charleston started with a hint of light peeping through the darkness. It soon widened and the pale color deepened into coral that gradually became a canary yellow. The mist burned away, its remnants visible only on the glistening beads of dew clinging to the leaves and blades of grass.

Sitting near the window at a desk, Sheila wrote in her journal as she nibbled on a bagel with cream cheese. Every now and then, she would take a sip of hot tea.

When she finished writing in her journal, Sheila sat there contemplating what she could do to keep from being bored. She couldn't stomach sitting in the hotel suite all day long—she had to find some activity.

Yesterday, Sheila had done the final walk-through on her house before the closing on Friday. She couldn't wait to move out of the hotel. She was ready to unpack and settle down in a home for good.

Sheila rubbed her left temple with one hand and held her bagel with the other. She was yearning to drive over to Madison-Moore and pop in to see how things were going.

She was dying to know if things were moving smoothly without her. Sheila was a bit surprised that she hadn't received more phone calls concerning the clients. She assumed Marla and Randy were calling Jake.

After her light breakfast, Sheila showered and dressed in a pair of linen pants with a matching top. She pulled her hair into a ponytail and selected a pair of white gold earrings and a matching necklace to wear.

Nicholas's words jumped into her mind as she eyed her reflection in the full-length mirror.

He doesn't know what he's talking about, she told herself. *He's never even seen me without my makeup.*

Sheila picked up her purse and the keys to her rented automobile, grateful that she was still able to drive. After she closed on her house, Sheila intended to buy a new car.

Her dream car. A Jaguar.

Fifteen minutes later, Sheila pulled into the parking lot of Madison-Moore and turned off her car. She felt a sense of joy just sitting there, admiring the modern four-story building that housed the company she and Jake had created. The name, Madison-Moore Creative Visual Solutions Inc., greeted her in bold burgundy and gold letters.

It's been a long time since I've been in there, she thought. *I've missed it.*

Sheila opened the car door to get out. She yearned to go through the revolving glass doors of Madison-Moore and reconnect with her employees.

She had reached the sidewalk when she heard someone call her name. She bit her bottom lip when she caught a glimpse of Jake walking up behind her.

She turned around when he neared.

"Hey . . . I thought that was you."

Sheila pulled at her jacket. "I was a little curious to see how things were going."

"Things couldn't be better, Sheila. I can't complain. By the way, I told Marla and Randy not to bother you anymore—they can bring any issues that come up directly to me. I wanted you to enjoy your leave."

"I'm sure," Sheila murmured softly. She swallowed hard, trying not to reveal her anger. Jake was already trying to cut her out of the company.

"Are you back in Charleston this time for good?"

"I'm back." She met his gaze straight on. "Hey . . . don't worry, Jake. I won't be bothering you or your little family. I've got more pressing matters on my plate. But even if I didn't—I'm certainly not interested in revisiting the past."

"I'm real glad to hear that, Sheila." He pointed toward the door. "You going inside? I'm sure the employees would love to see you."

Sheila glanced down at her watch and shook her head. "Actually, I have an appointment. I didn't realize it was so late."

He shrugged. "Well, I won't keep you."

Sheila felt her temper rise in response but she strode off without saying another word. She needed to put some distance between them before she cussed him out.

She didn't look back until she reached her car.

Jake was gone.

It came as no real surprise to Sheila. She hadn't really expected to find him standing there, wearing his heart on his sleeve. He had never loved her—never had any feelings for her outside of friendship.

Only now they weren't even friends. They were two people who happened to own a company together. They were partners.

Reluctant partners.

A part of her just wanted to stomp into the building after Jake and announce that the partnership was over.

In her fantasy, Jake would fall to his knees, begging her to stay because Madison-Moore would no longer be successful without her presence.

It was just a stupid fantasy.

Jake would probably shout for joy if she wanted out. Sheila was pretty sure of it, because he'd brought it up twice.

Both times came after her move to New York. Jake wanted nothing to do with her—he was reluctant to even open the New York office.

No, she would not give him that satisfaction. Sheila wanted Jake as miserable as she was.

Maybe even more, because he was the one who was married. Jake had done nothing more than play with her emotions.

"I hope you burn in hell, Jake Madison."

Tori met Jake at the front door. "How was your day, honey?"

"Great," Jake responded. "We landed the Tanner BMW account this afternoon."

Tori embraced her husband. "The new dealership that just opened up? Congratulations. I'm so proud of you. This should put a smile on your partner's face."

"I saw Sheila today right before the meeting. But yeah . . . this will make her happy."

Tori folded her arms across her chest. "So she's still in Charleston? I thought she went back to New York."

Jake nodded. "I know she went back, because I communicated with her while she was there. But she's here for now—for how long, I don't know. She didn't say a whole lot and I didn't push. Sheila acted like she was in a big hurry."

"Well, I'm not too surprised," Tori muttered.

"I don't care where she stays, as long as it's far away from us, if you want to know the truth."

Tori nodded in agreement. "I'm going to check on the children."

He eyed his wife as she made her way up the circular stairway. Jake could tell from the stiffening of Tori's body that his news about Sheila disturbed her.

"Baby, you have nothing to worry about," he whispered. "I love you, Tori, and I'll do whatever it takes to keep my family together—even sell my shares of Madison-Moore to Sheila. I won't ever let that woman come between us again."

Tori stood outside her son's room and began to pray. "Lord, please help me get past this. I don't like the woman I'm becoming. I know what Your Word says about forgiveness. I can't forgive her. This is not me—this is not the way I want to be. I trusted You with my marriage when Jake left me. I trusted You when Sheila did everything she could to try and break us up. Father, I'm trusting You now. I know that You honor marriage and I give You my marriage yet again. Keep us strong and give us wisdom where needed. All this I pray, Father God, in Jesus' name. Amen."

She breathed in deeply, then exhaled slowly before opening her eyes. She stayed in the hall until she felt much better.

Tori walked into her son's room with a smile. "What are you two up to?"

"Watching cartoons," JJ responded.

Her daughter toddled over, her chubby arms outstretched.

"Hey, sweetie pie. Are you watching cartoons?" Tori leaned over to pick up Brittany. "Your daddy's home," she said.

"He is?" JJ asked.

Nodding, Tori said, "He just got here a few minutes ago. Why don't you come downstairs and say hello? Dinner will be ready soon."

"Can I watch for one more minute? Please?"

"Peeze?" Brittany echoed.

"What? No hello for Daddy?" Jake strode into the room.

He planted a kiss on Brittany's forehead before taking her from Tori.

JJ pushed up from the floor and ran over to Jake. "Hey, Daddy."

"Hey, son. Have you been a good boy?"

"I think so. You have to ask Mommie."

Both Jake and Tori burst into laughter.

They had a quiet dinner together and then spent time with the children before bedtime.

Jake went off to his office to do some work while Tori decided to study her Bible. She really needed to spend some time with God to help her deal with what she was feeling.

Tori sat in the middle of her bed with the Bible on her lap.

"Lord, forgiveness is so easy to talk about but difficult to practice. I know that I have to forgive Sheila." She could forgive her husband, her mother . . . anyone but the woman who set out to destroy her marriage.

She picked up her journal and opened it. Tori found her notes on forgiveness from an old sermon.

"*If we confess our sins, he is faithful and just to forgive us our sins, and to cleanse us from all unrighteousness . . .*" Tori closed her eyes a moment to meditate on the verse she'd just read, First John 1:9.

She opened her eyes and continued reading.

" 'What is forgiveness? The word *forgiveness* means to pardon, to remit, to absolve from blame, to cease to feel resentment against an offender on account of a wrong done, to abandon a claim against a debtor.' "

Tori turned to the sixth chapter of Matthew. She read verses nine to fifteen. "Forgiveness also involves restoring a personal relationship that has been interrupted," she murmured. "Thank you, Father, for this revelation. Your Word tells us to exercise forgiveness toward those who offend us, and we complain about how hard it is for us to do—yet we beg You to forgive us of our sins."

Her notes led Tori to turn to the eighteenth chapter of Matthew and read verses twenty-one and twenty-two.

Then came Peter to him and said, "Lord, how oft shall my brother sin against me, and I forgive him? till seven times?" Jesus saith unto him, "I say not unto thee, until seven times: but, until seventy times seven."

Then she turned to the book of Jeremiah and read the thirty-fourth verse of the thirty-first chapter.

> And they shall teach no more every man his neighbour, and every man his brother, saying, Know the LORD: for they shall all know me, from the least of them unto the greatest of them, saith the LORD: for I will forgive their iniquity, and I will remember their sin no more.

Before she ended her study for the evening, Tori added another entry in her journal.

> Forgiveness awakens love for God.
> Forgiveness removes mistrust.
> Forgiveness brings peace of mind.

Her last thought before she went to sleep was, *Lord, I know what You desire of me, but I'm gonna need some help from You. Please help me forgive Sheila, because I can't do it without You.*

CHAPTER TWELVE

～

S heila was grateful that Nicholas was able to accompany her to meet her new neurologist, Dr. Patricia Daniels.

She was impressed by how well the doctor had done her research. She was already familiar with Sheila's medical history and had spoken to Dr. Hill several times to discuss the case.

After their initial conversation, Sheila felt comfortable in building a relationship with Dr. Daniels.

She would be fine with her new doctor, Sheila decided.

Dr. Daniels performed a thorough exam before sitting down with Sheila and Nicholas to discuss further treatment.

"Do you have any questions for me about anything?" Dr. Daniels inquired. "Are you having any difficulties?"

Sheila fingered the fringe-edged hem of her tropical skirt. "The Copaxone seems to be working fine, but I've been having some stiffness in the mornings lately, and I'm still always so tired. I used to be very active. Now I get tired just walking from my bedroom to the living room." She stole a peek at Nicholas before adding, "Sometimes I'm so tired that it actually hurts to move. Is there anything I can take to help with that?"

"I'll write you a prescription for Amantadine. There are some other medications available if this one doesn't suit you," Dr. Daniels said. "I'll also give you a prescription for Zanaflex. It should help with the stiffness."

Sheila nodded. "Thank you so much."

An hour later, Sheila and Nicholas walked out of the doctor's office and toward the car.

"More prescriptions," Sheila sighed. "I hate taking medicine."

"I don't like taking pills," Nicholas admitted. "I can deal with liquids or injections, but swallowing pills is not my favorite thing to do."

"I really hope the meds will help with my exhaustion," Sheila said, waving the prescription. "I never feel like exercising anymore. I'm always so tired. I know that it probably doesn't make sense to you, but it really does hurt."

"Are you still taking naps?"

"It's all I seem to do these days. I'm trying so hard just to function, Nicholas. And it's hard because I'm not used to lying around doing nothing. I like to keep busy. It keeps me from thinking so much."

Nicholas inquired, "Do you like to read?"

"Well, you already know how much I love mysteries."

"How about reading my manuscript?"

Sheila halted, shocked. "The one you're working on now?"

"I'm almost finished, but I could use your opinion."

"Really?"

Nicholas smiled. "Yeah."

"I love your books; I'd be more than happy to read it." Her voice rose an octave in her excitement. "I've been wanting to know what happened to LeVert's wife. Is she really dead? I don't think so." Sheila suddenly stopped talking. "I'm sorry . . . I'm rambling, but I'm so excited."

Nicholas laughed. "I hope you'll enjoy it."

"I know I will." Sheila gave him a hug. "Nicholas, thank you so much. You've really made my day."

She couldn't believe he was actually going to allow her a sneak peek at his next book. Her excitement dwindled, however, at the thought of Nicholas letting Tori read his projects before they reached the bookstores.

"This is something I've never done," he said, as if he'd heard her thoughts. "Now, don't tell anyone about the story. I want this book to come out with a bang. I must warn you, though. You're going to view Magda in a different light after reading the manuscript."

"I won't tell a soul," Sheila promised. "I'm so excited."

She climbed into the car, smiling.

Nicholas got in and started his BMW. "If I'd known you'd be so happy about it, I'd have let you read it a long time ago."

Sheila was still wearing the silly grin. The fact that Nicholas didn't even let Tori read his manuscripts made his offer much more appealing to Sheila.

Too bad she couldn't rub this in Tori's face, Sheila mused.

I bet she'd really be hurt.

Saint Tori probably thought she and Nicholas were the best of friends—if they were, why wouldn't he let her read his manuscript?

"Hey, where'd you go?" Nicholas prompted.

Sheila gave him a sidelong glance. "Huh? Oh . . . sorry."

"What were you thinking about?"

Staring out the window of Nicholas's car, Sheila responded, "Nothing in particular."

She was still trying to figure out a way for Tori to discover the manuscript in her possession when Nicholas turned on her street.

To go to Tori's bookstore would be too blatant. It had to be completely by accident. A thread of guilt traveled down her spine. She really couldn't hurt Nicholas in that way. He had been too good to her.

Sheila was stunned by her own feelings. A few short months ago, it wouldn't have bothered her at all to betray him.

"We're here," Nicholas announced before parking the car. "You sure are preoccupied with something. You didn't say a word the entire time I was driving."

"I'm so sorry, Nicholas. I was just thinking of what Dr. Daniels said."

Nicholas escorted her into her house.

"I'll drop off the prescriptions when I leave," he said. "And arrange to have them delivered."

Sheila nodded her thanks. "You're not leaving right now, are you?"

"Not if you want me to stay."

"I could use the company." Sheila took a seat on the sofa in the family room.

His gaze was as soft as a caress, forcing Sheila to fan back and forth with her hand.

"You okay?" he questioned, sitting down beside her.

"Hot flash," Sheila murmured. He was disturbing to her. She was by no means blind to his attraction, and struggled to hide it.

She didn't want Nicholas unlocking her heart and soul. It was just too painful. Besides, she still wasn't sure whether or not he was working with Tori against her. Sheila was beginning to consider that she might be wrong in her thinking.

Smiling, she said, "I would make us something to eat but, besides the fact that I'm too tired, I have to be totally honest—I can't cook."

"Why don't you let me make something for you?"

Surprised, Sheila felt her mouth drop open. "You cook?"

Nicholas nodded. "I love cooking."

"I'm impressed. I don't think I've ever met a man who knew how to cook, much less admit to love cooking."

"You need to get out more," Nicholas teased.

Grinning, Sheila acknowledged, "You're probably right." She almost pinched herself to see if this was real. Nicholas was actually going to cook for her. No man had ever done that. Sheila was amazed at the thrill she felt whenever she was around Nicholas.

When she caught him watching her, a new and unexpected warmth surged through her, but Sheila was determined not to let her emotions get the best of her.

Nicholas rose to his feet. "I'm going into the kitchen to see what you have."

"Not a whole lot, I'm afraid," Sheila apologized. "I mostly eat out or order in."

Shrugging, he responded, "I'll run out to the store if I need to."

"We can order something," Sheila protested. "You really don't have to go to all this trouble."

"It's no trouble. Besides, I'm sure you could do with a home-cooked meal."

Sheila stretched out, making herself comfortable on the sofa. "Okay. I'll just rest here then."

"Sounds good," he said.

His smile melted some of the ice surrounding Sheila's heart.

*   *   *

Nicholas got up at the crack of dawn the next day. He went straight to his computer and began typing his thoughts.

Early morning was his favorite time to write. His fingers flew across the keyboard, trying to keep up with the images forming in his mind. His books came to him as movies playing in his head.

He wrote until seven.

Nicholas left the computer, showered and slipped on a pair of jeans and a T-shirt. Last night, after he returned home, he had come up with an idea to surprise Sheila with something he hoped would ease some of the MS symptoms she'd been having.

Nicholas knew she was an early riser, so he'd made plans to be at her house promptly at eight thirty a.m.

She was stunned to see Nicholas outside her door, but he could see that the woman standing beside him surprised her more.

"What's going on?" Sheila demanded.

"I hired a masseuse," he quickly explained. "I thought maybe Rosa could give you a massage to help relax your muscles."

Sheila moved out of the way to let them enter the house. She pointed to the end of the hallway and said to Rosa, "You can set up in there."

To Nicholas, she said, "Thank you for being so thoughtful. I really appreciate it." She was touched by his kindness.

"I'm hoping it will help some. I'd read somewhere that massages can help with poor circulation, relax your muscles and relieve some of your MS pain. It might even help with your depression."

"I hope it'll help, too. I woke up all stiff this morning. I wasn't sure I'd be able to make it out of bed."

"I've explained to Rosa that you have MS. I thought she should know, because I didn't want her accidentally doing anything to cause you more pain."

"I guess I better go back there."

Nicholas nodded. "I'll wait for you here. See you shortly."

Sheila came out of her bedroom an hour and twenty minutes later.

"How do you feel?" Nicholas inquired. "Did the massage help at all?"

"Actually, I think it did." Sheila stretched. "I feel a lot better. Rosa is wonderful. I told her that I plan to have her come on a regular basis. She's really great with her hands."

Nicholas smiled. "I'm glad."

Sheila sat down beside him. "You are so good to me. Nobody's ever treated me the way that you do."

He chuckled. "I haven't really done anything."

"Nicholas, you've done a lot," Sheila countered. "More than all the people I know. Outside of my mother. She did her best for me."

Sheila glanced over and found him watching her. "What?"

"You shouldn't wear so much makeup. You have a beautiful face."

Sheila put a hand to her face. "No, I don't."

Nicholas pulled it away. "You're beautiful, Sheila."

"Thank you," she whispered. She wanted so much to believe him.

"What are your plans for the rest of the day?" he asked.

"I don't have anything planned. I'll probably just park myself right here on my sofa and surf the Internet on my laptop." She gave him a side-long glance. "What are you doing? Writing?"

"I'm fleshing out an idea for a new book." Nicholas met Sheila's gaze. "Why don't you invite some of your friends over?" he suggested.

"I don't really have any friends. I have associates."

"Sweetheart, you know you can't make it on your own. God created us for relationships—I'm not just referring to dating and marriage. I think it'll be a good idea for you to find some friends. Good friends."

"To do what?" Sheila asked. "I have you—we're becoming friends, I guess. I don't need any more. Besides, how will making friends help my condition?"

"I have a core group of friends whom I can call on whenever I get up-set, frustrated or just lonely. I even call on them when I have something to celebrate."

"Hooray for you, Nicholas. I don't happen to be so lucky."

"With that attitude, I can see why," he blurted.

Sheila's mouth dropped open. "I can't believe you just said that to me."

"You want me to be honest, don't you?"

"Not to the point of rudeness."

"All I'm saying is that in order to have friends, you have to be willing to be a friend. Friends love each other unconditionally."

Sheila shrugged. "Whatever . . ."

"I need to get going." Planting a kiss on her forehead, Nicholas said, "See you later, Sheila."

"Will you give me a call later?"

Nicholas nodded. "Sure." He rose to his feet. "Just stay there," he told her when Sheila made a move to stand up. "I'll see myself out."

The place where his lips touched her skin stayed warm long after Nicholas was gone.

He was a good man, Sheila silently acknowledged. And brutally honest. Despite vowing to keep her distance, Nicholas was getting to her in ways no other man ever had.

Just yesterday he'd made a delicious lunch for her, and even baked a chicken dish for Sheila's dinner before leaving.

And this morning, bringing a masseuse . . . he was very good to her. Nicholas must really care about her, she decided.

Too bad I didn't meet him first. Maybe I wouldn't have been such a fool for Jake.

Nicholas was still heavy on Sheila's mind two days later. Her attraction to him was growing, and she could no longer fight it.

She clasped her hands to her head and groaned. "I can't believe this . . . I'm supposed to be using Nicholas. Not falling for him."

Reaching for the telephone, she muttered, "This is crazy." She hung up before Nicholas could answer.

"I'm just bored," she told herself. "I need to find an outlet, and it can't be Nicholas."

Sheila missed working. She had spoken with Marla earlier just to see how things were going in the New York office.

Nobody seemed to miss her, however.

Both the New York and the Charleston offices seemed to be running smoothly. The fact that Madison-Moore *could* function without her brought on a bout of depression.

"Maybe I should go back to work," she mumbled. "I can't have Jake thinking he can run the company without me."

The ringing telephone cut into her thoughts.

"Hello . . ."

"Hello, beautiful," Nicholas greeted. "I'm calling to check up on you. How're you doing?"

"Okay, I guess."

"You don't sound okay. What's wrong?"

"Jake's already cut me out of Madison-Moore. He doesn't want the employees reporting to anyone but him. He told them not to bother me."

"This should make you happy, Sheila."

"It doesn't," she snapped.

"I don't think Jake's trying to move you out—he can't, sweetheart. You're his partner."

"I *created* Madison-Moore. I just let him put his name on it because I thought . . . anyway, I'm not going to let him just take it away from me. The company belongs to me, Nicholas."

"Madison-Moore belongs to both you and Jake. Sheila, it's really up to you whether or not you take this leave. You can go back to work any-time you're ready. Remember, you're the one who made the decision to leave. You can't blame Jake."

Sheila was a bit taken aback by Nicholas's tone. She didn't like it.

He was wrong.

She could and did blame Jake for everything. It was because of him that her life had turned out so pathetic. It was because of Jake that she was alone and unhappy.

CHAPTER THIRTEEN

Early Saturday morning, Sheila drove along Route 21 singing softly. She'd been back in Charleston for two weeks now but this would be the first time seeing her mother since her return.

She dreaded the conversation they would have, because Sheila knew her mother would try to pressure her to move back home.

She hated Frogmore.

Although Nicholas insisted she should feel a sense of pride, Sheila felt anything but proud of her roots. She wanted nothing to do with the place that had caused her so much heartache.

When she left for college, Sheila had vowed that she'd chopped her last piece of firewood and washed the last piece of clothing in that tin tub—and no more cooking on her mother's cast-iron stove.

As she neared her childhood home, her foot involuntarily hit the brake as if her body was telling her, "It's not too late! Get away!"

The trouble was that she had nowhere else to run. The only person who truly loved her lived in that rundown house at the end of the road.

Sheila forced herself to drive the last few yards, and parked in front of a wooden shanty that sat up on short columns of brick and cinder block in a dirt yard.

She stepped out of her brand-new platinum-colored S-type Jaguar. Like it or not, Sheila was home.

Taking in her surroundings, Sheila stood rooted in place, trying to rid herself of the dread she felt rolling around in her belly. A dull throb of pain bloomed in her left eye, deepening with every heartbeat.

She truly detested this old broken-down house. Sheila wasn't sure if she was feeling sick from the medication or from the sight of the splintered and rotting wood around the doorjambs and windows, where the fading haint blue paint was supposed to keep the evil spirits away.

As far as Sheila was concerned, the house in its current shape was enough to keep Satan away.

Sheila heard a door behind her open and close. She glanced over her shoulder to the green and white house across the dusty road, knowing instinctively that it was her mother's nosy neighbor, Minnie Davis. The stocky little woman just had to see who was visiting Essie Moore.

Sheila reluctantly raised her hand and waved in greeting.

"W'y you don' come'yah tuh see yo' maamy?" the old woman yelled from her perch.

"New York is not exactly around the corner, Miss Minnie. I kept telling Ma that I'd get her a plane ticket, but she scared to fly."

Sheila didn't wait around to hear Miss Minnie's response. It was probably something sarcastic anyway. The old bat had a smart mouth.

Her mother came out the front door, broom in hand.

"Uh thought Uh heard yo' voice. W'y you don' call me tuh say you comin'?"

Sheila refused to speak Gullah. "I need to call before I come or something, Ma?"

"Don' be smaa't." Essie beckoned. "In yah cah sid down."

Turning up her nose at the smell of the old house, Sheila gave her mother a brief hug before taking a seat on the sofa. "I didn't call because I wanted to surprise you."

Nothing had changed. The air inside felt warm and smelled musty. A faint whiff of furniture polish throttled Sheila instantly back to her childhood—back to those early Saturday mornings when she had to wipe down the coffee and end tables with orange oil polish, summoning a shine bright enough to see her reflection.

Sheila felt a hot flash coming on. It was hard to be without air-conditioning even for a short while. Waving her hand back and forth, she used it as a fan.

She smiled in gratitude when her mother turned on the small oscillating fan sitting in the middle of the floor.

"Uh been t'inkin' 'bout you. Minnie say you be comin' home."

The pain in Sheila's left eye stabbed through the back of her skull. "How many times did she tell you that, huh?" Sheila grumbled. "And I never showed up. Humph . . . that old woman don't know nothing about telling the future. I don't know why you always listening to her."

"Eb'ryting she say come tuh pass, Sheila. You know'um true."

"I didn't come out here to argue with you. I was hoping we could have a nice visit for a change."

Essie surveyed Sheila's face. Shaking her head, she uttered, "Nusso. Mek you duh rarry so?"

Sheila wasn't surprised that her mother could read the worried look on her face. Essie knew her well. "Ma, I need to tell you something. Come sit down."

Sheila waited while her mother propped her broom in a corner and sat down on the tattered love seat across from her.

"Now I don't want you getting all upset, Ma," Sheila began. She took a deep cleansing breath. "I found out not too long ago . . . a little over a month ago, actually . . . anyway, I found out that I have primary progressive MS. Multiple sclerosis, Ma."

Unexpected tears stung the backs of Sheila's eyes. She didn't know if they were tears of sadness for herself or her mother.

Tears sprang into Essie's eyes as well. Pressing a hand to her chest, she wailed, "Lawd . . . no."

"You don't have to cry. I'll be fine, Ma. I'm going to beat this disease."

Essie wiped her eyes.

"I'm doing everything the doctor tells me to do. I'm even eating healthier. Walking is going to be difficult sometimes, but Ma . . . I'm not a quitter. I won't let this disease get the best of me."

"You don' look sick," her mother whispered.

"This is a good day for me. Ma, some days I'm in a lot of pain."

"W'y don' you come home? Uh kin tek care of you."

Sheila's face twisted into a frown. "Are you kidding me? Oh no . . . I'm not coming back *here*."

The hurt in her mother's eyes might have made Sheila feel guilty if she didn't resent her mother so much.

Essie had always been too wrapped up in her own issues to help her hurting child. Sheila couldn't forgive her for that.

Essie rose and walked the short distance to the kitchen. "You hongry?"

"Naw," Sheila responded. "I'm okay."

Black iron skillet in hand, her mother approached her. "You hab tuh eat, Sheila. Uh kin make you swimp 'n' grits."

"No thanks, Ma. I'll eat," she promised. "When I'm hungry. I'm alright for now."

"Huccome you be so mean, chile? Uh didn't do nuthin' tuh you. Jis' tryin' tuh help, iz all."

"Ma, I don't want to fight. I only came to tell you that I'm back in Charleston. For good."

"Well, Uh'm glad to know you be close." Essie set the skillet back down on the counter. "Uh'll come up dey if you need me."

Sheila gave her mother a tiny smile. "Thank you, Ma."

When Essie sat back down on the sofa, Sheila shifted the focus off herself by inquiring, "How have you been feeling?"

Her mother had aged in her absence. She was a tiny woman, but now she looked more frail than before.

"Uh'm doin jis' fine. Uh hab a few days my gout was actin' up. Other than dat—Uh bin good. T'engk Gawd."

Sheila and her mother continued to make small talk over the next hour or so.

Checking her watch, Sheila pretended she was in a hurry. "I have to attend a launch party this evening, so I need to get back home and rest. I'll give you a call tomorrow, Ma."

Essie sighed in resignation.

"Don't be that way," Sheila pleaded. "I'd like to visit with you longer, but I've got some things to do later this afternoon and then an event tonight." She rose gingerly to her feet. "I just wanted to tell you face-to-face what's going on with me."

"Uh don' t'ink you should be livin' alone."

"Ma, you can move closer to me."

Essie inclined her head. "What good dat do?"

Shrugging, Sheila answered, "I don't know. Ma, we'll talk about it later. Okay? I've got a lot on my mind right now and I haven't sorted everything out yet. Please, just bear with me."

Essie reached out and hugged Sheila, surprising her with this rare show of affection. "The Lawd—He watchin' ober you. Don' you forget it."

"I need to get going," Sheila muttered uneasily. She was eager to step out of her mother's weak embrace.

One and a half hours later, Sheila released a soft sigh when she pulled into her driveway. The drive had exhausted her, and she was glad to be home.

Brightly colored petunias lined the edge of the path. The vivid profusion of violet, pink and white made a stream of color against the spring green grass. By the house was a large circular flower bed. Delicate pink and white flowers dotted the shiny green foliage.

Sheila glanced from the vivid bursts of color spread all over the yard to the crepe myrtles near the entrance.

"It's beautiful," she murmured. Sheila loved her new house and hoped to spend time working in her yard to plant more flowers. She loved roses especially and desired a rose garden.

Sheila also wanted to have an outdoor kitchen built off her deck. Although she wasn't much of a cook, she enjoyed grilling during the summer months.

Maybe I'll even host a Fourth of July pool party, she thought to herself. *Just depends on how I'm feeling at that time.*

Sheila navigated to her kitchen and hastily slapped mayo and spicy mustard onto two slices of wheat bread, then laid several layers of ham and Swiss cheese before topping it with lettuce and tomato.

She pulled a cold Sprite from the refrigerator and fled to the solitude of her family room to watch television while she ate.

When she finished eating, Sheila placed a call to Nicholas. When he didn't answer at home, she called his cellular phone.

Still no answer, so she hung up without leaving a message.

"Nicholas, where are you?" she whispered, feeling insecure.

Maybe Nicholas had grown tired of her ways already. Maybe he was just avoiding her. Or maybe he was somewhere sniffing after Tori.

Sheila wondered if he'd talked to Tori about their budding friendship. She felt no guilt in using Nicholas to get at Tori—he was most likely using her for the same exact reason.

She believed that, deep down, Nicholas still hoped to win Tori's affection.

As the hour of the launch party drew near, Sheila debated whether or not to attend. Vectors Records was Jake's client, so she didn't really need to be in attendance. She wasn't in the mood to play nice with her partner tonight.

Her face began to hurt.

Sheila took a couple of painkillers and lay back down. She decided to stay in for the evening.

After a few minutes of quiet, though, Sheila's thoughts drifted irresistibly to Nicholas. She missed him.

Sheila really did enjoy his company. They had a lot of fun together—much more than she'd ever anticipated. Whenever Nicholas wasn't writing, he would come by to pick her up so that they could go walking on the beach.

Sheila's jaw, teeth and eyes all began to throb at the same time from her pain.

Why does MS have to hurt so much? she wondered.

Nicholas drove to the Penn Center museum.

He'd wanted to visit for a while, but hadn't taken the time to do so until now.

The idea came to him during his drive back to Charleston three days ago. He'd been in Brunswick for the weekend.

The old faces of Gullah stared from Penn Center's museum walls. Nicholas eyed the image of the woman with a hoe slung across one shoulder, basket balanced on her head, walking to a field.

His eyes traveled to the photo of the man and woman in front of their one-room shanty. All these people were probably resting peacefully in a graveyard, charging their Gullah descendants to keep their history alive.

Why would Sheila want to erase the work of her ancestors? Nicholas just couldn't fathom any reason why.

He would never understand Sheila's way of thinking where her heritage was concerned. She must have been terribly hurt in the past, Nicholas surmised.

She could be a very loving person if she allowed herself to be. She was also very devoted—the way she had pursued Jake was proof of that.

Nicholas wished he could've gotten through to Sheila back then. Maybe she wouldn't be so angry and bitter now.

He hoped one day those feelings would evaporate. Sheila deserved some happiness. She wasn't a bad person. A little shallow and self-centered, but he liked her. They had a lot in common.

Nicholas couldn't deny that he really enjoyed spending time with Sheila. She had a great sense of humor when she let her guard down, which wasn't too often.

Sheila was afraid to trust him. Nicholas could tell by the way she reacted to him at times.

He wasn't offended, however. Sheila was a victim of her past.

What she needed most was a good friend and confidant.

She had a huge battle ahead, and Nicholas vowed to stand by her side every step of the way.

Without telling her, he had already begun attending support meetings for friends and families of people dealing with MS. Nicholas wanted to learn ways to help Sheila.

He was looking for any suggestions to help her cope with the pain and combat her bouts of depression.

When he stopped by Sheila's house Sunday evening after returning from Brunswick, Nicholas found her crying from the pain racking her body. He did what he could to calm her. Then he went to the kitchen and walked out carrying a bowl of soup. "Try this," he encouraged.

Sheila shook her head. "I hurt too much to eat." She cradled her head in her trembling hands.

"Honey, you haven't eaten all day . . ."

"I can't," Sheila managed.

Nicholas set the bowl down on top of a magazine and dropped down beside her. He began gently massaging the muscles in her shoulders.

"Is this helping at all?" he inquired after a few minutes passed.

She nodded. "I don't think I've ever had pain so bad. I can just sit still and a wave of agony comes on me. This is maddening."

Sheila suddenly collapsed against him.

Holding her close to him, Nicholas asked, "Hey, you okay?"

"Yeah. The pain is gone, finally."

Nicholas held her until she fell asleep.

He eased her up and moved out of the way before laying her down on the sofa. He covered her with a blanket before leaving.

Sheila would probably sleep through the night. Nicholas prayed it would be pain-free. It broke his heart to see her suffering.

Sheila was depressed again, but she was too stubborn to ask for help. To her, it was another weakness, and she would find a way to get through this episode on her own.

She'd confided once to Nicholas that she was depressed and he'd suggested she see a therapist. Sheila wasn't interested in sharing her feelings with a shrink and she didn't want to take another pill, especially if it made her feel weird or gain twenty pounds, or gave her a dry mouth.

When the telephone rang, she glanced at the caller ID. It was Selma calling from Madison-Moore. "What does she want?"

Sheila debated whether to answer or let it ring.

It could be important.

She took a deep breath before picking up and saying, "Hello . . ."

"Sheila, it's Jake."

"I know," she responded dryly. "How did you get this number?"

If she'd known it was Jake calling, Sheila doubted she would've picked up the telephone.

"Selma gave it to me," he responded. "I hope you don't mind."

Sheila decided to get to the heart of the matter. "Did you need something?"

"I'd like to meet with you . . . today, if at all possible."

"Why?"

"We have a lot of things to go over. You're still my partner, Sheila."

"You don't have to remind me," she spat out. She instantly regretted her remark. "Jake, I'm sorry. I didn't mean to snap like that. I'm not in the best of moods today."

"I'm sorry to disturb you, Sheila, but if you could come to the office for a couple of hours, I would really appreciate it."

"Are you listening to me, Jake? This just isn't a good time for me."

"Sheila, I don't know what's going on with you, but we still have a business to run."

"I'm taking a leave of absence," she reminded him. "Remember?"

"I wouldn't bother you if this didn't concern you. It's Knight Electronics. They want to hand over their new division—only they want you to personally manage the account."

"They recently launched a specialized division—the Technical Market Development Group."

"Exactly. Knight Electronics has been your baby from the beginning, so it's only natural they'd want you on board."

"I'll see you shortly," Sheila said. "Bye."

She muttered a curse before rising to her feet. The last thing she wanted to do was be forced to deal with Jake, on today of all days.

Sheila walked into her closet, searching for something to wear. She didn't feel like getting dressed, but she couldn't go into the office looking like a ragamuffin.

She finally decided on a pair of navy blue pants with a matching navy and white twinset.

Sheila pulled her hair into a ponytail and tied a navy silk scarf around it. She slipped on a pair of navy and red low-heeled mules.

After putting on a pair of red and platinum earrings with matching necklace and bracelet, Sheila strode back into her closet to retrieve a navy handbag.

She studied her look in the large full-length mirror that sat in one corner of her bedroom. She smoothed her brow with both hands and fluffed up her ponytail with her fingers.

Satisfied, she left the room and headed to the front door.

If I don't leave now—I won't leave at all.

A few minutes later, Sheila was on her way to Madison-Moore.

"I'm not looking forward to this," she mumbled. "I've got enough to deal with right now. Today is a bad day for me."

Her cell phone rang. It was Selma.

"Hello."

"Miss Moore, I was just calling to see if you were on your way."

"I'm in the car now. I should be there in about ten minutes."

"Great. I'll let Mr. Madison know."

You do that, she wanted to respond, but Sheila would never be so unprofessional. "Thanks, Selma."

"I told that jerk I'd be there," Sheila complained aloud after she clicked off her cell phone.

She sat in her car for a few minutes to compose herself. On this day of all days, why did she have to face Jake Madison?

CHAPTER FOURTEEN

S heila eyed the plate of sandwiches and pitcher of iced tea on the conference table. Since she hadn't eaten breakfast this morning and didn't have a chance to grab lunch before the meeting, she was hungry.

As soon as Sheila sat down, Selma set a plate in front of her.

"It's so good to see you, Miss Moore."

She pasted on a smile. "Thank you, Selma. I'm glad to be back home."

"I ordered smoked ham and Swiss sandwiches just for you. I even made sure the deli used that spicy mustard you love so much."

"You didn't forget."

"I never forget a thing," Selma announced proudly. "How long are you going to be in Charleston?"

"I'm back permanently."

Tossing her blond hair across her shoulders, Selma clapped her hands with glee. "I'm so glad to hear that. When will you be—"

Jake's entrance silenced Selma. She immediately went back to work, preparing for the meeting.

"Sheila . . . good you're here."

You ordered me here, didn't you? Sheila yearned to utter the words out loud, but held her tongue. She was acutely aware of Selma watching her, so she kept her expression blank.

Office gossips had gone around speculating on what transpired between Sheila and Jake shortly after they announced that she would be opening an office in New York, and Sheila was determined not to give them anything new to buzz about.

While they waited for everyone to arrive, Jake tried to engage Sheila in small talk.

"Marla seems very excited about her new position."

Pretending to study her hands, Sheila nodded. She didn't have a thing to say to Jake Madison.

She couldn't believe he was still running his mouth, trying to have a conversation with her.

"She told me that her husband was happy about moving back to New York. He's from Brooklyn. They—"

"Could you please pass me a napkin?" Sheila interrupted, cutting him off.

"Sure," Jake muttered. He eyed her a moment before turning his attention to the people walking through the doorway.

Sheila made sure there was a big smile on her face when the CEO and the senior vice president of Knight Electronics entered the conference room. She pushed away from the table and stood up.

"Greg, it's so nice to see you," she greeted. "Good seeing you again, George."

Sheila shook hands with both men.

Greg and Jake spoke politely but neither had really warmed up to the other since their initial meeting nearly six years ago. Sheila didn't know why the two men didn't like each other and she didn't care. Instead, she decided to use it to her advantage.

"Why don't you take the chair beside me, Greg?" she suggested. "We can catch up while we're waiting for the others."

Jake quietly observed the two of them. Sheila wanted to burst into laughter at the pathetic look on his face.

Now he knew firsthand what it felt like to be an outsider.

As long as Sheila was a part of Madison-Moore, the company would be successful. She had made the company into the success it was. Because of her love for Jake, she'd groomed him to take the reins, but he would not be able to stand alone—Sheila vowed she would destroy the company before she let him take it from her.

She continued to taunt Jake by soaking up all of Greg Knight's attention.

"So, how is your father doing?" Sheila inquired.

"He's great. He wanted me to give you his regards. He'd planned to come to the meeting with me, but Mother hasn't been feeling well since her heart surgery."

Jake noisily cleared his throat. "It's time we get started..."

Together, Sheila and Jake came up with an impressive marketing plan and promotional Web design idea for Knight Electronics' new division.

"How about holding a Web site launch party and invite advertisers, key press contacts, industry analysts, editorial and investors of course," Sheila suggested. "We could develop opportunities to promote the Web address, or even provide showcase for advertisers."

"I like it," Greg stated. "I'd like to maintain a regular presence in trade discussion groups, newsgroups, e-zines and other online forums."

Jake nodded in agreement. "We could also arrange cross-promotional links with sites that have attractive and complementary readership demographics."

"I think it would be advantageous to expand the site to several languages," Sheila suggested.

For the moment, they were once again a team.

The meeting went on for almost three hours. Sheila waited until everyone left before she stood up to leave. Without so much as a good-bye, she grabbed her purse and walked toward the door.

"Wait, Sheila," Jake called out. "I'd like to talk to you."

Turning around, she strolled back to the conference table without saying a word.

"I thought we'd see you at the Vectors launch party last Saturday."

"I had a previous engagement," Sheila lied. "I heard everything went well, though. Adam Spears is a great speaker." Selma had given Sheila a minute-by-minute report the following Monday.

Jake nodded in agreement. "It was nice. Everyone was asking about you."

"I hope you reassured them that I hadn't left the company—just on a personal leave."

"I did," Jake confirmed.

"I'm sure you didn't call me back here to discuss the launch party." Sheila pulled out a chair and sat down. "Is there something else?"

"Sheila, I want to apologize. I take full responsibility for my share in what happened between us. I—"

Frowning, Sheila interrupted him by saying, "Let's not go back there, Jake. You made a fool of me and I'm not going to let you off the hook that easily. I loved you with my entire being and I thought you had feelings for me. *You didn't.*" She spat out the words contemptuously. "I'm glad you've been able to move on, you and your lovely little family, but don't expect me to be your friend."

"Sheila, I'm not looking for us to be friends. You abused that privilege a long time ago." Jake paused for a moment. "Look, I'm just trying to get rid of some of this tension between us."

Sheila released a harsh laugh. "That'll never happen. Give it up, Jake. I don't even know what I ever saw in you. You're no different from any other dog walking around. You are just another user. All I feel for you now is hate—pure hatred."

She resisted the urge to smile at the flash of pain she glimpsed in his eyes.

"I'm sorry you feel this way," he said quietly.

"But I bet Tori will be ecstatic," Sheila shot back.

Jake didn't respond to her comment about his wife. Instead he said, "We're partners, Sheila. We have to find a way to get along or dissolve the partnership."

"This company is a success because of me—I'm not going anywhere. If *you* want to leave, then I'll be more than happy to buy you out." Sheila rose to her feet, swaying slightly.

"You okay?"

"Don't pretend to be concerned," Sheila snarled. She held up a hand.

"Just leave me alone, Jake. I know that you'd like nothing better than to take this company away from me. I'm not going to let that happen."

Jake seemed surprised by her accusation. "Sheila, I'm not trying to push you out of Madison-Moore. I just don't like all this tension between us. I'm sure everyone else in the meeting noticed it, too."

"I really don't care." Sheila walked gingerly toward the door. "I need some air."

"Sheila, we really need to talk this out."

She stopped walking and turned around, facing him. "When I wanted to talk to you, Jake, you practically slammed the phone down in my ear. You set all the rules—don't call you at home unless it's an emergency. Don't call you at work unless it's strictly business—"

"Sheila, things got crazy between you and me. You were—"

"I'm not anymore," she interjected. "Trust me."

Sheila didn't bother waiting around to see if Jake dared to respond. She strode out of the conference room, heading for the elevators.

Sheila was seething by the time she reached her house.

Jake sat in that conference room, tall and proud as if he had done nothing wrong.

How dare he try to shift all the blame on me, she thought. He'd used her—only he wasn't man enough to admit it.

She blew into her house, blazing a trail straight to her bedroom. She removed her clothing, changing into a comfortable pair of sweats and sneakers.

Still a little hungry, she walked to the kitchen and retrieved an orange from the refrigerator.

Sheila sat down at the breakfast table with her snack, forcing Jake from her mind as she ate.

She had just eaten the last slice of orange when the doorbell rang.

"Okay, who can this be?" Sheila muttered as she rose to her feet.

Her mouth turned upward when she opened the door to Nicholas.

"What are you doing here?"

"I was at the Barnes and Noble down the street," Nicholas responded. "So I thought I'd stop by and check on you."

Sheila stepped out of the way so that he could enter the house.

"I'm happy to see you," she murmured. Her dark mood brightened just from seeing Nicholas. He had a strong effect on Sheila—there was no denying that.

He followed her through the house to the family room.

"Were you busy?" Nicholas asked. "I probably should've called first."

"You're welcome to come by here anytime. You know that," Sheila responded. "I had a meeting at Madison-Moore earlier and just got back a little while ago."

"How'd it go?" Nicholas asked as he took a seat on the sofa.

"The meeting went okay. Jake wanted to talk afterward, but I really wasn't in the mood to deal with him. Besides, he is still not quite owning up to the way he used me."

"Are you?"

She swallowed hard, lifted her chin and boldly met his gaze. "Am I what? Owning up to my part?"

"Yeah," he said smoothly with no expression on his face.

Nicholas's question sent Sheila's ire into a tailspin. "I only did what I did because Jake was sending me mixed messages. If he wanted Tori so much—why did he cheat on her?"

"Why don't we change the subject?" Nicholas suggested. "How about taking a drive with me to Port Royal?"

"When?"

"Tomorrow. We can drive down early and have dinner at the Dockside Restaurant. We'll drive back after dinner."

"I love Port Royal," Sheila said. "Have you been there to watch the dolphins playing in the ocean?"

Nicholas shook his head no.

"We have to go to the observation tower, in that case. I love watching them."

"Let's plan to leave around ten. How does that sound?"

Grinning, Sheila responded, "It's a date."

She walked him to the door. "I'll see you tomorrow morning."

He hugged her. "Bye, sweetheart."

She watched him drive away before going back into the house. She could still feel the warmth of Nicholas's arms around her. She shook off her turbulent emotions. She would not confuse friendship with anything more.

The next day, Nicholas arrived promptly at ten to pick her up. They made small talk during the hour and a half drive from Mount Pleasant to Port Royal.

"I thought about buying a house in Port Royal," Nicholas told her. "I love the atmosphere here. People are so friendly."

"Why didn't you?" Sheila wanted to know.

"I really liked the house I'm living in now."

"I can see why you fell in love with your house. It's gorgeous."

Nicholas nodded. "I didn't find anything in Port Royal that I liked better." He added, "In my price range, that is."

He parked and asked, "How are you feeling?"

"I'm fine right now," Sheila pointed to her feet. "I wore my Keds for walking. My other shoes are in my tote."

"Let me know when you start to feel tired. Okay?"

Sheila gave a short laugh. "You don't have to worry."

They began their day on the boardwalk.

"I love it out here," Sheila murmured. "My mother used to say I should've been born a fish because I love the water so much."

Nicholas chuckled. "My parents probably felt the same way. My mother told me that I walked straight into the ocean during one outing when I was about four years old. She said I was convinced I knew how to swim. She put me in swimming lessons right after that."

"I love the water, but I never learned to swim."

He was surprised. "Really?"

Sheila nodded. "I'm going to learn one day." She laughed, then admitted, "I've been saying that for years."

They left the boardwalk twenty minutes later and went to the observation tower.

Nicholas and Sheila weren't there long before he said, "You look like you're getting tired."

"I am," she said, surprised that he'd noticed.

"Let's head back to the car. I booked a hotel room so that you could take a nap."

Another surprise. "You did?"

"I knew you'd need to rest before dinner."

Sheila didn't quite know what to make of Nicholas. He just seemed too good to be true. Her blood coursed through her veins like an awakened river when he took her by the hand.

When they were back in the car, Sheila turned to him, asking, "Why are you being so good to me?"

He laughed and responded, "Why not? Everybody deserves to be pampered."

"I'm not complaining. Don't get me wrong."

While he drove, Sheila appraised him with more than mild interest.

Nicholas pulled in the parking lot of the Days Inn. "I'm afraid this isn't a five-star hotel."

Sheila laughed. "It's really okay, Nicholas. We're only going to be here for a few hours."

She was grateful to finally lie down on the queen-sized bed. Sheila was asleep before her head hit the pillow.

She slept soundly for three hours.

Nicholas was sitting on the other bed watching television with the volume turned down low when Sheila woke up.

She sat up in bed rubbing her eyes, before stealing a peek at the clock on the nightstand.

"Hey, beautiful . . ."

Sheila swung her legs out of bed. "I can't believe I slept so long."

"I hope you feel rested."

"I do," Sheila confirmed. "I really needed that nap. I was tired."

She stood up and stretched. "I'm going to freshen up for dinner."

Nicholas went to the bathroom after Sheila came out fifteen minutes later.

They left for the Dockside Restaurant shortly after he came out and soon were there.

"I love eating here," she said happily. "Have you tried the jalapeño-stuffed shrimp before?"

"Yeah. I like the sunset shrimp better though. It's easier on my stomach. And I like the steamed seafood pot."

"I like that, too," Sheila agreed. "The crab legs, shrimp, oysters and lobster, mmmm . . . I think I'll have that tonight."

Nicholas put down his menu. "Have you ever eaten at the Gullah House?"

Sheila shook her head no. "Nope, and don't plan to. It's not a place I'd want to go."

"I thought you loved jazz."

"I do. But I don't want to go there," she burst out. "Now can we drop it?"

Nicholas nodded. "Sure."

"I'm really not trying to be evil," Sheila explained. "I just don't want to eat at a place called the Gullah House. Okay?"

"I understand."

"Hey, I'm having a pretty good day. Mostly pain-free, too. Let's enjoy it." Sheila moistened her dry lips. "I'm in desperate need of a good time."

"Think you'll feel up to a little walk after dinner?" Nicholas inquired.

Shrugging, Sheila replied, "I don't know. We'll see."

They finished their meal and Nicholas signaled for the check.

Sheila was too tired for a moonlight walk so Nicholas decided to drive back to Charleston.

By the time Nicholas turned on Woodlake Drive, Sheila was fast asleep.

CHAPTER FIFTEEN

J ake and Tori dined at Robert's of Charleston on the evening of June
seventh. For the past year, this was how they always spent the first
Friday of each month—celebrating each other.

"I'm really glad Charlene and Shepard offered to keep the children tonight," Jake said. "It'll give Aunt Kate a break. I know she loves Brittany
and JJ, but she watches them for us during the day."

"She acted a little miffed when I picked them up this afternoon, but
she'll be okay. I told her that Charlene and Shepard just wanted to spend
some time with them."

Jake chuckled. "They're probably wanting to practice their parenting
skills."

"On Tuesday, Charlene will be in her third trimester. Our little niece
will be here in under three months. Can you believe it?"

"They better get all the rest they can right now," Jake said. "Once the
baby comes, their life is gonna change drastically."

"I do love this place," Tori murmured. She surveyed the room, feasting
on the warm, golden hue on the walls, a color that reminded her of a
beautiful sunset. Tori inhaled the aroma of fresh roses that the owner,
Robert, had placed on every table.

Jake agreed. "I didn't eat lunch just so I have an appetite for dinner."

They enjoyed crusty, warm bread and Jake sampled chilled Chardonnay while Tori drank water.

The server came around to explain how the courses were going to be served.

While they waited for the first course to arrive, Jake said, "I need to update your Web site with the new information for your upcoming heritage tour."

"Yeah, we need to do that. The one for the bookstore needs to be updated, too. I'm thinking we really should have you set us up for online ordering. Charlene and I discussed it this morning."

"I've been telling you that for a while now. I'm glad y'all are gonna try it, at least. It can only grow your business."

"I'm gonna need a full-time person to manage the online orders and also maintain the Web site."

"I've got the perfect person for you, in regards to the site. You only need to have someone fill the orders and ship the products. Plus you can have your distributors do direct shipping."

Tori agreed.

Their conversation came to a halt when Tori turned her head to watch Robert coming through the rear entry, two plates perched in midair, floating through the restaurant singing *Oliver*'s "Food, Glorious Food."

As always, hearing the owner sing made the hairs on her arm stand up.

"Robert can really sing," Jake complimented.

Tori nodded in agreement.

The first course was a warm sea scallop mousse, a favorite of Jake's. Tori looked forward to the next course, the roasted breast of duckling served with Oriental rice noodles and orange ginger barbecue sauce.

While Jake and Tori waited for the next course, they continued discussing the Web site for the bookstore.

After the duckling the entrée, a succulent chateaubriand, was delivered to their table, again with a song by Robert.

Slicing off a piece of meat, Tori announced, "Oh, I went to the doctor this morning and he checked me out. He says that everything looks good. We can start trying, Jake. He even told me to get started on prenatal vitamins."

"So we could even get pregnant as early as tonight?" Jake asked.

"Well, maybe not tonight, but pretty soon, I guess. I just stopped taking my birth control pills last month." Tori broke into a grin and leaned forward. "We can get started trying tonight, though. Who knows—we might even get lucky."

Jake took a bite of his filet mignon, chewing slowly. "Another baby . . . wow."

"Are we crazy?" Tori asked with a laugh.

Nodding, Jake replied, "We must be. I'm almost forty-three years old. Most of my friends have children in high school or college now. We have a couple of toddlers running around."

"I don't care. We'll just pray that the Lord will keep us healthy and energetic enough to keep up with them." Tori pierced a shrimp with her fork. "I'm so excited, Jake. And very happy. Nothing can change that."

"I haven't been here since I moved to New York," Sheila murmured. "I used to come to Robert's at least once a week."

"How often did you come home?" Nicholas took a bite of his chateaubriand, chewing slowly.

"Not too often." Sheila put a forkful of beef in her mouth, savoring the butter-tender meat and the woodsy flavor of wild mushrooms. She swallowed before adding, "Maybe two or three times during the four years I was gone."

"Your mother must have missed you."

"Nicholas, Jake humiliated me and I was heartbroken. I didn't want anyone around here seeing just how bad a shape I was in."

Nicholas sliced off another piece of beef. "I need to know something, Sheila. Are you truly over Jake?"

Sheila's eyes traveled the restaurant. She stiffened when they landed on Jake and Tori.

Turning her attention back to Nicholas, she asked, "Where is this coming from?" She watched him with a trace of suspicion in her eyes, wondering if she was being set up. "Did Tori put you up to this?"

"No. She doesn't have anything to do with this. I simply asked because I wanted to know."

"Nicholas, I don't have any feelings for Jake Madison. Trust me . . . I hate the man." Her gaze discreetly sought out Tori. *But I hate her even more,* Sheila added silently.

"Jake had me making a fool of myself while he had full intentions to win Tori back. If she hadn't taken him back . . ." Sheila's voice died.

"What?" Nicholas prompted. "You think he would've ended up with you?"

Sheila didn't like the way Nicholas threw the question at her. "Yeah. Especially if Tori had gotten involved with you."

Leaning forward, Nicholas said, "Sheila, I need you to listen to this. Tori's heart always belonged to Jake and his to her. I knew that and you did, too. There's no point in sitting here being angry. Let it go."

"When I'm good and ready, Nicholas, I will. But not a minute before. I'm entitled to my anger."

"What does being angry get you?" he asked her.

Sheila didn't respond.

"All you're doing is walking around accumulating resentments. These resentments will end up controlling your life and hindering your ability to experience joy."

"Being angry is a part of life, Nicholas. I'm sure you've been angry once or twice, so don't take that high-and-mighty tone with me."

"Yeah, I've been angry—I just don't let my anger consume me."

Sheila reached for her glass and took a sip of water. "Alright, Dr. Washington . . ."

"Sweetheart, when you're a child, it's okay to bury your pain, but as an adult, all your buried pain is like a weight anchored to your feet. You cannot be free until you dig into the deep hole of your suppressed anguish. Sheila, you've got to be willing to forgive."

"So you're saying that forgiveness is the only way out? That's the key to my being free?"

Nodding, Nicholas said, "Forgiveness allows you to free yourself from the past. Anger is a bondage to the past."

Silently, Sheila hoped Tori would glance in their direction. She really wanted the cow to see her with Nicholas. Tori would probably choke on her expensive meal.

She'd heard every word Nicholas said, but there was no way she could forgive Tori and Jake for the way they'd treated her.

Tori glanced in their direction a few seconds later, prompting Sheila to look away quickly. She pretended to be engrossed in Nicholas's conversation. She could almost feel the heat of Tori's gaze on them.

Sheila picked up her water glass and took a sip. Tossing her hair over her shoulder, she hoped she and Nicholas looked like they were out on a romantic date, instead of two friends having dinner.

She kept his attention on her, because she didn't want Nicholas spotting Tori and Jake having dinner across the room.

Although she never looked back in their direction, Sheila continued to feel Tori's eyes on her and Nicholas.

She almost burst into giddy laughter at the thought of Tori green with envy over Sheila being in such a romantic setting with Nicholas.

It would serve Jake right if Tori suddenly decided she wanted Nicholas after all. He deserved to suffer the same heartache he'd put her through.

Bitter, miserable and alone.

"What in the world is he thinking?"

Jake glanced up from his food. "What is it?" He followed Tori's gaze and squinted. "Is that Nicholas and Sheila over there?"

"Nicholas has lost his mind," Tori snapped in anger. "I thought maybe he'd come to his senses after the charity ball, but obviously he hasn't."

Reaching out, Jake grabbed her by the hand. "Honey, I know Nicholas is your best friend, but he's also a grown man. He can take care of himself. If you don't want to lose his friendship, you need to stay out of his business."

She nodded after a moment. "You're right. And you and I are supposed to be spending quality time together." Tori wiped her lips with the corner of her napkin.

Deep down, she was ready to spit nails. She couldn't believe Nicholas was still hanging around that snake!

"Tori," Jake prompted, drawing her attention back to him.

"Huh?"

"Honey, I want you to promise me that you'll stay out of this. If Nicholas wants to date Sheila—"

"They're not dating," Tori interrupted. "Sheila probably found out we were having dinner here."

"But how would she have known that?" Jake questioned.

"Who knows?" Tori responded. "We did make reservations."

"Honey . . ."

Tori grinned. "Okay . . . maybe I was reaching with the reservations, but I'm almost positive that she manipulated this dinner out of Nicholas. Why else would he be here with Sheila?"

"He may enjoy her company," Jake pointed out.

The thought that there might be a grain of truth to his words made Tori lose her appetite. She couldn't even enjoy the rich chocolate cake with whipped cream.

Tori reached for her water glass. She took a sip, then another, before saying, "Don't ever say that again."

"It might be true, honey. No matter how much you want otherwise."

"I don't think I want to discuss this any further. Sorry." Leaning forward, Tori asked, "Are you ready to get out of here? I can't sit here and watch Sheila make a fool of Nicholas."

Sheila used anger as a protection against pain, Nicholas realized the more he listened to her talk. She hid her emotional pain from others because it made her feel vulnerable.

That pain had evolved into anger.

Nicholas wasn't concerned with the fact that Sheila was angry. It was an emotion everyone experienced from time to time, including himself. But what did bother him was that Sheila used anger as a plate of armor against her suppressed emotional pain.

Sheila had a lot of emotional baggage. Anger had become as natural to her as breathing—he'd bet she didn't even notice it most of the time.

What Nicholas couldn't figure out was why she was such an angry and unhappy person. What had happened to her? Surely this couldn't be just about Jake.

He was curious about Sheila. Nicholas wanted to get to know her better. The challenge, however, would be getting over and around the brick wall Sheila had erected to protect herself.

She didn't fully trust him, but it didn't bother Nicholas much. Sheila didn't really know him that well.

In time, she would see that he meant her no harm.

CHAPTER SIXTEEN

Walking, Sheila pulled the folds of her sweater together. "Cold?"

"It's a little breezy, but I'm fine. I love being out here on the beach."

Nicholas agreed. "I like coming out here in the evenings. Not a lot of people."

She looked up at him. "You come down here often?"

"In the evenings?" he asked. When she nodded, he replied, "Not really. I'm here maybe twice a month, I guess."

"Is this where you bring all your lady friends?"

Nicholas shook his head no. "You're the first woman I've ever brought here."

Surprised, Sheila stopped in her tracks. "Really?"

"Why do you look so surprised? I'm not some gigolo, you know."

Sheila laughed. "I know that. I just figured this was a very romantic place to bring a date. You know . . . moonlit walks and all."

"So you consider this romantic? Our walking on the beach in the moonlight?"

She gave him a playful slap on the arm. "Not between us, silly. Of course not. We're not a couple."

"C'mon, Sheila . . . you like me, don't you?"

"Yes, I like you, Nicholas. As a *friend*."

Sheila savored the sultry sounds of Nicholas's laughter. Sexy through and through . . .

"So Nicholas . . . do you like me?"

"Very much," he responded. "I like all my friends."

Laughing, Sheila rubbed her arms through the sweater, trying to ward off the goose bumps from the brisk ocean air. At least, she assumed they were from her surroundings and not caused by the sexy chocolate man walking beside her.

Nicholas wrapped an arm around her. "Better?"

Nodding, Sheila replied, "Much better."

Her eyes traveled to the moonlit sky. "Nicholas, why do you think God allows bad things to happen?"

"That question is ages old—nobody can really come up with an acceptable answer other than David. If you read Psalm eleven, David says, *When all that is good falls apart, what can good people do? The Lord is in his holy temple; the Lord sits on his throne in heaven*."

"Okay, so what does it mean exactly?"

"God isn't altered by what happens to us. Things may fall apart around us, but God has not, Sheila. He remains faithful."

"I just don't understand how God can be for us and let all these terrible things happen. I'm not supposed to look at my MS as a punishment, but I don't know how else to feel about it."

"Sheila, it's important to remember that God's thoughts are not like our thoughts. His ways are not like our ways. They are so much higher than ours. God uses pain to bring peace, my pastor always says."

"But who is God? Is He really in control?"

"If you really want to know who God is, just look at all He's done. I always look at it this way—what is impossible with man is possible with God. To me, that says it all."

Sheila considered Nicholas's words. "You're very passionate about this."

"I love the Lord, Sheila. I wouldn't be anywhere without the Man Upstairs." Nicholas pointed upward. "I'm here today because of Him. The knowledge that God is who He says He is gives me the confidence to face an uncertain future."

Sheila didn't know how to respond. She'd had no idea Nicholas was such a religious man.

After their walk along the sandy shoreline, she and Nicholas sat down on a huge beach towel that he'd pulled out of the trunk of his car, talking about their dreams as they watched the waves tossing to and fro.

When Sheila started to shiver again, Nicholas took her home.

She went to bed right after he left and slept throughout the night.

Sheila sent her mother a bouquet of flowers for her June eighth birthday. She'd originally planned to drive out to Frogmore to take her to dinner, but she didn't feel up to making the drive.

She'd felt fine last night, when Nicholas had taken her out for their moonlight stroll on the beach.

This morning though, Sheila woke up feeling depressed. Getting out of bed had been a struggle, and even now, three hours later, she hadn't been able to get dressed or comb her hair.

Nicholas showed up at her door just before noon. She'd completely forgotten he was coming over.

"I'm not in the mood for company," Sheila said when she opened her front door. She knew she was being rude, but really could care less at the moment.

He gave her a once-over. "I can see that."

He brushed past her and into the house. "Why don't you go take a shower?"

A wave of embarrassment washed over Sheila. Folding her arms across her chest, she asked, "Why? Do I stink?"

"I wouldn't say that, but you *do* need to take a bath. I think we need to get you out of the house for a little bit."

"Nicholas, I don't feel like going anywhere," Sheila whined. "I know you're just trying to help, but please, just leave me alone today."

Nicholas shook his head no. "You need some fresh air," he insisted. "We don't have to go anywhere in particular—just around the neighborhood."

Drained, she dropped down on her sofa in the living room. Running her hands through her hair, Sheila muttered, "I look a mess."

"You look like you're sick, Sheila. Now, are you going to let this disease get the best of you?"

"I haven't been sleeping too well for the past couple of days. The pain is getting worse. I'm tired all the time." A lone tear rolled down her cheek. "I don't feel like doing anything. I couldn't even go visit my mother. Today is her birthday."

Nicholas sat down beside her, wrapping an arm around her. "Sweetheart, I'm so sorry. I wish there was something I could do to make things better for you. I'm telling you, Sheila. You can't just give in to the disease. You've got to keep fighting."

Sheila wiped her eyes. "You might not want to get too close to me. I stink, remember?"

He laughed. "This will just show you what a good friend I am."

Sheila put a hand to her mouth, covering up her laughter. "You're crazy."

He rose from the sofa. "Sit here and I'll run your bath."

She made a move to stand. "Nicholas, you don't have to do that."

"Just sit down," he instructed a second time. "I'll come back and get you when it's ready."

Sheila sat there, stunned. Nicholas was actually down in one of the guest bathrooms, running water for her bath. Deep down, Sheila wanted to protest but just didn't have enough fight in her.

When he returned, Nicholas assisted her off the sofa. She remained silent as he escorted her to her waiting bath.

"I'll be right outside the door if you need me."

She smiled. "I think I can manage from here." Sheila paused in the doorway. "My robe is hanging behind the door of the bath in my room. Could you get it for me, please?" She knew Nicholas would not venture into her bedroom without permission, which was why he'd run the bath in the nearest guest bathroom.

He nodded.

By the time Sheila bathed and dressed in a skirt and halter top, she needed to sit down for a moment. Although the bubble bath had been soothing, she still felt tired.

She rested for about fifteen minutes, then stood up. "I'm ready. Please don't try to walk me around the whole neighborhood."

Chuckling, Nicholas vowed, "I won't, sweetheart. Just let me know when you're ready to come back home."

Sheila made it down four steps, then stopped suddenly.

"Why'd you stop?" Nicholas asked. "Something wrong?"

"I just need a minute." Sheila wasn't ready to admit she was having some problems navigating the last two steps, but she didn't want to fall on her face in front of Nicholas either.

"Hold on to my arm."

She pushed an errant curl away from her face. "I don't like what this disease is doing to me." Silently, she wondered, *What else is this disease going to do to me?*

"Your doctor told you to quit being stubborn, Sheila. I agree with her. Let's get that cane before you fall down and hurt yourself."

"You're the one who's always telling me not to give in to the MS." Sheila had spent a lifetime building this image of herself, and she needed more time to reassemble the pieces of her self-image in her mind before that image changed.

"That's not what you'll be doing. I think using a cane is actually a way to take back some control." Nicholas slowed his pace when it seemed Sheila couldn't keep up. "Look at it this way, you only have to use it when you need it."

"Nicholas, I know how I am. I find it strange to see a young person in a wheelchair or using a cane. I don't want people doing that to me."

"Then wear a sign that says, 'I have MS, so what's your problem?'"

Sheila burst into laughter, breaking the tension that was building between them. "Nicholas, you're crazy."

"Maybe a little. But the point is this, sweetheart . . . if you need assistance with walking—get it. If you don't, you're going to mess around and fall. And if you break your leg or your hip, what do you think you're going to use then?"

"People won't think twice if I'm wearing a cast. They can see something's wrong with me."

He sighed. "Do me a favor. Go with me to an MS support meeting. There's one tonight."

"Why?"

"I just think it'll be a good idea for you to meet other people dealing with MS. My aunt was recently diagnosed with a lump in her breast. She's having surgery in a few days. She found a support meeting for women with breast cancer. She needed to know what to expect and how to deal with the possibility of having cancer."

"Nicholas, I don't feel like sitting around in a room somewhere listening to a bunch of sob stories. I have my own issues."

"They're not always sad—sometimes the stories people share are inspirational and motivational."

The tender expression on his face made Sheila relent. "I'll go this time, Nicholas. But I'm only doing it for you."

"I don't want you doing anything just for me, Sheila. This has to be about you."

"I said I'd go."

Nicholas coerced her into going out for lunch. They didn't go too far from Sheila's house since she tired easily.

"I've been thinking of wearing my hair short," Sheila blurted once their meal had been served.

"I think you'll look beautiful."

She gave a short laugh. "Nicholas, you're just saying that. You've never seen me with my hair short."

"I happen to like short hair." He picked up his sandwich and took a bite.

"I'm only thinking about it because I'm having some trouble with my hands." Sheila pushed her hair behind her ears. "This morning I had a hard time using the curling iron. I almost called you to help me after I burned myself here." She showed him the small blistering souvenir left where her curling iron nicked her.

"I've never curled hair, but I could give it a try," he responded with a laugh.

"Well, you're no help at all."

They returned to Sheila's house after lunch.

Sheila lay on her sofa while Nicholas relaxed in the love seat, watching a movie.

She rose gingerly around five o'clock. "I need to freshen up and change my clothes if I'm going to this meeting with you."

"Sheila, you look fine."

"Thanks, but I'm still changing," she answered.

Nicholas gave a slight nod. "No problem."

Sheila navigated to her bedroom and selected a black dress and a pair of low-heeled black mules. She pulled her hair into a ponytail, securing it with a black and white barrette.

An hour later, they were on their way.

When Nicholas pulled into the YMCA parking lot, Sheila glanced over at him. "The support group meets here?"

"Yeah. Once a week. I found out about it when I came to sign up for the men's basketball league."

"Oh," Sheila mumbled.

She blinked twice when she strode into the room. Most of the people in the room seemed much younger than she was. They were using walkers or canes, and a couple of them were in wheelchairs.

"I can't believe I let you talk me into coming here," she whispered after a moment.

He tried to hide the irritation in his voice. "Sheila, don't be negative."

"Nicholas, I'm just not feeling this. It was a mistake coming here."

"We just got here. Give it a chance. Please."

Sheila sighed in resignation. "I'm only doing this for you."

"Thank you."

She gestured toward a couple of empty chairs. "Let's get this over with—"

Nicholas pulled her into his arms, kissing her softly on the lips.

Sheila glanced around to see if anyone was paying attention to them. "What was that about?"

"My way of saying thanks."

"I like the way you show gratitude." Sheila gave him a big smile. "What else can I do for you?"

"Watch out now . . ."

Nicholas and Sheila took a seat. They made small talk while they waited for the meeting to start.

Ten minutes later, the meeting began.

Sheila introduced herself, followed by Nicholas. This was about as much participation as she planned to give. She would not be sharing the pitiful details of how MS was affecting her life.

The young woman sitting beside Sheila began talking. "There were so many emotions that I had to deal with when I was first diagnosed with MS. There was fear, sadness and a lot of anger. I was only twenty and I had my whole life ahead of me. But it was Jesus Christ who helped me cope with all of these emotions. My greatest fear was being in a wheel-chair."

Several of the people in the room murmured in agreement.

"I had memories of how my life used to be, and dreams of how my life was going to be. It just wasn't fair . . ."

Sheila could really relate to what the young woman was saying.

". . . Being a believer in Jesus Christ, the first thing that helped me was prayer and meditation on the Word. I have never given up my faith that Jesus will be true to His promise when He said, *I will never leave thee nor forsake thee.* I trust Him with my life."

"Very well said," another woman responded. "I think of my MS as a gift. If I didn't have this disease, I don't think I'd value my life the way I do now. I'm not gonna let MS rob me of my peace and joy in life."

Stunned, Sheila couldn't believe she'd heard them correctly. They were actually sounding like they were happy about having MS. It had to be the medication talking.

Frowning, she stole a peek at Nicholas.

Across from where Sheila sat, a young woman in a wheelchair spoke. "When I found out I had MS, I just sat down and started giving God the praise. The second verse of the first chapter of James tells us that we should count it as joy when we face trials of every kind. I thank God for my condition, because it's brought me closer to Him. He has been so faithful— He even guided me as to what treatments to take in order to manage my symptoms. Like Krystal just said—I trust God completely. For those of you who are newly diagnosed or if you're here for the first time tonight— you can find rest in the Lord. I'm telling you what I know to be true."

Sheila had heard enough. She rose to her feet and walked toward the nearest exit.

Nicholas joined her a few minutes later in the hallway.

"Why did you walk out?"

"Did you hear what they were saying?" Sheila asked him. "They're in there acting like having MS is a gift or something. And that other woman—the one in the wheelchair. She actually thanked God for allowing MS to come into her life. Said it brought her closer to Him. Nicholas, these people are crazy."

"They're not crazy, Sheila. They just trust the Lord. Verse twenty-eight in the eleventh chapter of Matthew plainly says, *Come to me, all you who are weary and burdened, and I will give you rest.*"

"Well, I'm not happy about having this disease and I won't pretend that I am. I hate it."

"I don't think anyone is *happy* to have MS—what they are saying is that they are not going to just give up on life because of it."

"I don't care, because I'm not going back in there. I'm not good at coping with illness in the first place, Nicholas. It depresses me to listen to their stories."

"Is that the only reason?"

"What do you mean?"

"I believe that you don't want to go back inside because you believe that you're going to end up like them in a matter of months. Am I right?"

"Yes," Sheila whispered. "Nicholas, I can't do this right now. This disease is tearing down my body and I'm powerless to do anything about it." She shook her head sadly. "Please take me home. I can't go back in there."

Nicholas wrapped an arm around her. "Okay, sweetheart. Let's go. I'll take you home."

Sunday after church, Nicholas hit I-95 south to Brunswick. His aunt was due to have surgery Monday morning. She was nervous whenever it came to doctors and hospitals, so he wanted to be there to comfort her.

But today, the twelfth of June, was also his aunt and uncle's wedding anniversary. She didn't want to celebrate until after the surgery, so Nicholas planned to surprise them with a cruise. They would board the *Emerald Princess* next month for a cruise to Puerto Rico.

While he drove, Nicholas couldn't get Sheila out of his mind. He'd hoped the meeting last night would help—maybe it could have if she hadn't stormed out the way she did.

Sheila was stubborn. She wanted nothing to do with God because she blamed Him for the MS. Nicholas prayed Sheila would come to understand that only the Lord could get her through this ordeal. MS was not an easy road but with Jesus in her life, Sheila would come to know that He would make up for all she had lost.

"Father God, please open Sheila's heart to You," he whispered. "She desperately needs You in her life. She just hasn't realized it yet."

He exited the interstate and made his way through town to Amherst Street, where his aunt Lily and her husband Pete lived. He parked in front of their house and got out.

His uncle met him at the front door. "Hey, son. Lily Belle was just calling yo' house to see if you was on the road yet."

"I told her I was coming after church. We had a meeting after the service today." Nicholas walked into the house after his uncle.

"I'm here, Aunt Lily," he called out.

A slender woman with salt-and-pepper hair strolled out of the kitchen. "I just called your house."

Nicholas embraced his aunt. Sometimes it pained him to look at her, because she looked just like his mother, Lulu Mae. They were identical twins. She was the only family he had left on the East Coast. He had never been close to his father's West Coast relatives.

"How you feeling, Aunt Lily?"

"I'm okay. Just ready to get this over with."

He knew she was referring to the surgery. His aunt was scheduled to have a biopsy because a lump had been discovered in her breast.

"Aunt Lily, if we ask anything according to God's will, He hears us. And because we know He hears us, whatever we ask—we know that we have what we asked of Him."

"Amen," Lily murmured. "Thank you for that reminder. My peace only comes from Jesus."

Nicholas nodded.

"I made some chicken, collard greens, macaroni and cheese. You hungry?"

"Starved," Nicholas answered.

Over dinner they continued talking. Nicholas presented them with the cruise tickets right after dessert was served.

"So is there a special lady in your life?"

Nicholas shook his head no. "No, ma'am. Not yet."

"I been praying for you to find a wife," Lily announced.

He laughed. "Thanks, Aunt Lily. I know I don't have to worry about a thing with you and God on the job."

His uncle chuckled.

"Alright, mister. At least you won't have to worry if she's marrying you or your money."

Three hours later, Lily had turned in for the evening while Nicholas and Pete settled in the den to watch television.

That night, Nicholas prayed for his aunt and for Sheila.

His aunt had a successful surgery the next morning. Nicholas stayed with her most of the day before going home with his uncle.

Nicholas made dinner for the two of them. Pete didn't have much of an appetite.

"You're worried about Aunt Lily." It was a statement.

"I can't lose her. I saw what it did to you and Lily when your mother died . . . I don't know if I can be as strong."

Pete looked like he wanted to cry. He truly feared losing his wife.

Nicholas offered what comfort he could.

CHAPTER SEVENTEEN

Nicholas remained in Brunswick for two more days before leaving for home, but not before promising to return the following weekend.

One of the first things he did upon his return was check in with Sheila. He'd missed her.

"How did everything go?" she inquired after they exchanged pleasantries.

"Great. We're waiting to hear the results of the biopsy. I'm believing that Aunt Lily's test comes back cancer-free, though."

"I know you were really worried about her. The two of you seem really close."

"We are."

They talked for a few minutes more before Nicholas hung up to start work on a project.

A couple of hours later, the incessant buzzing of the doorbell distracted him. Nicholas typed in one last word before getting up to answer the front door.

"Tori . . . hey," he greeted. "What are you doing on this side of town?"

She tried to look past him into the house. "I was just about to leave— it took you a while to answer the door. Did I interrupt anything?"

"No." Nicholas moved aside. "C'mon in."

"I thought maybe you had company or something."

Closing the front door, Nicholas broke into laughter. "You thought Sheila was here, didn't you?"

"It's a possibility, right? Jake and I saw y'all the other night at Robert's."

Tori took a seat in the burgundy leather chair in the living room. "What's really going on between you and Sheila?"

Folding his arms across his chest, he said, "Tori, don't start this again . . ." There was a critical tone to his voice.

"Jake didn't want me to say anything to you about this, but you know me—I just can't keep silent. You're my best friend and I care about you, Nicholas. I don't want Sheila hurting you, too."

Nicholas sat down on the arm of his sofa, facing her. He spoke calmly, saying, "Tori, I told you that there's nothing for you to worry about."

She disagreed. "I wish I could believe that. Nicholas, you just don't know Sheila like I do."

"I've spent some time with her, Tori," he countered. "Sheila's not the same person. She's changed quite a bit."

Shaking her head, Tori responded, "She's an actress. Sheila knows how to play the game well. Trust me on this."

Nicholas stood his ground with her. "This is not a game."

Frustrated, Tori fluffed up her hair. "Tell me the truth, Nicholas. Do you have feelings for Sheila?"

"Yeah," he replied after a moment.

"Are you in love with her?"

Nicholas shook his head no. "I wouldn't call it love, Tori. But I do care a great deal for her."

She sighed in resignation. "You two are becoming close then?"

"I think so."

Tori gave him a sad look. "Nicholas, I have to be honest—I think you're making a big mistake. I just want to go on record saying that Sheila is not the woman for you."

"It's not your decision, Tori. If you remember, I told you a long, long time ago that Jake wasn't the man for you—yet you've proved me wrong."

Anger flashed in her eyes. "My situation is totally different and you know it."

"The point is, I didn't believe Jake was the one for you until a few years ago. He made mistakes. Sheila is flawed, but so am I. Nobody's perfect."

"Nicholas, I hear what you're saying. Really I do."

"Why don't we just agree to disagree on this subject?" Nicholas suggested. "My relationship with Sheila is my business, Tori. I'd like for you to respect that."

"You're right," she conceded. "You'll just have to find out for yourself, so I'll back off. Just don't be expecting me and Jake to go double-dating with y'all."

"Understood." Nicholas relaxed. He and Tori would be alright, although she wasn't happy about his relationship with Sheila. Their friendship was safe now, but if he and Sheila actually fell in love—could Tori handle that?

Tori arrived at the Wentworth Mansion two hours after Jake summoned her. As soon as she walked into the hotel, she felt like she'd been transported back to the Gilded Age, a time of refinement. Wentworth Mansion was unlike any other hotel Tori had ever visited.

The hotel was the former home of a wealthy cotton merchant and featured original Louis Comfort Tiffany glass windows, which Tori loved. The hotel also boasted crystal chandeliers, marble mantels and elaborate fireplaces.

She'd been trying to get Jake to book a romantic weekend getaway at the Wentworth Mansion for years, but he considered it a waste of good money.

Her husband met her in the lobby a few minutes later.

"You look beautiful," Jake murmured after greeting her with a kiss.

Tori eyed Jake from head to toe. "When did you get this suit? I don't remember ever seeing it."

"That's because I bought it earlier today."

"It looks great on you, Jake. Like it was made just for you."

Smiling, he said, "I'm glad you like it."

"Are we eating at Circa 1886?"

Jake nodded.

As they waited to be led to their table, she glanced around. "I thought this was a dinner meeting with some of your clients."

"No," Jake responded. "It's just the two of us tonight."

"But—"

Jake cut Tori off. "I wanted to surprise you."

"You and my mother were in on this together, weren't you? I wondered why she insisted on coming up this weekend." Tori broke into a smile. "You're such a sweetie. Thank you."

Jake embraced her. "I have another surprise for you."

Tori laughed. "I don't think you'll be able to top this. Do you remember the first and only time we came to Circa 1886?"

He nodded. "When we got engaged. My mother brought us here to celebrate the engagement."

"I wanted to have our wedding here in the hotel, but Mama insisted we had to have it in a church."

They were seated within minutes of arriving.

Tori settled in across from Jake, admiring how handsome her husband looked.

They both decided on the spicy grilled shrimp over fried green tomatoes as the first course.

"Two date nights in a month," Tori began. "I'm not sure I know how to act. This is really sweet, Jake."

He leaned forward, saying, "I love you, honey, and I want you to know it."

"I do," she assured him. "And I love you, too."

"Lately . . . since Sheila's been back, you seem kind of—"

Tori cut him off. "Hon, I'm not worried about Sheila. I know you love me. I've never doubted that. I just don't want Sheila back in our lives."

"I love you enough to leave Madison-Moore, if I have to," Jake told her. "You and our children mean more to me than that company. I mean it."

Tori had waited a long time to hear those words. *Thank you, Father God.*

Meeting his gaze, she said, "I appreciate the thought, but I know how much you love Madison-Moore. That's not an easy decision to make."

"But a necessary one, nonetheless, if I have to choose between my marriage and the company."

"Well, if that time comes—we'll discuss it."

After dinner, Jake led her toward the elevator.

Puzzled, Tori asked, "Where are we going now?"

"I booked a suite for us," he announced.

"Wow, you're really doing it up good."

"I know how much you've always wanted to stay here. I called your mother and she's watching the children for us until we come home tomorrow."

Tori embraced Jake. "You are such a sweetheart. That's why I love you so much."

When Jake unlocked the door to their suite, Tori gasped.

"Oh, my goodness," she exclaimed. "This room is stunning." She felt like she'd walked into a piece of heaven.

Tori went over to the fresh floral arrangement and sniffed, inhaling deeply.

"We're scheduled to have a couple's massage," Jake announced. "In half an hour."

She broke into a big grin.

"We have chocolate strawberries and a bottle of champagne. I wanted tonight to be perfect."

"It is," Tori murmured, her eyes tear bright. "The perfect night to make a baby."

Jake wrapped his arms around her. "That's the idea."

Sheila gave herself an injection of Copaxone. Since the first injection, she hadn't experienced the tightness in her chest or any problems with her breathing.

She was sick and tired of being sick and tired. Sheila was the type of person who ignored ailments, but with MS constantly in her face—she couldn't deny it.

Sheila was no longer in control of her life.

Her condition could do whatever it wanted to her and she was helpless to do anything about it, but Sheila had never been one to quit.

Until now.

This is one battle I'm not winning and it's driving me crazy. I'm depressed, she decided. Her doctor had offered to prescribe Prozac, but Sheila refused the prescription. She was already taking about twenty pills a day.

Okay. Maybe not exactly twenty. But more than one was too many.

The next morning, Sheila cringed at the thought of getting out of bed. She was in no mood to face the world.

Nicholas had suggested she see a therapist, but Sheila wasn't having it. She didn't need a shrink—she just needed to feel normal again.

Nicholas was due to arrive shortly, and Sheila still hadn't showered. She sat on the edge of her bed, trying to summon the strength to move. She wondered if Nicholas's broad shoulders ever tired of her burden. He was always so patient with her.

It took Sheila a full ten minutes to make it to the bathroom and into the shower. She turned on the water and stepped beneath the spray, wishing the drops could rinse away the fatigue that tormented her body.

Sheila became painfully aware that her skin craved the sensual touch of a man. She craved sex, no denying that.

But what she missed most was simply feeling a man's arms around her. Jake was the only man she'd ever really wanted. Now she didn't even want Jake—hadn't since he treated her so badly.

Sheila turned off the water and had just begun to dry herself when her mind suddenly conjured up a flash of Nicholas lying naked in her bed.

"No," Sheila blurted. "Not him."

Great. How am I supposed to face Nicholas now? Lusting for him like this.

Determined not to go there, she pinned her hair into a bun at her nape and decided to forego makeup. She simply didn't care how she looked today.

Nicholas had told her on many occasions that she was beautiful without it—well, he was in for a rude awakening this morning.

She had just slipped on her Keds when the doorbell sounded. Perfect timing. Sheila slowly made her way to the front door.

Nicholas took one look at her and said, "Your skin is flawless, Sheila. You don't need all that makeup."

She didn't buy it. It was easier to believe all the kids she'd grown up with—the ones who constantly teased her for being skinny as a rail—for being dark and ugly. She believed her father—the man who left because she was way too dark to be his daughter.

"You had a rough night?" he asked out of concern.

"Sort of," Sheila responded. "I woke up feeling so stiff and out of sorts. I wish I could just lock myself in a room and never come out."

"You have a swimsuit?"

"Yeah," Sheila said, confused. "Why?"

"We can go swimming in your pool. I think it'll help with some of the stiffness."

"I can't swim, remember?"

"We won't get in the deep end. Besides, I'll save you."

"I don't know . . ." Sheila brushed back her hair with her hand. The image of Nicholas in swim trunks with the outline of his body straining against the fabric filled her mind.

His words cut into her musings. "You don't trust me?"

"Nicholas, don't . . . that's not it at all." Sheila rose to her feet and moved to stand in front of the fireplace. "When I was sixteen, I wanted to be friends with a certain group of girls and boys in my school. Anyway, they invited me to join them at a pool party, and two of the guys threw me in the pool. I almost drowned."

"How did you get out?"

"One of the girls eventually jumped in and pulled me out. The others thought it was funny."

"Didn't they know you couldn't swim?"

"I can't remember how it all started, but I know the boys decided they were going to throw all the girls in the water. The girls all kept screaming they couldn't swim but they did know how to—I was the only one who didn't."

Sheila placed a hand over her rapidly beating heart. "Just thinking about it even now brings on anxiety. I never had anything to do with any of them after that."

Nicholas got up. "I'm sorry you had to go through something like that."

Sheila waved her hand in dismissal. "It was just one humiliation after another in high school."

Nicholas walked over to her. "Whatever happened back then made you strong. Look at the woman you are today, Sheila."

He always seemed to know just what to say. She eyed him, recalling the fantasy of him in her bed.

Get a grip, Sheila chided herself. *Or I'm not going to be able to look Nicholas in the eye.* Her ears commenced to throbbing with every heartbeat.

Sheila came out of her lapse to find Nicholas peering at her, his brows drawn together.

"Are you okay? Your breathing's kind of funny."

Mortified, Sheila felt a tingling erupt that left her hands and legs feeling weak. "I'm fine. Just having another hot flash."

"Maybe a dip in the pool will cool you down," Nicholas suggested.

Semihysterical laughter erupted from her mouth. She needed a dip in her pool all right.

He peered at Sheila in concern.

"I think that I will try getting into the pool. I'm trusting you, Nicholas. I had nightmares for a long time after I almost drowned back then."

"I promise to keep you safe, Sheila."

His hand firmly on her elbow, Nicholas guided her to the hallway. "Go put on your swimsuit."

Smiling, Sheila did as she was told.

She returned a few minutes later. "I guess I'm ready."

"I'll get my swim trunks out of the car and change."

Sheila stood in the doorway watching Nicholas, admiring the way his jeans fit his body.

Great. I've got the hots for him. Sheila groaned at the thought. She walked past the mirror in the hallway, pausing long enough to hiss "Traitor" at her reflection.

Sheila woke up Sunday morning feeling a strong sense of accomplishment. Nicholas had been very patient and understanding while teaching her to swim.

She couldn't really call herself a swimmer yet, but at least she wasn't afraid to put her face in the water anymore. With Nicholas's help, she'd conquered that fear.

Just the thought of him made Sheila flush warmly. She tried to convince herself that her lust for Nicholas was just that—lust for male companionship and intimacy. She would feel this way about any man.

Liar.

Sheila glanced nervously around, as if the accusation had been spoken aloud.

She was attracted to Nicholas and could no longer deny it.

He would never know. Sheila vowed to make sure of it. She would never allow herself to be humiliated again.

CHAPTER EIGHTEEN

~~~

The congregation applauded when Nicholas finished his solo. He returned to his place in the choir stand and sat down.

Pastor Henry stood at the podium saying, "Thank you, Brother Washington, for that song. 'Amazing Grace' . . . a song like that really ministers to my soul." He paused a moment to gather himself.

"I would like to talk to you right now about how God is the God of second chances. In life, there aren't always second chances given to us. Too many times, people don't give us a second chance in life to make things right. Now, why is that?"

He paused a heartbeat, then said, "Because people are quick to judge us. God, however, is slow to judge us because He knows what's in our hearts already, whereas people don't. I want you to know that God sees each of us as His favorite, and because of this He will give us a second chance when we make a mistake . . ."

Sheila came to Nicholas's mind as his pastor continued with his sermon. He had invited her to church on several occasions, but she always refused. He wished she'd come to hear this particular sermon.

After church, Nicholas went home and took a nap. He'd stayed at Sheila's house until one in the morning.

They'd rented three movies after her swimming lesson and watched all of them back-to-back.

When Nicholas woke up a short time later, he got up and made dinner. He was just about to sit down and eat when Sheila called.

"How're you feeling?" Nicholas asked.

"Today is a good day. I think the water might have helped. I'm thinking about getting back in today. Not the deep end."

"Maybe you should wait until someone's there," he suggested. "To make sure—"

"I don't hurt myself, and can get out safely," Sheila finished for him.

"I promised to keep you safe, didn't I?"

Nicholas could almost feel the warmth of her smile. "Why don't you wait until I can come over?"

"When?"

"I was just about to eat dinner. I can come afterward."

"Okay. Sure."

"Have you eaten yet?"

"No," she answered. "I don't have much of an appetite these days."

"I'll bring you a plate. I made smothered chicken and a spinach salad."

"Sounds delicious."

"I'll be there within the hour."

Nicholas hung up.

His feelings for Sheila were intensifying, wrapping around him like a warm blanket.

Sheila wasn't a bad person. She had issues, for sure. But she wasn't all bad.

Nicholas prepared two plates and covered them. He decided to eat with Sheila.

Half an hour later, Nicholas walked into Sheila's house carrying the plates.

"I made some lemonade," she announced. "It's about the only thing I make well."

He laughed. "One day I'm going to give you a cooking lesson."

Sheila shook her head as she accepted the plate of food. "Don't bother. I don't cook by choice. One day I plan to have enough money to hire a chef."

She took a bite of her chicken. "Nicholas, this is wonderful."

"Thank you," he murmured.

An invisible web of attraction was weaving between them. Nicholas felt it and wondered if Sheila felt it, too.

He wrenched himself away from his preoccupation. He had no right thinking of Sheila in this way. His getting involved with her could only make matters worse. Besides, Nicholas still doubted whether Sheila was over Jake.

An hour and a half after eating, Nicholas gave Sheila another swimming lesson.

He could tell from her excitement and laughter that Sheila was really enjoying herself. She actually looked happy.

Later in the house, Sheila sat toweling her wet hair.

"Thanks so much, Nicholas . . . for everything." She broke into a grin. "By the end of summer, I might be swimming like a fish. I'm going to enroll in private lessons tomorrow."

"See . . . the water isn't as bad as you thought."

Sheila nodded. "You're right. At least I can put my head under the water now. Yesterday, I could only put my face in."

Nicholas was caught up in her enthusiasm, and felt a certain sadness that their day was ending. It was almost eight and he could see that Sheila was wearing down. She looked tired.

"Sweetheart, you look exhausted," he said, rising to his feet. "I'm going to leave so that you can get some rest."

Sheila smiled. "Okay. I need to try and do something with my hair anyway." She got up and walked him to the door.

His fingers ached to reach over and touch her, but Nicholas maintained his control. He walked away, trying to ignore the strange aching in his limbs.

Sheila was nearly bored out of her mind by the time Wednesday came around.

She was tired of sitting at home and doing nothing but reading. Several times throughout the day, she'd been tempted to call Jake and ask for a project to work on at home; she just wasn't used to having so much idle time.

Sheila liked to stay busy. It kept her mind off her problems.

She'd hoped decorating her new house would keep her occupied, but it hadn't. She'd started painting one of the guest rooms, but couldn't finish because of fatigue.

Sheila answered the telephone on the second ring. "Hello."

"Hey, what are you doing?" Nicholas asked.

"Looking at this half-painted room over here. I started on it almost two weeks ago and I haven't finished it yet. It looked a lot easier in the books. It's not so much the actual painting itself—it's all the taping up stuff. It's working my nerves."

"I assumed you would've hired painters."

"I was going to, but since I'm home every day bored to death, I figured I'd just try painting it myself. I was trying to stay busy, but I'm too pooped to finish."

"Dr. Daniels changed your medication. It's not helping with the fatigue?" asked Nicholas.

"Not really," she answered. "Maybe it hasn't kicked in or something. Dr. Daniels checked my blood to see if there are some other problems like anemia."

"When will you know?"

"Hopefully soon."

It made Sheila feel good to know that Nicholas was so concerned about her. He was always inquiring about her health—almost as if he were keeping notes.

"I just don't get you," Sheila blurted. "Why do you care so much?"

"Because I do. Sheila, get used to it. I care a great deal about you."

It thrilled her that he cared, but Sheila wanted Nicholas to find her desirable.

They ended the call after he insisted on getting someone to finish the painting project for her.

The following Saturday, Sheila opened the door to Nicholas. Frowning, she asked, "What in the world are you wearing?"

She took a peek outside, glancing from one side to the other. "Get in here. My neighbors probably think you're some homeless person begging door-to-door."

Nicholas glanced down at his clothes. "I wore clothes I don't mind getting paint on."

"Paint? You came over here to paint."

"Yeah."

Sheila was touched beyond words. She cleared her throat, pretending not to be affected by his thoughtfulness. "I thought you were going to hire a painter. I didn't think that you meant to do it yourself."

"I painted my house. I enjoy painting."

Sheila surprised herself when she threw her arms around him. "Thank you so much, Nicholas. I really appreciate this."

She felt the electricity of his touch when he hugged her back, and she thought she detected a flicker in his intense gray eyes.

His nearness kindled feelings of fire.

Sheila reluctantly broke the embrace. "I guess you should get started," she murmured.

She led him down the hall to the bedroom. Sheila stood in the doorway watching him as he set up. She couldn't tear her gaze from his profile.

The man is fine.

She left the room, heading to her bedroom where she changed into an old T-shirt and a pair of shorts.

She went back to join Nicholas.

"What do you think you're doing?" he asked when she picked up a roll of blue painter's tape.

"I'm helping you," Sheila responded.

"I don't need any help. You can stay to keep me company though."

Sheila dropped down on the covered queen-sized bed. "Works for me. I didn't really feel like painting anyway."

Nicholas laughed.

While he continued going around the room, taping and covering furniture, molding and baseboards, Sheila watched him in silence.

Around noon, she heard her stomach growl. She got up, saying, "I'm going to make some sandwiches."

Nicholas nodded, but continued painting.

She walked to the kitchen, her heartbeat throbbing in her ears. Nicholas was so compelling, his magnetism so potent.

Initially, Sheila had intended to use him to try to get back at Tori, but now she wanted Nicholas—the man.

Okay . . . I must be crazy to even think about him in this way. He's only being nice to me because I have MS. He would never look at me otherwise.

Sheila heard footsteps and turned around.

"Lunch ready?" Nicholas inquired.

"Almost," she answered. She piled on ham and pepper jack cheese, then laid lettuce and tomato before topping it with a slice of wheat bread.

She handed the sandwich to Nicholas.

Sheila could hardly eat, his nearness was so overwhelming. She was forming an attachment to Nicholas, and the thought of being rejected by him took away her appetite.

Sheila silently chided herself. She had a disease that would worsen over time. Nicholas would never want to be saddled with a woman like her. She could not afford to be carried away by her emotions.

Besides, this was all about getting back at Tori, she reminded herself.

Determined to stay focused, Sheila pushed her growing feelings for Nicholas to the back of her mind.

Three days later, the rest of the bedrooms were painted and decorated.

Sheila and Nicholas went from room to room, admiring their efforts.

"It looks great, Nicholas," Sheila murmured. "You did a wonderful job."

Smiling, Nicholas replied, "I'm glad you're pleased with the results."

He and Sheila had gone shopping earlier, and he'd even offered suggestions to help her decorate. Nicholas noted that he and Sheila had very similar taste in colors and furniture.

"I love it," Sheila stated as they toured each bedroom. "Now this house truly looks and feels like mine. My personality is all through it."

Nicholas agreed. "It looks really nice. Now we should go over to my house and do something to it."

"Feeling inspired, huh?"

He nodded. "I am. I've been wanting to do something to the guest rooms. I want to take out all that wallpaper."

"Let's do it," Sheila suggested. "I may not be able to help paint, but I can definitely boss you around."

They both laughed.

Sheila didn't have any idea of the power she held with that beautiful smile of hers. Nicholas never tired of looking at her—he enjoyed seeing her happy and pain-free.

That evening they went to dinner to celebrate.

"We make a great team," Sheila said. "Don't you think?"

Nicholas agreed. "Yeah . . . we do."

He was in love with Sheila.

Nicholas realized it at that very moment. This was no longer about friendship or lending support. His feelings ran much deeper than that.

For now, it would remain his secret. There was still much to learn about Sheila.

CHAPTER NINETEEN

～

"**P**astor Allen sho' preached this morning," Kate commented. "Didn't he?"

"He sure did," Tori agreed. "He was talking to me personally. Especially when he brought up the questions: How can I cope when I have ill feelings toward another? Should I trust someone I have forgiven? Or does forgiving imply forgetting? I have those same questions in my heart all the time." *Mainly where Sheila is concerned,* she added silently.

"Girl, you not the only one. I think we all feel that way from time to time. I know I do," Kate responded.

"I'm always saying I forgive, but I don't forget," Charlene contributed, "so I know Pastor was talking to me, too."

Smiling, Tori glanced over at her husband. "My heart was convicted when Pastor said forgiveness is something we have to do for ourselves because if we don't, we'll find ourselves filled with so much bitterness."

Tori was still struggling with forgiving Sheila. She just felt she couldn't forgive until the other woman acknowledged all she'd done.

"Yeah, he stomped on my toes a li'l bit when he said that," Kate admitted. "Now I know why I'm so ornery—I got a mess of people I need to be forgiving."

Folding her ample arms across her heaving chest, she stared pointedly in Jake and Shepard's direction while their wives burst into laughter.

Chuckling, Jake opened his Bible. "Aunt Kate, Pastor did offer some help with that. He said that if you didn't feel like forgiving, God could help you with it." He went through his notes. "Read the first chapter of Luke, the thirty-seventh verse."

"I have it memorized, so you don't need to look for it," Shepard announced with a chuckle. "It says, *For nothing is impossible with God.*"

Everyone broke into a round of laughter.

"Y'all was always a pair of smarty pants," Kate said with a chuckle.

"Leave my mama alone," Charlene said between bits of laughter. "She forgave your uncle a long time ago, and y'all for being such spoiled brats when she used to keep y'all. Right, Mama?"

"Now, I ain't saying all that," Kate stated. "I'm still a work in progress where the good Lord is concerned. I ain't gon' lie about that. I can hold on to a grudge better than I can a dollar. And you know I can keep money."

Her words sent them all into another wave of laughter.

While Jake and his brother settled in the family room, Charlene, Kate and Tori went upstairs with the children.

Tori considered calling Nicholas and inviting him to have dinner with them but changed her mind.

He was probably with Sheila. They seemed to be spending a lot of time together.

Frowning, Tori shook her head sadly. Nicholas was too good for a witch like Sheila.

Nicholas peeled a grape and popped it into Sheila's mouth.

"You'd better quit it—you're spoiling me," she warned with a small laugh. "I could get used to treatment like this."

"Peel your own grapes then."

She gave Nicholas a playful jab. "Don't be so mean."

He laughed.

Sheila eyed a group of children playing nearby. Nicholas seemed to really enjoy hanging out at the park on Sunday afternoons. They'd come out here a couple of times in the past three months.

When Sheila turned back in Nicholas's direction, she found him gazing intently at her. "What? Why are you looking at me like that?" She suddenly felt self-conscious—almost as if her soul had been bared.

"I like seeing you smile."

Sheila picked up an apple and bit into it, chewing thoughtfully. She swallowed before replying, "I haven't had a whole lot to smile about in my life."

Playing with the fringe on the end of the blanket they were sitting on, Sheila asked, "Have you ever felt like life just wasn't fair?"

Nicholas nodded. "A few times. But that was before I gave my life to the Lord. I was searching for something, but didn't know what it was until I got saved. I didn't know it at the time, but my heart was yearning for a relationship with God. That's what was missing in my life."

"God and me . . . I don't know . . ."

"What is it, Sheila?"

"I prayed for my relationship with Jake. I prayed for a relationship with my parents—one that children should have, a normal life—you know what I mean. Anyway, God never answered those prayers. He gave me a life of pain instead."

"I think we talked about this before, Sheila. Out of pain comes peace—you only have to trust the Lord and keep Him first. Seek Him first and all things will be added. But let me be clear—you will not always get what *you* think you want. You should ask instead for God's best for you."

Rolling her eyes heavenward, Sheila folded her arms across her chest. "So I'm just supposed to accept whatever is dished out to me?"

"That's not what I'm saying, Sheila."

"I always hear people saying that God answered their prayers for a house, husband, car—whatever. I only asked for two, no, three things and I didn't get any of them. He doesn't care about me."

"Sweetheart, God loves you. He *does*."

"Not enough to hear my prayers. That's why I stopped praying. There was no point."

Nicholas smiled.

"Why are you smiling?"

"Now I know one of the reasons why God brought us together. I'm supposed to show you the goodness of our Heavenly Father. Sheila, look around you and tell me what you see."

Confused, Sheila murmured, "A bunch of children laughing and playing. Parents walking around, talking to each other." Her gaze returned to him. "Trees, flowers . . . I'm not sure what you're asking me, Nicholas."

"Who could've created a better landscape than this?" he asked. "Imagine this on a canvas hanging in an art gallery."

Sheila observed her surroundings once more, slowly taking in the scenery before her. "If I were to paint an emotion, this scene would be the color of happiness."

"God is an awesome artist."

"Nicholas, how would you paint sadness?"

"When it rains, it reminds me of being sad, but it also gives me hope."

"Why do you say that?"

"Because there is always a rainbow at the end. What this tells me is that there will always be a brighter day after a storm. I look and live for those brighter days."

"Humph. I don't think I've ever looked at it quite that way." Sheila finished off her apple.

"You need to have some real fun," Nicholas decided.

Chuckling, Sheila agreed.

"Next Saturday, we're going to get up early and do something special."

"What?"

"It's a surprise."

"C'mon, Nicholas, tell me," Sheila teased.

She continued to plead with him until Nicholas reached over and pulled her into his arms.

"There's only one way I know how to shut you up."

Before Sheila could respond, Nicholas kissed her.

She responded hungrily, matching him kiss for kiss.

Her lips left his reluctantly. Sheila eyed him. "Nicholas, what are we doing?"

His gaze never left hers. "Exploring all of our options, I guess. Did I make you uncomfortable?"

"No . . . I just don't want to go back down Heartbreak Road again."

"I don't want to push you into anything, Sheila," Nicholas assured her.

"We're friends and I'm fine with leaving it at that. However, I'd like to see what develops. I know we're attracted to one another. Let's just take it one day at a time and see what happens."

"I'd like that," Sheila managed. She struggled to keep her thoughts unscrambled. She *really* liked Nicholas, but worried that she'd end up heartbroken.

He and Tori were very close. Sheila had a feeling that Tori would do whatever she could to ruin their relationship.

"Nicholas, how do you think Tori will feel about us?"

"She's not going to like it," he admitted. "But it's not about her. This only concerns you and me."

Pulling his face down to hers, Sheila kissed him again.

The feel of Sheila's lips was still imprinted on Nicholas's mouth. He didn't regret giving in to his feelings at all.

The more time Nicholas spent with Sheila, the more he wanted to see her. She was smart, witty and beautiful. If only he could get Sheila to see it for herself.

She felt defined by hair, physical attributes and wealth. Sheila depended on those things to make her happy. Little did she know that only God could give her the joy she craved.

He was all she needed in this world.

He'd invited Sheila to attend church with him several times, but each time she refused him. Nicholas continued to pray for her.

His lips turned upward at the thought of the upcoming weekend. He wondered how Sheila would react when she found out they were going deep-sea fishing.

Early the following Saturday, Sheila stood in her doorway eyeing Nicholas curiously from head to toe.

"Why are you dressed like that?" He'd told her to wear jeans but she hadn't expected him to look quite so casual. His pants looked as if he'd slept in them.

"I-I thought we were going somewhere today," she stammered in bewilderment.

"We are."

His response sent alarm bells ringing. "Where are we going with you wearing those jeans?" she asked, her hands on her hips.

"You'll see," Nicholas replied cryptically.

Sheila glanced down at what she was wearing: new jeans, a crisp white camisole top beneath a cropped denim jacket and matching denim mules.

"I told you to dress casually." Nicholas glanced down at her shoes. "Sweetheart, you might want to change into a pair of old sneakers."

Sheila became more uncomfortable by the minute. "Are we going slumming or something?"

Nicholas laughed, then shook his head.

Fuming, Sheila stalked off to her bedroom to change her shoes.

Where the hell is he taking me? she wondered. When Sheila returned a few minutes later, she resisted the urge to pull him into the laundry room and force him to iron those jeans he was wearing.

"Why won't you tell me where we're going?"

Nicholas embraced her. "It's a surprise, Sheila. I just need you to keep an open mind. Can you do this for me?"

Sheila nodded, although she was still wary. "This better not be some kind of prank. I don't have a sense of humor."

"I told you before—I don't play games."

During the drive, Sheila tried to figure out exactly where Nicholas was taking her.

When they pulled into the parking lot of Fish Call Charters at the Isle of Palms Marina, warning spasms of alarm erupted within her. "Nicholas, why did you bring me here? Don't tell me that you intend to fish . . ."

"*We're* going fishing."

"You've lost your ever-loving mind." Sheila folded her arms across her chest. She wrinkled her nose and shook her head. "*I don't fish.*"

"After this weekend, you won't be able to say that again." Nicholas got out of the car and walked around to open the door for Sheila.

"Humph," she muttered. "You mean to tell me that I went out and bought a new pair of jeans for this?"

"You didn't have to buy a new pair. You could have worn a pair of your old ones."

"I don't wear jeans, Nicholas," Sheila explained. "I didn't even own a pair until I bought these."

His eyes raked boldly over her. "They do look nice on you."

"I'm not fishing for compliments, Nicholas. In fact, I'm not fishing at all."

He embraced her. "This is going to be fun, sweetheart, and you're going to have a good time. I promise you."

"We're actually going to get on a boat and—"

"Go inshore fishing," Nicholas finished for her.

"I normally don't get on anything smaller than a cruise ship," Sheila stated with a slight grin of defiance.

Nicholas burst into laughter.

"I wouldn't do anything to bring harm to such a beautiful woman."

"Uh-huh." Sheila tried not to smile. "I have no choice but to trust you on this."

Eyeing the boat nearby, she pointed and asked, "Are we going fishing in *that*?"

"That's a 1720SE Hybrid flatboat," Nicholas answered, as if that mattered to Sheila. "It's really a nice little boat."

"How safe is it?"

"It's designed to keep us nice and dry—even in real choppy waters."

She could only nod.

Not too long after, they were in the boat, sailing away.

Sheila let her gaze drift over the wide expanse of sparkling blue-green water that drew her to the railing like a magnet.

She clung to the rail and leaned over, mesmerized by the way the boat split the tides with speed and diversity, taking them to the perfect location to cast their rods.

Sheila barely noticed the other boats with motors whining in the air ahead of them; she was caught up in the peaceful beauty of her surroundings.

"So what do you think?" Nicholas inquired, standing beside her.

Sheila glanced over at him. "It's beautiful, Nicholas." She swiveled slowly, her delight growing. "I love being out here on the water. It's so serene."

"Relaxing . . ."

"Yes," Sheila murmured. "It's very relaxing. You were right about this part. The fishing I don't know about . . ."

She and Nicholas sat down as the boat slowed its speed.

"I'll hold the pole for you. Put one hand down here and the other one on the base of the rod," Nicholas instructed. "Okay?"

She sighed. "This is not going to work."

"Sheila, just give it a try. You'll never really know if you like fishing until you actually try it."

"I can live with not knowing," she responded, abandoning all pretenses. "Honestly, Nicholas. It won't kill me to never know if I'd like fishing. It's just not something that'll keep me awake at night."

"I don't know why you keep saying you don't have a sense of humor—you're a funny lady. That's one of the reasons I like hanging out with you."

"After today, you might be changing your mind."

Nicholas shook his head no. "I doubt it."

She swung her head around to look at him. "I can't believe you really expect me to do this. I'll just watch while you fish. Okay?"

"C'mon, Sheila, you promised to keep an open mind. Remember?"

Tossing her hair across her shoulders, Sheila said, "You set me up and you know it. You knew I wouldn't be caught dead out here trying to catch a fish."

"You're the one always complaining that you're bored since taking your leave. Just look at it as an adventure."

"Well, I'm out here with nowhere to go." Sheila glanced out at the water. "I'm probably not going to catch a thing anyway."

"Give it time," Nicholas encouraged with a chuckle.

"How will I know if I catch something?"

"You'll feel a little tug on your line," Nicholas explained.

Sheila made a face. "I'm not touching it. I just want to make that clear right off the bat. I'm not touching any slimy fish."

Nicholas cast his fishing line into the water. "I sure hope we do catch something. That's dinner."

"Excuse me?"

"We're catching our dinner."

"I'm definitely not cleaning any fish."

"I'll do it," Nicholas responded with a laugh. "I'll even fry the fish."

"I have a feeling that we'll be having dinner in a nice restaurant some-where. Especially if you're waiting on me to bring the meal."

Sheila felt a tug on her line and squealed, surprising Nicholas.

"Honey, what's wrong?"

"The fishing pole!" Sheila shouted. "It moved! I felt it move, Nicholas. What am I supposed to do now?"

He reached over and checked her pole. There was a splash and he felt the strong tug of a hooked fish.

"I caught a fish!" Sheila screamed. "I caught one!" She was excited over her first catch—more than she ever thought she would be.

"Pull him in, sweetheart," Nicholas instructed.

Sheila held on to her rod as tightly as she could. "I can't. It's trying to get away and take my pole with it."

Together they reeled in Sheila's catch.

"You caught a redfish," Nicholas stated. "A good-sized one, at that. You're lucky it didn't bend the rod."

Sheila squealed and jumped out of the way of the flopping fish. "Oh, my goodness," she murmured. "It's huge."

Nicholas embraced her. "You did good, baby."

Sheila was grinning from ear to ear. "I caught a fish. I can't believe it."

"A real good catch, sweetheart," Nicholas said with a big grin on his face.

"I want to do it again." Sheila pointed to the pole. "But I'm not put-ting bait on that. You have to do it, Nicholas."

Not long after, Sheila caught a smaller one just as Nicholas felt the fa-miliar tug on his rod. She felt a sense of pride at being able to reel in her fish by herself this time.

They decided to call it a day when Nicholas caught his tenth and Sheila her eighth fish. She was getting tired.

When they were back in the car, Nicholas asked, "So what do you think of our little adventure today?"

Sheila smiled. "It wasn't as bad as I thought it would be—I had a great time with you."

"So, do you think you can trust me from now on?"

She nodded.

"Ready to try crabbing?"

Sheila burst into laughter. "Not really. Let me get the hang of this fishing thing first. Okay?"

Nicholas smiled and gave a slight nod.

An hour later, they were back at his house. Sheila watched Nicholas in awe as he expertly cleaned all the fish they'd caught.

He offered her the knife. "Want to give it a try?"

"No, thanks," Sheila replied. "I only want to touch my fish after it's cooked."

CHAPTER TWENTY

S he sat so near Nicholas that she had to feel the quickened rising and falling of his chest.

Nicholas often considered Sheila a ticking time bomb, but today he'd seen something else. She'd actually let her hair down enough to enjoy herself on the boat.

Sheila sampled the redfish she'd caught. "Mmmmm...this is so good." Her eyes traveled to Nicholas. "You're really a great cook. Homemade potato salad, coleslaw and hush puppies. Wow." She forked up a bite of potato salad and put it in her mouth, chewing slowly.

"I saw a different side of you today."

"What side was that?" she asked without looking up from her plate.

"Your adventurous and competitive side. You were starting to get upset when I caught more fish than you."

Sheila laughed. "I wasn't getting upset. I just wanted to be the one to bring home more fish. At least I caught the biggest."

"I'm very proud of you for being such a good sport about this."

"I actually had a good time, Nicholas. And we have something in common." Grinning, she added, "You're a little competitive yourself."

"I think we have a lot in common," he replied. "We like the same types of music and movies. We like a lot of the same foods..."

"We do have quite a bit in common," Sheila acknowledged. "For example, you're the perfect gentleman. The type of man who marries the girl next door. Me . . . well, let's just say that I'm not that girl."

Sheila wiped her mouth on a napkin, then laid it on her plate. "What are you doing, Nicholas?"

"I'm taking it one day at a time," Nicholas answered.

"What are you talking about, exactly?" Sheila didn't want to make the wrong assumption. "Are you trying to keep me distracted so I won't go after Jake?"

His face went grim. "Sheila, I'm not into playing games."

"Don't be mad. I'm just trying to be honest with you."

"I'm not angry, but I figured you knew me better than that."

"It's me, Nicholas. I have some huge trust issues—just blame it on my father and my mother."

"This is the first time I've heard you speak of your father."

"For good reason, I assure you. He's not worth the words that'll come out of my mouth. My daddy left us two days after my fifth birthday. After he left, my mother became so depressed she couldn't even function without pills and alcohol. For the next five years, I basically raised myself and took care of her."

Sheila's eyes filled with tears. "I had to hold in my pain to take care of her. She should've been taking care of me." She wiped away a tear. "I needed her."

"What about the men in your life? Other than Jake."

She let out a short laugh. "There were no other men. Jake and I went to college together. I've loved him since the first day I met him. In high school, nobody hardly even talked to me except to make fun of the way I talked and looked, or to get my class notes. It was pretty much the same way in college—Jake was the only person who treated me like I was somebody. He was nice to me."

Sheila stopped. "I didn't mean to tell you that."

"Why not? Still trying to shut me out?"

"Nicholas, I just want to forget everything that's happened. Do you understand what I'm saying?"

He nodded. "I believe I do."

She looked over to see if Nicholas was serious. He seemed to be.

"Okay, I shared my sad story with you. Tell me if you've ever been heart-broken."

"What do you think?"

"I don't think so," Sheila responded quickly. "Not the golden boy."

"You're wrong. I've had my heart broken a few times."

"Who in the world would hurt you?"

"There was a young lady I went to college with. I knew I always wanted to be a writer, but she had it in her head that I should be a doctor. She had planned on becoming a lawyer. Her mother was a lawyer and her father a doctor."

"She wanted the two of you to be just like them?"

Nicholas nodded. "She said I was being stubborn and unrealistic when I refused. She then made it clear that she wasn't interested in taking care of a man."

"So what happened?"

"We broke up."

"I wonder what she thinks of you now."

"She thinks that we'd make a great team."

Sheila's brows rose in surprise. "You've talked to her since college?"

"Yeah. About a month ago."

"Are you thinking about getting back with her?"

Nicholas shook his head no. "The fact that she had no faith in me and my dreams really hurt me. She didn't really love me back then, and I doubt anything has changed."

"What about your ex-wife?"

"We outgrew each other."

"From your tone, I take it that you don't want to talk about your marriage."

"I'd prefer not to discuss Alexis at all."

"Okaay . . . Sounds like you don't forgive easily."

"I wouldn't say that. I forgive because it's the right thing to do. I just try not to make the same mistake twice."

"I like that," Sheila said.

"What are you doing on the fourth?"

"That's next Monday, huh?"

Nicholas nodded.

"Nothing. At one time I'd thought about having a pool party but I just haven't had the energy to plan one."

"I'm driving down to Brunswick. My family always hosts a big barbecue for Independence Day. You think you'd be up to the trip?"

Sheila broke into a big smile. "As long as I'm not driving—I should be okay."

"Good. You'll get to meet my family."

"You sure you want to introduce me to your family?"

"Yeah, why not? Would you believe I want to show you off? I have quite a few teenage cousins and I want them to meet you—you'd be a great role model for them. You're smart and you worked very hard to achieve your dreams."

Sheila burst into laughter. "Okay. If you say so."

"But there is one condition." Nicholas held up one finger. "You've got to promise me that you'll leave all your troubles here in South Carolina."

"I'll try."

The hope spread from Nicholas's mouth to his eyes and as he fixed them on her, Sheila raised a warning finger.

"I'm not making any better promise than that. When are you planning to leave?"

When Nicholas moved forward to kiss her, Sheila's lips were already on his and her arms clung tightly around his neck.

Sheila woke up early on the Fourth of July. She climbed out of bed, showered and hurriedly dressed in a pair of denim walking shorts and a yellow cotton shirt. She tied a multicolored scarf around her waist, then checked in the mirror to see how she looked.

She and Nicholas had driven down to Brunswick yesterday. She'd met his aunt and uncle briefly before going to the hotel. The drive had worn her out.

This morning she felt energized—how long it would last was the million-dollar question.

Sheila hadn't seen much, but it was enough to fall in love with Jekyll Island. Nicholas had promised to take her on a tour of Saint Simons Island as well before they left Georgia.

Nicholas reserved a room for her in the Jekyll Island Club Hotel, in-stinctively knowing she would prefer staying on the island.

He knew her too well.

Sheila had a light breakfast because she wanted to take a walk along the ten-mile beach before it became too hot for her.

She strolled along the ocean's edge, loving the pungent smell emanat-ing from the water. For a brief moment, Sheila wished she'd invited Nicholas to join her. He would enjoy being surrounded by fresh air, sandy beaches and miles of ocean.

Sheila had almost asked Nicholas to stay with her at the hotel, but didn't want to rush whatever was going on between them.

Things had changed the day Nicholas took her fishing. They had grown closer over the past few months, but Sheila had never really antic-ipated they would become more than friends.

After her walk, Sheila returned to her room to take a short nap. She planned to be well-rested by the time Nicholas picked her up for his family's barbecue.

His aunt and uncle were nice people, and welcomed Sheila with open arms. It was obvious they loved each other very much, giving hope to Sheila that romance was still alive and well. It was also very clear that they adored Nicholas.

As hard as she tried, she couldn't imagine what it would be like to have such a close family. Her mother had been an only child; her father had siblings, but Sheila didn't know them or where they lived. He also had other children, but Sheila had never met them either.

"Honey, why you over here sitting all by yourself?" Lily asked, bring-ing Sheila's attention from the past. "Come on over here with us."

She was so warm and friendly, Sheila couldn't help but comply.

"Do you play any sports?" Lily inquired.

"I used to . . . not anymore."

"We usually have a game of basketball. The young folks in our family think they can whup up on the old folks. They's the ones who gets whupped on though."

"That's because Grandpa cheats," a young woman sitting beside Sheila commented.

"We don't cheat. Y'all can't count too well," Lily teased.

"When you gonna get out there, Grandma? You talking all this stuff."

Lily pointed to herself. "You don't want none of this . . ."

Sheila burst into laughter. The lump in Lily's breast had not been can-cerous, and it seemed she was feeling well enough to be cocky. Sheila en-joyed the lighthearted bantering going on between Lily and her granddaughter.

"Thank you, Miss Lily, for including me," she said when they were alone. "I'm really enjoying myself. I've never been around a family that's so close like this."

The woman surprised Sheila by hugging her. "Honey, we glad to have you. Nicholas told me so much about you that I feel like I already know you."

Sheila looked over her shoulder at Nicholas. "He's a very sweet man."

He was standing beside the grill talking to his uncle. When he caught her watching him, Nicholas winked and smiled.

"Nicholas is a lot like my sister, his dear mama. She was always a gen-tle spirit. Like her, he really cherishes everybody he cares about."

Sheila smiled. "He's been a wonderful friend to me."

Lily surveyed her face. "I have a feeling that there's more going on be-tween you two."

"We're just taking one day at a time."

"Well, I think you two look good together," Lily stated. "Friendship is a great foundation for something more."

One of Nicholas's cousins walked over. "Aunt Lily, I need your help with something."

Before leaving, Lily told Sheila, "Honey, get yourself something to eat. We'll sit down and have ourselves a good talk later."

Sheila navigated over to the table laden with picnic supplies and picked up a plate.

"Having a good time?"

She stole a peek over her shoulder. "I'm having a great time, Nicholas." She pointed to the food. "You getting ready to eat?"

He nodded and picked up a plate.

Sheila piled her plate with baked beans, macaroni salad, corn on the cob and chicken fresh off the grill.

"You must be hungry," he observed.

"I am."

She and Nicholas found a seat at one of the picnic tables beneath a towering shade tree.

"What's on your mind?" Nicholas asked when he sat down beside her.

"Just thinking about family." Her eyes flicked over the scene, taking in the happy and laughing faces of his family. "It must have been so nice growing up in yours. I know I've had a great time today with them. I would probably be a different person if I'd grown up in a family like this—close and very loving."

"Do you have any other relatives outside of your mother that you were close to?"

Sheila was almost tempted to unburden herself, but she fought the urge. "Not really. My father has two sisters and three brothers. My dad married again and has more children, too, but I've never met any of them."

"Have you considered looking them up?"

Frowning, she gave him a sidelong glance. "What for?"

"Aren't you at least curious about them?"

Sheila feigned nonchalance. "Not really. They never bothered to find me. Besides, my dad knows where to find my mother. She's right where he left her."

A heaviness centered in Sheila's chest. "Nicholas, I told you that my dad left, but not the reason why. It was because of me."

"Because of you . . . how?"

"My father was what you call high yellow. He had curly black hair—he was a very handsome man. He left my mother because he didn't believe I was his child. I was too dark, and I had a head full of nappy hair. He was very jealous, always thinking my mother was cheating on him. He didn't like her speaking Gullah because he didn't know what she was talking about—thought she was sending messages to one of her lovers."

Sheila shook her head sadly. "You should see my mother. To tell you the truth, I don't even know how she ever got my father. She's not an attractive woman at all."

Running a hand through her curls, Sheila continued. "My mother was pregnant with a girl before she had me. That baby was very light-skinned and had mounds of curly black hair. I saw a photo of her. She was a beautiful little girl."

"What happened to her?"

"She died when she was three. She was sickly, and she just couldn't fight anymore when she developed a bad case of pneumonia. My mom became pregnant with me six months after Leann died."

"And your father did this when you were only five? I think that's what you mentioned before."

"I was five," Sheila confirmed. "I overheard them fighting one night about how I didn't look like Leann. My father said he wasn't raising nobody else's child. At the time though, I didn't really understand what he was talking about. I blamed my mother for his leaving until she told me it was my fault. She broke my heart, and I won't forgive her for that."

"Sheila, we've talked about forgiveness."

"Yeah, and I told you that I'll forgive when I'm ready," she countered icily. "For now, I want to hold on to my anger. It keeps me from being hurt like that ever again."

"Sheila, you are not doing what Jesus would do. You shouldn't allow anyone to take you away from the path of God. Ephesians one and six says, *To the praise of the glory of His grace, wherein he hath made us accepted in the beloved.* You see . . . He won't ever reject us."

She settled back with her arms folded across her chest. "Don't preach to me, Nicholas. God has so many things to worry about—I seriously doubt He cares about the little black girl whose father never loved her."

"God does care for you, Sheila. He loves you more than anybody else could ever love you. The same way you hurt from being rejected—God hurts when you reject Him."

Sheila remained silent, lest her rebellious emotions get out of hand.

"You make a great basketball coach," Nicholas complimented during the drive back to Charleston the next day. "My cousins loved you."

"I wanted to play but my legs weren't cooperating." Sheila rubbed her left arm. "I've been having some pain in them and this arm."

"You take anything?"

She nodded. "Your aunt Lily can really play. Some of the younger kids couldn't keep up with her."

Nicholas laughed. "I'm surprised you don't want children. You're very good with them."

"I don't have anything against kids—I just don't think I'm mother material. I have way too many issues."

Reaching over, Nicholas took her hand, squeezing it. "No one is without issues, sweetheart."

"Well, it's out of the question for me right now . . . the MS . . ."

"Have you talked with your doctor about having children?"

Sheila shook her head no. "What's the point? I don't even have a man in my life." She stole a look at him. "Unless you're proposing."

His laughter sent goose bumps down Sheila's spine. "Not at this moment. Maybe tomorrow."

"Alright . . . don't play . . ." Sheila warned with a laugh.

Three and a half hours later, they pulled in Sheila's driveway.

"I'm in the mood for a movie," she announced. "Would you like to join me?"

"Are you asking me out on a date?"

"Yes, I am," Sheila confirmed.

"I think we just took our relationship to another level."

"So, is it a date?"

Grinning, he nodded. "It's a date."

"I can't believe I'm not pregnant yet," Tori complained while shopping in the baby department at Belk's with her cousin. "I'm usually as fertile as a rabbit."

"I keep telling you not to stress out over this," Charlene reminded her. "That's probably why you haven't conceived."

"I know." Tori picked up a little dress off the rack. "This is so cute."

"Ooh, I love it."

"You should get it for your little princess, Charlene. She'll look so darling in this."

"I'm gonna hold off. I don't want to buy too much right now. I'd rather wait until she gets here."

"Are you still worried about losing the baby?"

"Kinda. One of the couples in my Lamaze class lost their son last week. She went into labor early and he didn't make it because the cord was wrapped around his throat." Charlene pressed a hand to her belly. "When she gets here, I'll go on a wild shopping spree but until then . . . I just want to wait."

Tori embraced her cousin. "Honey, it's going to be alright. I just feel it in my spirit."

Charlene nodded. "I'm just gonna get a few things that we'll need in case she decides to come early."

"So you just want to buy the necessary items?"

"Yeah. A few T-shirts, some socks—things like that. Just a pack of each."

Tori understood her cousin's fear. She hadn't lost her daughter to a miscarriage, but imagined the hurt was the same.

It had taken Charlene years to conceive, so it was understandable that she'd worry about carrying to term.

She selected a pack of receiving blankets. "You'll need these."

"I haven't seen Nicholas around much. Is he traveling?"

"I spoke to him briefly last week." Frowning, Tori said, "He took Sheila with him to Brunswick. You know his family always throws a big Fourth of July barbecue."

"What's going on between him and Sheila?" Charlene asked.

Tori released a long sigh. "Girl, I honestly wish I knew." She detested the idea of her best friend hanging out with Sheila, but Nicholas wasn't listening to her. Tori suspected he wasn't thinking with his head.

It was the only thing that made sense. First Jake and now Nicholas. Sheila had seduced him, too.

Tori was sure this had been Sheila's plan all along. She prayed Nicholas would come to his senses soon.

CHAPTER TWENTY-ONE

Their friendship had progressed into something deeper. Sheila and Nicholas were officially dating. It didn't really occur to her what it truly signified until they ran into Tori shopping at the mall, a few days later.

She and Sheila literally bumped into each other.

"I'm so sor—" Tori stopped short when she realized it was Sheila.

"Hello, Tori."

"Sheila," she answered dryly.

"You're looking well."

Tori didn't respond. She just stood there, eyeing her.

Sheila glanced around for Nicholas, who'd stepped away to check on something in the store across the aisle.

"Looking for someone?"

Sheila gave a subtle lifting of her chin. "Actually, I am. Nicholas. We decided to do some shopping for his bedroom." She waited for her words to sink in.

Tori paled. "I don't believe you. Nicholas wouldn't have you anywhere near his bedroom."

"You're wrong, Tori. Nicholas and I are a couple now."

"You are a big liar, Sheila."

"Nicholas and I are officially dating," Sheila confirmed with a smile.

"Nicholas is a very nice man and he doesn't need yo—"

Interrupting her, Sheila shot back, "I know exactly the type of man he is . . ." Her voice died when pain exploded through her brain, taking her completely by surprise. She put a hand to her forehead. "Tori, I'm not in the mood to argue with you today. Can we table this discussion for another time?"

Tori's eyebrows rose in surprise, but Nicholas appeared before she could respond.

"What's going on?" he asked, looking from one woman to the other.

"Nothing." Sheila almost moaned out the word, her head hurt so badly. "Tori and I were just saying hello." Taking Nicholas by the hand, she said, "We should leave." In a lower voice, she added, "I'm not feeling well."

"Nicholas . . ." Tori began.

"I'm sorry—we really need to be going."

"Can you give me a call later?" Tori inquired. "We need to talk."

He nodded and kept walking.

Sheila was in too much pain to gloat. She just wanted to leave the mall before she passed out. By the time they reached the Jag, she was in tears.

"It hurts," she moaned over and over. She held her head all the way home.

As soon as Sheila walked into her house, she headed straight for her medicine cabinet. She needed something strong—something to knock her out while chasing away the pain.

Nicholas brought Sheila a glass of water, which she practically snatched out of his hand. She threw a couple of pills down her throat, and then drank the water.

The last thing she remembered before drifting off to sleep was the tender way Nicholas stroked her face as she lay on the sofa.

Two weeks later, Sheila spent the morning working in the yard. She placed her flowers in rows that ran north to south to take full advantage of the sunlight.

She'd had her gardener plant climbing roses at her fence posts to soften the rustic lines, and lavender to provide fragrance.

Around noon, Sheila decided to go back inside the house. Her vision blurred and she missed a step, causing her to fall down on the porch, scraping her knee.

Sheila released a string of curses between moans.

Her neighbor across the street yelled, "Hey . . . you okay, Miss Moore?"

"Yeah. I was just trying something new." She let out a forced laugh. "I'll be okay."

Once inside the house, Sheila allowed her tears to flow freely.

She wept aloud, rocking back and forth until no more tears would come.

If this had been her first time falling since her diagnosis, Sheila wouldn't have been so upset. But the truth was that she'd had several close calls in the past.

The neurologist had warned her that she would experience episodes like this. Sheila was afraid of losing her ability to walk altogether, and dreaded the need for a wheelchair.

She stared down at the darkening bruise on her knee and the small cut on her arm, wondering, *Is this a definite need—to—buy—a—cane—or—something warning, or just one of those things that can happen to anybody?* Sheila didn't want to make too much of it if it wasn't necessary.

Most days she did fine, but there were those days when she seemed to bounce from one wall to the other.

She tried to reach Nicholas, who was out of town, but was only able to leave a voice mail message for him. It wasn't like him not to call her back, so this sent her insecurities into a tailspin. She worried that she'd chase him away with her attitude.

Her leg hurt for the next two days.

Nicholas had called yesterday but couldn't talk long. Sheila had immediately jumped to the conclusion that he was with someone—another woman.

Now he was due home later today, but Sheila could care less. She was furious with him.

Maybe I need to lighten up some. But then, if Nicholas truly cared for me—he would be here no matter what. Jake and Tori had taught her this much, if nothing else.

Sheila rubbed the area surrounding her bruise. It was still puffy from the swelling.

I probably should have gone to the doctor, she thought.

The sound of her doorbell ringing drew Sheila from her musings. She limped all the way to the front door, throwing it wide open.

Nicholas reached for her, but Sheila pushed him away.

"Don't try to hug me."

"What's wrong with you?"

"I guess you . . . your phone didn't work," Sheila sputtered.

Nicholas looked confused. "What are you talking about?"

"You usually call to check on me. I guess you got pretty *busy* this time." Sheila pointed to her knee. "I fell," she announced. "Outside."

He was instantly concerned. "Are you okay?"

She nodded. "Not that you care." Sheila sat down, nearly collapsing into the chair as her knees buckled. "You couldn't even hold a decent conversation with me the *one* time you actually called me back."

"Sheila, they kept me busy. By the time I had a free minute—it was late."

Nicholas sat beside her and brushed a stray curl from her face. "You sure you're okay? It looks pretty bad." He pulled out his phone.

"Who are you calling?" Sheila wanted to know.

"Your doctor."

"For what?"

"Sweetheart, you fell down. It might happen again. It's time for you to get a cane or something to have on hand—just in case you need help walking."

"NO!" yelled Sheila. "I'm not doing it. I don't need anything to help me walk."

At the sight of the quad cane, Sheila burst into tears.

"Sweetheart," Nicholas murmured as he held her in his arms. "It will be okay."

"No, it's not." Sheila retrieved a tissue from her purse and dabbed at her eyes. "Until now, I might have been able to pass through any public place without attracting a second glance. If I have to use that thing—it tells the world that I'm not perfect. That something is wrong with me."

"Sheila, people use canes all the time. Put your pride on the back burner."

"And people, even children, wonder what's wrong with them. Especially if the person using the cane is under the age of seventy." Shaking her head, she said, "I don't want to use a cane. I can't do it, Nicholas."

"Sweetheart, you need some assistance with walking. Remember what Dr. Daniels said. Let's face it. If you won't use the cane, then you will have to get a wheelchair."

"But what if I get better and can walk around on my own?"

"You only need to use the quad cane whenever necessary."

Later at home, Sheila eyed the cane that stood propped up in the corner of her bedroom.

Rolling her eyes at Nicholas, she said, "I don't want to use that thing. Who's going to want a woman with a cane? I might as well throw on an old lady dress and a gray wig."

Nicholas chuckled.

"It's not funny."

"Honey, it shouldn't be a big deal to start using the cane. Don't let this disease rob you of your independence. The cane is supposed to add a bit of stability and balance to your walking. That's all."

"What it means is that I'm a cripple, Nicholas," she replied with tears in her eyes. "No man in his right mind will ever want me like this."

"You're wrong." Nicholas wrapped his arms around her. "Sheila, haven't you realized by now that I'm crazy about you?"

She saw the heartrending tenderness of his gaze and smiled in response. "We're going out, so I kind of figured you liked me a little bit."

Moving closer, he shook his head and smiled. "I like you a lot, Sheila."

"Don't play with me." She pulled away from him, using the back of her sofa as support.

Nicholas kissed her, his lips more persuasive than Sheila cared to admit.

Raising his mouth from hers, Nicholas gazed into Sheila's eyes. "Do you still think I'm playing with you?"

"No," she responded. "I believe you. You like me a lot."

Burying her face in his neck, Sheila felt safe—something she hadn't felt in a long time. "I'm beginning to really care for you, Nicholas. Please don't hurt me."

"I would never intentionally hurt you, sweetheart. That's why I don't want to rush things between us. I like this pace."

Giving him a sexy grin, Sheila said, "It's okay."

She relaxed while Nicholas prepared dinner for them. Sheila couldn't believe how lucky she was—a gorgeous man was in her kitchen cooking for her.

When it was ready, they ate by candlelight.

"I missed you," Nicholas confessed.

"I missed you, too." Sheila took a drink of water. "I was so mad at you, Nicholas. I'd gotten used to hearing from you all the time. I thought that maybe you were seeing someone."

"That's not the case. I said I'd be here for you."

"I know . . ."

Sheila sampled the short ribs. "This is delicious. You know, if you keep this up, I'm going to be gaining weight like crazy," she pointed out. "We don't want that."

"That's why we're always taking walks." Nicholas put a forkful of food in his mouth. He chewed and swallowed.

"Oh, I want you to reconsider having your mother come stay here with you," Nicholas added. "You keep telling me how much you want her out of that old house—have her move in here with you."

Sheila considered his suggestion. She couldn't deny she was afraid to live alone with everything that was going on with her. "I'll think about it."

Nicholas ran her out of the kitchen while he cleaned up.

He stayed until after Sheila showered and dressed for bed. And when she fell asleep, she dreamed of becoming Mrs. Nicholas Washington.

"I hope you're not seriously considering marrying Sheila," Tori said.

"Whoa!" Nicholas's head snapped up. "Where did that come from?"

"Thank God, you haven't totally lost your senses. I was worried for a moment."

"Let's change the subject, because if you insist on having this conversation—we're going to end up arguing."

"Nicholas, we hardly talk anymore. The only time I really see you now is when you come into the bookstore."

He gave a short chuckle. "Well, now you know how I used to feel. Remember how you used to treat me when Jake came to town?"

"We were teenagers. But I do know what you mean—you're right. I guess because you're seeing Sheila . . . Nicholas, I'm feeling a bit betrayed."

"I'm still your friend, Tori, but I have to live my life the way I want. I can't let you or your feelings make choices for me. I care for Sheila a great deal. It's not what I set out to do, but it happened. I don't regret it."

He waited for Tori to respond, but she remained silent. In truth, there was nothing she could say—his heart belonged to Sheila.

CHAPTER TWENTY-TWO

ould Nicholas be falling in love with me? Sheila dared to wonder.

She'd worked hard to stay grounded where Nicholas was concerned, because she didn't want to make the same mistake twice.

But it appeared she and Nicholas were becoming very close. Maybe this time her luck would take a turn for the better.

The thought of her and Nicholas as a couple put Sheila in such a good mood that she didn't mind calling her mother and asking for help.

"Hey, Ma. Did I catch you at a bad time?"

"Naw. Jis sittin' here readin' my Bible. 'Smattuh, gal?"

"I fell down the other day," Sheila told her. "The MS is progressing . . . I-I need you to come stay with me, Ma." She paused to clear her throat. "If you can't do it—"

Essie interrupted her daughter. "When you want me dar?"

"My friend and I will come pick you up on Saturday morning if that's okay with you."

"Dat be fine. I'ma be ready."

Satisfied, Sheila made the arrangements and hung up the phone.

The automobile carrying Nicholas and Sheila neared the dirt road where her mother lived.

"She lives in a shanty, Nicholas, but the house is clean," Sheila explained.

He reached over, grabbing her by the hand. "Sweetheart, you don't have to be embarrassed."

"I just didn't want you to think . . ." Sheila's voice died. "I hope I'm doing the right thing. Maybe after living with me, she'll want to stay in Charleston."

"Don't push her, Sheila."

"You can park over there." Her stomach felt queasy at the thought of Nicholas meeting her mother. Sheila was embarrassed by her.

He parked the car. "Here we are . . ."

"Yeah," she muttered.

Her mother opened the front door and walked out on the porch wearing a dress that had clearly seen better days.

Sheila was mortified. She'd never wanted Nicholas to see her poverty-stricken roots.

Nicholas got out of the car and walked around to the passenger side where he opened the door for her.

She stepped out.

"You look like your mother," he observed.

"Humph . . . no, I don't." She couldn't believe he'd said something like that to her.

Nicholas wisely let the matter drop.

Essie came down the rickety steps to assist Sheila, almost sending Sheila into hysterics. To anyone watching, they must look absurd.

Sheila waved her mother's efforts away. "I can manage, Ma."

She breathed a sigh of relief when she reached the porch. Sheila didn't want to go inside the house—she couldn't stomach the smell.

"I think I'll just sit out here," she said firmly. "Are you all packed and ready?"

Essie nodded. "Jis' need to get my suitcase."

Sheila was thankful her mother hadn't lapsed into her Gullah dialect. She'd suffered enough humiliation already.

Nicholas held the door open. "I'll bring out your luggage," he offered.

Sheila couldn't help smiling. Nicholas was always a gentleman.

After he placed her mother's suitcase in the trunk of the car, they were ready to leave. No one was more ready to leave than Sheila.

At least for now, she wouldn't have to come back out here, with her mother living in her house.

"The order came in for the book club," Charlene announced when she strolled into the office. "I'll call Margie in a few minutes to let her know."

Tori glanced up from the computer monitor. "Great. I was worried the books might not arrive in time. They're having the author come in for the meeting in three weeks, I think."

Charlene released a groan and leaned forward clutching her stomach. "Oooh..."

Tori pushed away from her desk and rushed to her cousin's side. "Charlene, what's wrong?"

"I just had a sharp pain." Tears formed in her eyes. "I can't lose this b-baby...please God..."

Placing her hand to Charlene's stomach, Tori began to pray. "Heavenly Father, I come to You with the assurance that You have a special love and concern for little children. Father God, You know the anxieties within Your daughter, Charlene, concerning her unborn daughter. But from Your Word, I am assured that You love this little girl more than we do, and we commit this child into Your loving and protecting hands. We ask that You keep her safe until it is time for her to leave the protection of Charlene's womb."

Charlene placed her hand over Tori's. "Loving Father, I humbly ask that You place this blessing that You've given me under Your mighty wings and protect this baby from any kind of virus or any other attack that would seek to destroy her life. Let Your precious blood cover my unborn child at all times. We thank you, Father God, for listening to our innermost cries and for sending Your angels to keep guard over my little one. Thank You for the peace You have given me. In Jesus' precious name, we pray."

"Amen," they murmured in unison.

Charlene wiped her eyes. "I'm going into the bathroom to freshen up."

"Okay...I'll be right here if you need me."

Five minutes later, Tori heard Charlene cry out. She rushed into the bathroom.

"I'm spotting!" Charlene's eyes were wide with fear.

"Let's get you to the hospital." Tori didn't waste any time getting Charlene out of the store and into the car.

Tori continued to pray while driving as fast as legally allowed.

When she neared Charleston Memorial Hospital, Tori reached over and patted her cousin's trembling hand. "We're almost there."

Charlene had tears streaming down her face, bringing Tori to tears as well.

As soon as they arrived at the hospital, Tori jumped out of her parked car and rushed around to open the front passenger door.

"How are you feeling now?"

"Okay. Thanks so much for coming with me to the doctor. I'm so scared something's wrong."

"Honey, your baby is fine. I'm sure of it. It's too bad Shepard's out of town."

"Tori, he's really excited about this baby. I am, too. We didn't think we'd be able to conceive . . . now I don't want to have a miscarriage." Charlene's eyes filled with unshed tears. "If we lose this one, we may not be able to have another."

Charlene didn't have to wait long to see a doctor, who diagnosed her condition as premature labor.

"I can't have this baby now," she whispered. "It's too soon."

Tori nodded, unable to speak at the moment. She raised her eyes heavenward. "Father God, I stand before You asking You to bless and protect this little baby in her mother's womb. Grant Charlene a safe and easy delivery at the right time and bless her and Shepard with a normal and healthy child, Heavenly Father. I ask that You also keep Charlene in peace and perfect health . . ."

She couldn't explain it, but suddenly Tori began to feel warmth surrounding her. It was the peace that comes from knowing God is who He say He is. With tears in her eyes, she said, "I give You all the glory for answering this prayer. Thank You, Father God. Thank You."

Tori glanced over at Charlene and stated, "It's done . . ."

When the doctor allowed them to hear the baby's strong heartbeat, both Tori and Charlene sighed with relief.

"Thank You, Jesus," Tori murmured over and over. "Thank You . . ."

The doctor left the room after assuring them the baby was fine.

"Praise God," Charlene gasped in relief. "I'm so glad my baby girl is doing good—I just want her to stay inside for a little while longer. You hear me, sweetie? Don't be so fast to want to come out."

Tori chuckled as a nurse walked into the room.

Tori stood by silently as they administered an intravenous magnesium sulfate drug treatment, to decrease Charlene's uterine contractions.

"I'll call Shepard," Tori announced, retrieving her cell phone from her purse.

"No . . . just wait and see if this works. I don't want to scare him."

"Okay, but I'm calling Aunt Kate and Jake."

Charlene nodded.

Tori walked out of the room and down the long, sterile hallway to the nearest exit, where she punched in her aunt's phone number.

"Aunt Kate, Charlene and I are at the hospital. Calm down . . . she's okay. She went into premature labor and they're giving her medication to stop her contractions," Tori explained.

"No, ma'am. You stay home and I'll call you later if anything changes. I feel in my spirit that everything will be alright. Now don't go getting all upset."

Next, she called Jake but got his voice mail. "Honey, I'm at the hospital with Charlene. She went into premature labor and the doctor's got her on medication. I'll call you back if anything changes. Oh, and don't say anything to Shepard if you talk to him—Charlene doesn't want to scare him unnecessarily. Love you."

When she returned to the room, Charlene had dozed off. Tori tiptoed across the room and sat down in the empty visitor's chair.

Hours later, Charlene was released with strict instructions to stay off her feet as much as possible and to keep herself well hydrated.

"I told you to drink more water," Tori fussed. "You know I'm gonna be on your back."

"Girl, this scared me to death! You don't have to worry—I'm drinking water until I burst."

"The goal is to keep the baby inside you until she's big enough," Tori said with a laugh.

"You know what I mean."

"And you can forget about coming back to work. Girl, I can manage the store until you have the baby. I'm hiring more help—we'll be okay."

Charlene sighed in resignation.

"I'm taking you to Aunt Kate's house. You should stay there until Shepard comes home."

Rubbing her belly, Charlene inquired, "Did anyone ever tell you that you're very bossy?"

Laughing, Tori held the car door open for Charlene, then walked around to the driver's side and climbed inside.

"Thank You, Jesus," she murmured once again.

"Tori, isn't that Sheila?" Charlene asked as they were about to pull out of the parking space.

Tori followed her cousin's gaze. "Yeah, that's her. Is she walking with a cane?"

"Looks like it."

Tori watched Sheila slowly make her way over to a nearby car.

"That must be her mother with her," Charlene commented.

"Wow. She looks like an older version of Sheila," Tori mumbled. Her eyes traveled back to her nemesis. "I can't believe what I'm seeing. Sheila using a quad cane."

"I wonder what happened to her."

Shrugging, Tori responded, "She could've hurt her leg or something."

"Or got beaten up for messing with somebody's man. She good for that." Charlene placed a hand to her stomach. "Lord, please forgive me for that. I'm wrong and I know it. Here I am talking about that woman like that."

"I'm just as bad. You know, we should be ashamed of ourselves. God just gave us the blessing of your child's life, so enough about Sheila," Tori said. "We need to focus our attentions on your little one. With that in mind, let's get you to Aunt Kate's house."

"My car is back at the bookstore."

"Shepard or Jake can pick it up. You're going straight to bed."

"The doctor said partial bed rest, Tori. I just have to stay off my feet as much as necessary. Not all the time."

"Staying in bed can't hurt you, Charlene."

"Alright, bossy . . ."

"Call Aunt Kate...she's probably about to have a nervous break-down."

Tori didn't get home until after eight. She'd stayed with Charlene and her aunt to make sure her cousin had everything she needed.

Brittany and JJ were hungry so she waited until Aunt Kate could feed them before driving home to Edisto Island.

Jake met her at the door. He picked up Brittany, who had fallen asleep, and carried her up the stairs. JJ and Tori followed.

After the kids were settled in their beds, Jake and Tori went to their bedroom.

"I called your aunt's house but you'd already left. I called your cell and left a message. How is Charlene?"

Tori sat down on the edge of her bed and removed her shoes. "She's doing fine. They were able to stop her contractions. She's on partial bed rest and she has to drink lots of water—she was dehydrated. Shepard's coming home later tonight. He went to Texas to speak at some conference."

"Is everything okay with the baby?"

Rising to her feet, Tori nodded. "Jake, I'm so glad they were able to stop her contractions. Charlene's terrified of losing this baby and not being able to have another. You know how much they went through to get pregnant."

"I said a prayer for them as soon as I got the message."

"I was praying the whole time I was there, too." Tori rubbed her arms to remove the slight chill she felt. "The doctor says the baby's heartbeat is normal and thinks Charlene just needs to slow down some. I told her to stay home until after the baby's born. I'll hire another person to work in the store."

"Shepard's gonna be happy."

"I know," Tori responded. "I think if Shepard had his way, he'd have Charlene home full time."

"Have you two talked about it—you and Charlene?"

"Yeah, we have," Tori confessed. "I'm only in the store two days a week and even then it's only a half day. Charlene plans on doing the same kind of schedule. We have a pretty good staff."

"If Sheila weren't on leave right now, I'd take some time off to help out bu—"

Tori cut him off by saying, "Oh, I saw her today. Jake, she was using a quad cane to help her walk."

"Really? The last time I saw her she was walking fine."

"Not today."

"Hmmm . . . that's interesting."

"Not enough for me to dwell on," Tori said. "I could care less."

CHAPTER TWENTY-THREE

※

"Nicholas . . . hey," Tori greeted.

He leaned over to embrace her. "The store is looking good. Especially the window."

She laughed. "You saw your book display, huh?"

"Thank you, Tori. I really appreciate the push you give my books."

"Hello, good-looking," Charlene said as she joined Tori and Nicholas.

Her hands on her hips, Tori demanded, "Charlene, what are you doing here?"

"I ran out of books to read. Mama drove me here to pick up a couple of books, then I'm going back home to prop my feet up and read."

"If you'd called me, I would've brought some books to you. Charlene—"

Charlene cut her off with, "*Point of Deception* is wonderful, Nicholas. I've read it at least three times now since I've been banned from working. I love it."

"You ladies make me feel good." Nicholas broke into a wide smile. "Don't stop."

Charlene and Tori laughed.

"Are you looking for something special?" Tori asked him.

"Yeah. I need to pick up a new Bible. Mine is falling apart, so I want to get the Quest Bible."

"We just got some in a couple of weeks ago," Charlene told him. "We have them in black, navy and burgundy."

"I'll take the navy leather—it is the leather-bound, right?"

"Yeah. I'll get it for you."

Charlene walked away.

"You're in a good mood," Tori observed.

"I'm always in a good mood."

"I know. It's just that you seem happier than usual."

Nicholas laughed.

"Here it is." Charlene returned and held out the Bible to him.

"Thanks."

"Nicholas, we saw Sheila a couple of days ago," Charlene said. "She was walking with a cane. Is she okay?"

"She sounded fine the last time I spoke to her." Nicholas walked over to the cash register.

Tori and Charlene followed him.

Tori knew Nicholas well. His response was an evasive one. While she strode around the counter to ring up the sale, Charlene continued to probe. "Why is she using a cane?"

Nicholas pulled a credit card out of his wallet. "I guess she needed some help in walking. It's not a big deal, I'm sure."

"If it's not a big deal, then why are you being so evasive?"

Nicholas didn't respond.

"Charlene, leave it alone," Tori interjected. "Can't you see Nicholas isn't going to tell us anything?"

"I'm not trying to be difficult. It's just not my place."

"I can't believe you're being loyal to that snake," a voice said from behind him.

He turned around and greeted Tori's aunt. "How are you doing, Miss Kate?"

"Nicholas, what's gotten into you? You know good and well that tramp can't be trusted."

"Aunt Kate . . ."

She quieted Tori with a wave of her hand. "The truth is the light. That girl ain't nothing but trouble with a capital T."

"It's not our business," Tori told her aunt.

"It may not be my business, but Nicholas . . . you know I treat you like my own child. That Sheila Moore is a bad seed. Mark my word—she'll use you till you've got nothing left in you. Then she won't have nothing to do with you."

"I hear you, Aunt Kate. But you don't have to worry. I'm not going to let Sheila, or anyone else for that matter, manipulate me."

"Sheila Moore is the spawn of Satan. Listen to me, son. You might wanna check to see if she got them three sixes tattooed on her body somewhere."

Tori placed a hand to her mouth, stifling her laughter.

Nicholas released a soft sigh. "Aunt Kate, she's not trying to mess with anybody. Sheila's doing her own thing right now."

"I bet she is," Kate muttered.

Nicholas picked up his purchase and said, "I don't mean to be rude, but I need to get going. I'll talk to y'all later."

"I'll walk you out," Tori said. Nicholas knew more than he was saying and Tori intended to get to the bottom of all this secrecy.

As soon as they stepped outside of the store, Nicholas turned to Tori and said, "I hope you don't intend on grilling me." His mouth took on an unpleasant twist. "I've already told you that whatever is going on between me and Sheila is my business."

"Nicholas, I don't get it. You know what she did to me. How can you be involved with her?"

"She didn't do it alone, Tori. How can you be so forgiving of Jake?"

"He's my husband. Sheila tricked him."

"He slept with her, Tori," Nicholas reminded her. "Jake *willingly* went to bed with Sheila. Yet you can just forget all about that."

She winced. "I *know* what he did. I haven't forgotten it, but I am committed to my marriage and I want it to work." Tori's eyes filled with tears. "I can't believe you'd throw this up in my face after all this time."

"It doesn't feel good, does it?" Nicholas unlocked his car. "Tori, I'm glad you and Jake are together. But Sheila deserves a second chance, too.

She's not bothering you or your husband. Why can't you and your family leave her alone?"

"I can't believe we're standing out here arguing over Sheila Moore."

"Why don't you go back inside?" Nicholas suggested. "I need to be going."

Tori glared at him for a long moment before turning to walk back toward her bookstore. She wiped away a lone tear.

Nicholas was supposed to be her best friend, but apparently his feelings for Sheila ran much deeper than she first thought.

"Nicholas, is something wrong?" Sheila asked. "You haven't said much since you arrived."

He *hadn't* said much since arriving, but that was because Nicholas wasn't sure whether or not to tell Sheila about his argument with Tori. "I was thinking about something."

"What?"

"It's not important."

"C'mon, out with it, Nicholas. If it wasn't important, as you say, then you wouldn't be so consumed with it. This must have something to do with me, so you might as well tell me."

"Tori and Charlene apparently saw you with the cane one day while you and your mother were out."

"Great. I guess I was bound to run into them sooner or later. I'm sure they were curious. Did they ask you about it?"

He nodded. "Yeah, they wanted to know if something was wrong with you."

"Well, what did you tell them?" Sheila asked in a low voice.

"Nothing. Tori and I actually got into an argument over it. I said some things I probably shouldn't have." Sighing, he sat with his back straight and stiff.

Sheila gave his hand a reassuring squeeze. "Nicholas, I know you and Tori are tight. I shouldn't have placed you in this position. I'm sorry."

"You have nothing to be sorry about, sweetheart."

"I'm sure seeing me look so pathetic made their day." She closed her eyes, feeling embarrassed.

"I wouldn't say that, Sheila."

Her eyes were bordered with tears. Nicholas knew she'd hoped they would never see her with the cane.

"It doesn't matter what they think or what they know, Sheila. Your life hasn't ended."

"That's easy for you to say, Nicholas." Sheila was fighting tears. "You don't have to walk around with a cane."

"Having MS is not the end of the world."

"Spoken by someone who's never had it," Sheila shot back. "You don't understand, Nicholas, and you never will."

"I don't want to fight with you."

They sat in silence.

"I'm kind of tired," Sheila blurted after a moment. "I think I'm going to lie down for a little bit. Nicholas, I'll give you a call later. Okay?"

He nodded. "I debated whether or not to even mention this to you. I wish I hadn't." Sheila was clearly upset. He could tell by the sudden shift in her mood.

"I'm glad you did. I need to be prepared."

"I didn't tell you this for you to obsess over. You knew this could eventually happen."

He stood up. "Don't get yourself worked up. It's not good for you."

"You don't have to worry about me. I'll be fine. I'm just humiliated by the thought of Tori and Charlene seeing me."

"Sheila, sweetheart. It's not that big of a deal. You could've hurt your leg or something. They still don't know what's going on with you."

"But how long will that last? Jake's already trying to keep me away from Madison-Moore."

"You left of your own accord," Nicholas reminded her.

"I took a leave of absence," she clarified.

"And he's honoring that."

"I don't need you taking his side."

"I've had enough arguing for today." Nicholas headed to the door. "I'll talk to you later."

He sighed in frustration as he walked to his car. He wished he'd just kept his big mouth shut.

*　　*　　*

"T'engk Gawd for such a beautiful day," Essie commented. She and Sheila sat on the front porch, enjoying what was left of the afternoon.

Sheila watched the condensation pool up in the marble coaster after her mother set the glass down on the small table situated between the green rocking chairs.

The thought of Tori and that nosy Charlene spying on her had Sheila in a bad mood.

" 'Smattuh, Sheila?"

She took a sip of her iced tea. "Just leave me alone, Ma. I'm not in a very good mood."

Essie picked up her glass and took a long sip.

"I'm sorry. I didn't mean to be so rude." Sheila was so upset she wanted to scream. Tori was the bane of her existence. She was the major reason Sheila had allowed her anger and resentment to control her life, hindering her ability to experience any type of joy.

Sheila cut her eyes at Essie. Her mother was the other reason. All she'd ever done was humiliate and embarrass Sheila. She blamed her mother for almost everything wrong with her life.

"Sheila . . ."

"Ma, please . . . I just need to be alone for a while. I don't want to talk right now."

Shaking her head, Essie stood up and strode briskly into the house.

Sheila ignored the hurt look on her mother's face, just as Essie had ignored her when she was growing up.

She didn't care about my feelings, Sheila thought. *I don't care how she feels either.*

Sheila felt like crying. Why did Tori and Charlene have to see her with that cane? Hadn't she been humiliated enough?

She regretted pressuring Nicholas to tell her what happened. He knew this would upset her, so why bother to tell her? Unless he was trying to upset her.

But that wasn't like Nicholas at all.

"Uh'm mekin' red rice and swimp for dinner."

"I'm probably not gonna have any. I don't have much of an appetite."

"Gal, you need tuh eat."

"I'm not hungry, Ma."

"W'y you look so rarried?"

When they were inside the house and seated in the family room, Sheila answered her mother's question. "Jake's wife, Tori, and her cousin saw us."

Essie eyed her. When Sheila said nothing more, she prompted, "And?"

"And?" Sheila echoed. "Ma, they saw me using that thing over there." It was clear her mother couldn't comprehend what she was feeling. "Jake doesn't know that I have MS. Do you get it now?"

"W'y don' you tell him?"

"Because I didn't want him to know. He's trying to take Madison-Moore from me."

"Kin he do dat?"

"I'm not going to let him," Sheila vowed. "I'll see him dead first."

Essie put a hand to her chest. "Gal, don' talk like dat. You need tuh pray tuh the good Lawd tuh rid you of all dat anger."

Sheila put a hand to her face. "I'm sick and tired of everyone telling me that I need to let go of my anger. Maybe if all of you would do what you were supposed to do, I wouldn't be so angry. Ever think about that?"

"What you talkin' 'bout, gal?"

Her mother would never understand. Sheila sighed softly. "Nothing, Ma."

Using the quad cane for support, Sheila stood up and slowly made her way to the door. "I think I'm going to take a nap. I'm tired."

It was the first of August and Tori was still not pregnant. She inhaled deeply and exhaled slowly before walking out of the bathroom carrying the results of her latest pregnancy test.

"No baby," she murmured, wiping away a tear.

Jake was instantly by her side. "Honey, it's not the end of the world. We're just not pregnant yet."

She nodded. "I just thought . . ."

He wrapped his arms around her. "We're gonna stay positive. You know there's nothing wrong with you physically, and I'm okay healthwise. We've had three children already—when God decides it's time, we'll have our baby."

"I just have to be patient—that's what you're trying to tell me. Right?"

Nodding, Jake responded, "Yeah."

Tori held her tongue. It was easy for Jake to say that—apparently he wasn't worried about having another child. The thought occurred to her that maybe Jake didn't want a baby as bad as she did. But he would tell her—wouldn't he?

When Jake walked out of the room to check on the children, Tori fell to her knees and began to pray. "Father, please hear my plea and remove whatever is hindering the blessing of another child in my life. Please honor my request, dear Lord, by granting me another child for Your name's glory. I expect a miracle from Your mighty hand. And if it is not Your will for me to bring another child into this world, I still thank You even now, for making my life whole. In Jesus' name I pray. Amen."

Tori rose to her feet. She felt much better after praying. "Thank You so much, Father God. Whatever Your will—I am thankful."

She made peace with her decision to just trust God.

CHAPTER TWENTY-FOUR

"Stop obsessing about what people may or may not think about you using a cane," Nicholas demanded when Sheila refused to accompany him to a charity function on the following evening. "They have nothing to do with you and me."

"It's easy for you to say," Sheila mumbled. "You're not the one using this cane. With my luck, I'd run into Jake and Tori. That's all the ammunition he needs to push me out of the company."

"Why? Is it what you would have done to him if the situation was reversed?"

"Yes," Sheila blurted. "I would."

Nicholas seemed disappointed in her response.

"I never claimed to be a nice person."

"Jake can't just push you out of Madison-Moore. It won't be that easy. However, I don't believe he would be so callous."

"Oh, I forgot he and Tori were up for sainthood," Sheila sniped. "It must be so nice to be so wholesome and perfect. Poor Shepard and Charlene—how do they do it? It must be so hard for them to be around people who can do no wrong."

"Sheila, let's change the subject. I don't want to spend the evening talking about Jake, Tori or Charlene."

"What would you like to do instead?"

"How about this?" Nicholas leaned forward and kissed her.

His kiss was slow, thoughtful and sent spirals of desire racing through Sheila. "Mmmm . . . I love the subject matter."

"Now isn't this a more pleasant discussion?"

She nodded.

Reclaiming her lips, Nicholas crushed her to him.

Settling in his arms, Sheila laid her head on his chest. "Can you believe it's August?"

Nicholas nodded. "We're already two days into it." He stole a peek over his shoulder. "How are things going with you and your mother?"

Sheila shrugged nonchalantly. "Okay, I guess. She's trying. I guess she must really feel guilty over the way she treated me back then."

She moved closer to Nicholas. "Why don't you spend the night?"

"Sweetheart, your mother is here."

"I'm a grown woman," Sheila said in a loud whisper. "This is *my* house. I can do whatever I want in here."

"First off, I have too much respect for you and your mom to do something like that. Second . . . I'm practicing celibacy."

Anger flashed in her dark eyes. "Look, you don't have to tell me no mess like that. If you don't want me—just be a man and say so."

"Sheila, I said exactly what I mean. I don't have to lie to you. Besides, even if I weren't celibate, I wouldn't stay here with you while your mother is living here with you."

"Whatever . . ."

Nicholas eyed her for a moment. "Don't be this way."

"I can't believe I actually fell for your words," Sheila said bitterly. "I'm so stupid."

"Maybe I should leave," Nicholas said as he rose to his feet. "Sheila, I didn't mean to hurt your feelings in any way. I just wanted to be honest with you."

"Please leave."

Nicholas headed to the front door. "I'll give you a call tomorrow."

"Don't bother," she shot back. "I'll be busy."

*   *   *

Sheila woke up in the middle of the night soaking wet.

Night sweats combined with the dream of her father's leaving.

How long does menopause last? she wondered as she got up and changed her gown. She knew heartache lasted forever.

She went to the kitchen and drank a glass of water, hoping it would help cool her off, then went back upstairs.

She just felt so lost and lonely in the king-sized bed. "Nicholas, why didn't you stay here with me?"

After turning from one side to the other for two hours, Sheila swung her legs out of the bed and reached for her robe. Since sleep didn't seem to be forthcoming, she might as well get up.

She walked without assistance over to the French doors and stared out.

"Nicholas, I love you so much. I wish I could tell you, but I can't. I can't ever tell you how much you mean to me. I refuse to let myself be hurt ever again."

Her eyes filled with tears.

"I need you so much, Nicholas. I want to be loved. I just want to feel like a woman again."

Sheila wiped away the tears on her cheek. Her mother had ruined things yet again. "Thanks, Ma," she said bitterly.

A sudden thought entered her mind.

Hilton Head Island.

Maybe Nicholas and I could go away for the weekend. The idea brought a smile to Sheila's face.

"I need to get away," Sheila began. "I rented a beautiful house on the beach on Hilton Head Island for next weekend. The twelfth."

"That sounds like fun. Wish I could go."

"You could come with me. I don't mind." Sheila prayed he would join her. She didn't want to be alone.

"I can't go. I'm singing on Sunday."

"Singing? You don't want to go because you're singing in a church choir?"

"Yeah," Nicholas murmured. "Why? Does it seem strange to you or something?"

"I didn't know you were so involved in the church. I thought maybe you just went, listened to the pastor, then left until next Sunday rolled around."

"Why don't you like going to church, Sheila?"

"God and me—we never had too much to talk about. My mom used to try to make me go with her, but she eventually gave up."

"Why? What did you do?"

"Sometimes I went to sleep, and other times I just got up and walked out. I'd go outside and wait for her, or I'd just walk home."

"Sounds like you were something else."

"I had an attitude—I admit it."

"What would you say if I asked you to come to church with me on Sunday?"

"I'd say no, because you're singing in the choir. I don't want to sit by myself."

"Would you come if I weren't singing?"

"To be honest, I probably wouldn't. Nicholas, I'm not sure I even believe in God. Actually, I take that back. God probably does exist—but I know He has no love for me, because of what He's doing to me."

"God is not vindictive, Sheila."

"I think you'd better go back and read your Bible. My mother used to always tell me how God would punish me if I sinned. As much as she reads her Bible, I wouldn't be surprised if she has the whole book memorized."

"Have you ever read the Bible for yourself?"

"No," Sheila replied absently. "I didn't see any point."

Nicholas reached over and took her by the hand. "Sweetheart, what's running through your mind right now?"

Sheila turned her gaze to Nicholas. "Nothing much. Just thinking about all that's happened to me. My life really sucks. All I've tried to do was be happy."

"Are you saying you're not happy now?"

"Not really," Sheila admitted. "Look at what's happening to me. Why should I be happy about this?"

"Sheila, life is what you make it. You ha—"

She cut him off by saying, "I've heard it all before and I'm still not buying it. Nicholas, everyone in the world can have the man they want. They can go through life without all the drama . . . this just isn't fair."

"You still want Jake," Nicholas said without emotion.

"No, I'm not even thinking about Jake Madison. I wasn't talking about him. He is just another dog who plays with you, leads you on then tramples all over your heart. I will never forgive him for the way he treated me."

"Then who are you referring to?"

Sheila sighed. "Just forget it, Nicholas."

"No, I don't want to forget it. Were you talking about me?"

"Forget it."

"No, I don't think we should. Are you still upset with me because I wouldn't spend the night with you?"

She didn't respond.

"Look at me, please . . ."

Sheila met his gaze. "What!"

"You should appreciate the fact that I'm not trying to take advantage of you sexually."

"Nicholas, how do you really feel about me?"

"I'm crazy about you, Sheila." Nicholas held her face in his hands. "I'm . . . I care for you. I want to see where this takes us."

"You care so much for me, but you won't have sex with me," Sheila said skeptically.

"Don't think that I don't want to . . . I do. Sheila, I would love to make love to you, but only in the right way."

"The right way? What are you talking about?"

"I'm looking for a wife, and I'm going to be abstinent until I get married."

"You're really serious about this?"

Nicholas nodded. "But I'm very attracted to you."

"I'm still not buying it, and I'll tell you why. I tried to seduce you a few years back—remember that?"

When he nodded a second time, she continued. "You rejected me then, and I don't think it's because you were celibate. So far, you've rejected me twice."

"Sweetheart, I wish you wouldn't look at it like that."

"It's hard not to," Sheila responded. "I'll be okay though. You don't have to worry about me."

Tense silence filled the room.

Nicholas cleared his throat. "I don't want this evening to end on a bad note."

Sheila rose to her feet. "Everything's okay," she repeated. "If I get down to Hilton Head alone and fall ... oh well ..."

"Then why don't you take your mother with you?"

"Because if I wanted to be around her, I wouldn't be trying to get away. She and I need a break from each other."

Sheila was irritated that her scheme to have Nicholas join her in Hilton Head had failed.

Sheila didn't have a clue how badly he wanted to make love to her. His self-control was evaporating rapidly whenever he was around her, but Nicholas struggled to remain true to God.

When he gave his heart to the Lord, Nicholas had vowed the next woman he took to bed would be his wife. Even Sheila would have to come to understand his commitment.

CHAPTER TWENTY-FIVE

~~~

Sheila stared out the window of the house she'd rented for the weekend. She'd imagined Nicholas with her in the incredible four-bedroom cottage, with its fabulous West Indies décor.

From where she was standing, she had a fantastic view of the colorful flower garden, the ocean, and Daufuskie Island with houses on its shores, some of them stately mansions with sprawling decks.

Sheila turned away from the window.

This area is so beautiful, she thought. Her eyes traveled from the faux-finished stucco walls to the hand-painted furniture to the huge over-stuffed sofas.

"Nicholas, why didn't you come with me?" she whispered to the empty great room. "We could've had such a great time together. None of this means a thing without you."

She released a long sigh.

Her cellular phone rang, cutting through the silence.

She didn't answer after noting Nicholas's name on her caller ID.

Depressed, Sheila strode to the master bedroom and sank down on the king-sized bed. A hot tear rolled down her cheek. She'd never wanted to come to Hilton Head alone.

She briefly considered packing up and returning home, but that would mean Nicholas won. Sheila wasn't about to let that happen. She would stay here until Sunday evening, and she planned to enjoy herself.

After a lonely dinner, Sheila decided she'd had enough. She was here on a beautiful island and she would be insane to let it all go to waste.

"I'm going out to have a good time. The hell with Nicholas Washington."

Sheila showered and put on a very sexy dress that looked like it had been painted on her body. She styled her dark hair in long, flowing curls.

She made the drive to the Jazz Corner, a hot night spot.

Once she was seated, she scanned the menu and gave the waiter her drink order.

After her drink arrived, Sheila watched the people in the restaurant, who all seemed to be having a good time. She downed the rest of her apple martini.

Couples were gathered all around her, along with groups of single males and females, probably hoping to catch the eye of the opposite sex. She felt ice spreading through her stomach. Nicholas's rejection still hurt.

She decided on the angel hair tilapia for dinner, and gave the waiter her order. She continued to people-watch while she waited for her food to arrive.

Each time her eyes landed on a couple, a flash of loneliness stabbed at her. A bitter cold despair dwelt in the caves of her lonely soul.

Her meal arrived on a platter served with such flourish that Sheila felt she was back in Manhattan at one of her favorite posh restaurants. The flavor, appearance and texture of the tilapia, the accompanying pasta and braised vegetables both tantalized and satisfied her hunger.

After her meal, Sheila decided to stay and listen to blues vocalist Barbara Patterson.

When she put down her fork she felt sated, but the air of loneliness continued to embrace her in a thick fog of depression. Nicholas had given her a spark of hope, but then had quickly extinguished it by his rejection.

"Hello, beautiful."

Sheila glanced up from her second drink.

"Is this seat taken?"

"No, it's not," she murmured.

He sat down at the table. "You're not from around here, are you?"

"Probably half the people in this place are not from around here," Sheila answered. "I hope you have a better line than that. But to answer your question—I'm not from here. I live in Charleston."

"I see you have no problem speaking your mind."

"Weeds out the trash." Sheila signaled the waitress to bring her another drink. "Oh, I hope you have money to buy your own drinks, because I'm not that kind of girl."

He laughed. "Alright, pretty lady . . . I understand."

"Glad to hear it."

"Hey, did somebody make you mad or something? Or are you always so blunt?"

"I'm always this way, and I have no intention of changing."

"Do you mind telling me your name?"

"Sheila. Sheila Moore."

"My name is Derick Henderson."

"So Derick, what are you about?"

"I'm not sure what you mean."

"You know exactly what I mean," Sheila countered. "Look, I'm not in the mood to play like I'm some coy little girl. I'm a straight shooter and if you're not—leave."

"Someone did a number on you," he muttered.

"Nobody did anything on me. Derick, I'm just looking to have a little fun. I don't want a relationship—just sex. Is that clear enough for you?"

He broke into a smile. "You *are* direct."

"Does it bother you?"

"No. Not at all. I've just never met anyone like you."

Sheila sat there talking to Derick until the club closed. She finished her drink, then reached for her purse.

"Derick, I'm about to leave. If you have a car, we can finish talking at my house. You can follow me there."

He tried to embrace her as they walked toward the exit doors, but Sheila wasn't having it.

She only wanted sex.

She needed sex to wash away the pain she was feeling.

Half an hour later, they arrived at the house she was renting. Derick was impressed. "You living large out here. Sea Pines Plantation." His eyes traveled the room, checking everything out. "Very nice . . ."

"Don't get any crazy ideas. I'm a black belt in karate and a very good shot. Not to brag, but I'm also deadly with a knife. Don't make me prove it."

She almost broke into a smile at the flash of fear shining in his eyes.

Sheila strode over to the wet bar. "Would you like a drink?"

"Naw. I'm cool."

She went straight to the point. "Do you have protection?"

"Yeah. Always keep it with me."

Sheila's cell phone rang. It was Nicholas.

She left it lying unanswered on the bar.

"Come with me," Sheila said without emotion.

In the bedroom, she removed her clothes and climbed into bed. She turned off the light when Derick joined her.

A lone, hot tear fell from her eye.

"Morning, beautiful," Derick greeted.

Sheila placed both hands to her head. "Do you have to be so loud?" She felt dizzy and a bit disoriented. *Probably from all the martinis I drank last night.*

He moved to kiss her but Sheila pushed him away. "Don't . . ."

Derick eyed her, then shrugged. "Whatever."

"I need to shower and dress," Sheila said. "So could you do me a big favor and leave?"

He had the nerve to look offended. "Excuse me?"

"We had a good time, Derick. It's over now and I want to be alone." Her hand crept beneath her pillow for her handgun.

Derick's eyes followed the movement. "Sure. Whatever."

Sheila eased out of bed and slipped the gun into the pocket of her robe as she put it on. She strode into the bathroom, locking the door behind her.

Sheila stayed in the bathroom until she thought Derick was dressed. The sex had been okay, but now she just wanted him gone.

"You a cold-hearted woman, Sheila," Derick muttered when she escorted him to the front door ten minutes later.

Feigning a smile, Sheila responded, "Thanks for the compliment. Goodbye."

She walked over to where she'd left her purse and pulled out a bottle of extra strength painkillers. She took two of them.

I drank too much last night. It had only been three drinks, but they really did a number on her.

An hour later, Sheila's head was still hurting. She didn't bother getting dressed—just lay on the sofa in her robe.

She drifted off to sleep.

The shrill ringing of her cell phone woke her up forty-five minutes later.

"Hullo?"

"Sheila, hey . . . this is Nicholas."

Her head was throbbing from the pain. "What do you want?"

"I wanted to say hello and I miss you, so I thought I'd call and check on you.

"I'm great. Couldn't be better. Well, I could have been better if you'd come with me to Hilton Head. But then you would actually have to spend time with me."

He sighed. "Sheila, I didn't call to fight with you."

"Then maybe you shouldn't have called," she shot back. "I need to go; I have things to do."

"Goodbye, Sheila." Nicholas hung up.

Slamming the phone down, she burst into tears.

Nicholas had a way of ruining things for her. It was his fault that she'd slept with Derick in the first place. She'd never been the type for one-night stands.

"I hate you, Nicholas Washington," she sobbed, but even as she said the words, she knew she didn't mean it.

Sheila took a stroll outside a couple of hours later. She would be leaving soon but wanted to admire the stunning garden one last time.

The cottage stoop was outlined in brilliant gold and orange petunias and other wildflowers with rust-colored markings.

In the far corner of the garden, a raised bed of daylilies with wide, ruffled petals spread its canopy of leaves and blooms over the ground, creating a barrier around the lilac bushes.

The landscape was breathtaking, but Sheila's admiration of the beauty before her waned as Nicholas continued to dominate her thoughts.

The time to leave Hilton Head Island drew near.

Sheila turned and strolled back into the house where she grabbed her overnight bag and purse.

Soon she was driving away from the island, her mind filled with thoughts of what should have been.

As far as Sheila was concerned, Nicholas was no better than Jake. He didn't want her either.

Her own father never wanted her—so why should anyone else?

Two hours after her return home, Sheila appeared at Nicholas's front door with a bouquet of flowers.

"I'm sorry for being such a jerk," she said as soon as he saw her. "Can I come inside?"

Nicholas held the door wide open. "Of course."

They settled on the sofa in his den where he'd apparently been watching television.

He lowered the volume of the TV. "I hope you enjoyed your weekend alone."

"It could've been better," Sheila admitted. "To be honest, I kept thinking about you."

"You were on my mind as well."

Sheila reached over, taking his hand in hers. "I hate when we fight, Nicholas."

"I feel the same way."

"I really wanted to go away with you."

"Sheila, I wasn't rejecting you. I really wasn't. I just don't want to compromise my beliefs. I'm building a close relationship with the Lord, and I want to do what's right."

"I'm trying to understand you, Nicholas. I really am."

"I have something for you," Nicholas announced suddenly.

"I love presents."

He rose to his feet and strode out of the room, returning a few minutes later with a beautifully wrapped package.

Sheila grinned from ear to ear as she tore into the present.

She inspected it quickly, then looked up suspiciously, her smile disappearing.

"A B-Bible . . ." she sputtered. "You bought me a *Bible?" What in the world am I supposed to do with this?* she wondered.

"It's a Quest Study Bible."

Disappointed, Sheila held her tongue.

"Sweetheart, you've been through a lot in your life. A seed of rejection was planted in your heart a long time ago. Through the years, that seed has sprouted and grown into bitterness and unforgiveness. It's my prayer that this Bible will help you find the healing you need."

"I never should have told you all those things about me."

"Sheila, God can remove all the pain and heartache you're feeling."

Struggling to keep her temper in check, she responded, "I don't want to discuss a relationship with God, Nicholas. I told you that before."

"Sheila . . ."

"NO!" Sheila snapped. "Look, I'm serious. I don't want to get into this. The way I see it—God is responsible for everything I've gone through, and everything I'm going through now." She rose to her feet. "I should be getting on to the house."

"You can't keep running from God, Sheila."

"Whatever . . ." she muttered under her breath.

Nicholas didn't try to stop her from leaving.

Her mother was in the kitchen cooking when Sheila arrived home.

"Hey, Ma," she greeted unenthusiastically.

Essie eyed the package in Sheila's hand. "You went out and bought yo'self a Bible?"

"No. It's a gift from Nicholas. I guess he couldn't think of anything better to give me."

"Uh t'ink it's a nice gift."

"I don't need it, so you can have it, Ma."

Placing her hands on her hips, Essie demanded, "Huccome you so mean and ungrateful? This a nice gift from a man who care for you."

"I'm not trying to be mean. I'm just being honest. Better he hear the truth from me than I lie about how much I love it, then return it to the store. Remember that, Ma? I'd spent all summer working to raise enough money to get you that suit."

"Chile, Uh loved dat suit but I hab nowhere to wear such a fancy outfit, iz all. W'y you keep bringin' up all this stuff dat happened so long ago?"

"Your rejecting my gift was like rejecting me."

"Uh neber rejected you, baby. Uh love you, Sheila."

"So you say," she retorted. Sheila dropped the Bible on a nearby table. "Those are only words, Ma. We all know that actions speak louder than words."

"You needs to get rid of dat bitterness in yo' heart. It's turnin' you evil."

"I don't care," Sheila snapped. "I like the person that I am. If you don't—leave."

Sheila stared at the dosage of Copaxone.

It's not doing anything for me—why should I waste my time injecting the crap in my body?

She opened the drawer to her nightstand and tossed her medication back inside. She was tired of taking medicine.

What she needed tonight was a drink. Sheila pushed off her bed and navigated to her walk-in closet.

She was going out.

Sheila was dressed and ready to go within the hour. She paused outside her mother's room. "Ma, I'm going out for a while."

Essie opened her door. "Where you going?"

"Out," Sheila repeated. "Don't wait up."

She walked into her living room, her eyes traveling to the cane propped near the front door. Sheila hadn't needed it in the past few weeks, so she picked it up and placed it in the hall closet.

Thirty minutes later, Sheila was seated at a bar ordering her first drink of the evening.

"I thought you'd be in bed by now," a familiar voice said from behind her. "Imagine my surprise seeing you in here."

Sheila turned around to face Nicholas. "What are you doing here?" she queried. "Are you following me?"

"Your mother called me. When I was driving by here, I saw your car outside."

Sheila pushed to her feet. "Wanna dance?"

Nicholas shook his head. "No, thanks."

"Well, I do."

She walked away from him, leaving Nicholas standing alone.

Sheila pulled a stranger standing nearby to the dance floor. She kept her eyes on Nicholas the entire time.

"What are you trying to do?" Nicholas questioned when Sheila returned to her table with drink in hand. "Kill yourself? How many of these have you had?"

"What does it matter to you?"

Nicholas's brows flickered a little. He took the drink from her and set it down on the table. "Sheila, you know that you matter a great deal to me. If you want me to spell it out, then I will. I love you."

"You love me, but you won't have sex with me . . . yeah, right."

"This is why you're drinking? Because I won't sleep with you? Because I want to have sex only with the woman I marry?"

"Whatever," Sheila mumbled. "I wan . . . want another drink."

He shook his head no. "You've had enough. I'm taking you home."

Sheila was abruptly caught by the elbow and firmly escorted to the nearest exit. Nicholas shook his head angrily. "I can't believe you're doing this to yourself. You once told me that you care about YOU. What happened to that?"

"Nicholas, don't be mad at me," Sheila begged brokenly. "I'm in pain."

"Drinking is not the answer. Especially with your medication. You're playing with fire, Sheila."

"I'm not tasking . . . oops, sorry." Sheila broke into a tiny laugh. "I think I'm a little bit drunk."

"Just a little, huh?"

"I'm not taking medicine. I don't like the way it makes me feel. Won't help me anyway."

"I can't believe you," Nicholas muttered. "Sheila, you don't care about yourself."

"Stop fussing at me."

"You need to be fussed at," he shot back. "What you're doing is reckless."

Nicholas followed Sheila to Woodlake Drive.

Essie met him at the front door. "Uh glad you found her. Nicholas, t'engk you for bringin' my gal home. I was so rorried for her."

"She's been drinking," he announced.

"Telling my mom on me," Sheila muttered. "She can't do a thing to me. I'm a grown woman."

"Then start acting like it," Nicholas practically shouted. "Act your age, Sheila. These tantrums have to stop."

"Go to hell," Sheila snapped. "Y'all don't care about me. Don't nobody care about me . . ."

"Go to bed, Sheila," Nicholas said. "I'll talk to you when you're sober." He turned to Essie asking, "Can you get her into bed?"

"Uh can do it. T'engk you for making sure she got home safe."

"Good night, Miss Essie."

Sheila's stomach suddenly felt queasy. She doubted that it was from the alcohol she'd consumed. Most likely it stemmed from the ache in her heart.

CHAPTER TWENTY-SIX

Nicholas arrived early the next morning.

Holding a hand to her head, Sheila reached the door before her mother. "What do you want?"

He brushed past her, saying, "We need to talk."

Her temple throbbing, she waved away his words. "I have a headache, Nicholas, so please don't start with me."

"Just tell me why, Sheila. Why are you carrying on like this? Are you trying to push me away?"

"Don't flatter yourself." She was so angry with Nicholas, despite the alarm bells going off inside her heart, telling her she had no real reason to be.

"What's going on in your head, Sheila?"

Pointing to herself, Sheila argued, "Nicholas, this is me. Okay? I'm not going to change for you—been there and done that. I did all that for Jake and look where it got me. Take me the way I am or leave me alone."

She continued to ignore the warnings that if she continued along this vein—things would only get worse.

"You shouldn't be drinking, Sheila, and you know it. Alcohol can cause blurred vision, dizziness—it can really mess up your coordination. Things you're already having some problems with. Remember?"

Sheila turned away from him. "I needed something to make me feel better."

He shook his head sadly. "This isn't the answer, Sheila." Nicholas stepped around her, forcing her to face him.

"I needed something, Nicholas. Something you couldn't give me. You can't possibly understand what I'm going through or how I feel."

"I'm trying, Sheila." He ached with an inner pain, wishing he could find a way to reach her.

"My head is killing me," she complained.

"Have you taken anything for your headache?"

Sheila shook her head no. "I don't think I can keep anything down right now."

Nicholas watched her a moment before saying, "You brought this on yourself."

Rolling her eyes, she responded, "I really don't need to hear this right now."

"Oh, I'm afraid you do," Nicholas countered. "You are too old for tantrums. Why do you act this way? Are you trying to run me off?"

"You can do whatever you want."

Nicholas didn't hide his confusion. "Sheila, what is really going on with you? I know you're always angry, but why are you so mad with me?"

"I don't need you trying to change me."

"I'm not trying to change you, sweetheart. I'm not."

"There are men out there who'd love to have a woman like me. Just the way I am."

She'd strayed into dangerous waters now—there was no going back.

"In fact, I met a man while I was in Hilton Head. We slept together."

His eyes never left her face, but he remained silent.

Sheila could tell from his expression that she'd gone too far this time.

Nicholas couldn't find the words for what he was feeling right now.

The woman he loved had just announced she'd slept with another man, a complete stranger, at that. She was breaking his heart.

Even now, Sheila refused to keep her mouth shut. She stood with her arms folded across her chest. "Why are you sitting there and not saying anything?"

"I don't have any words for you."

"What? You supposed to be mad?"

"I'm not mad, Sheila. There's no point in being angry."

"So what exactly are you saying?"

"I can't reach you, so I think it's best for me to leave," Nicholas said, numb. "I think it's best that I go home and mind my own business, as you suggested."

Sheila didn't respond.

"Honey, I care a great deal for you. I love you, Sheila. But you don't want my love—you only want to drown yourself in anger and bitterness." He shook his head dazedly. "I can't do this anymore."

"Then leave, Nicholas. I can't make you stay."

"Sheila, the world is not against you. I'm not against you. All I wanted to do was love and support you, but it's just not enough for you."

"Nicholas . . ." Sheila paused. "I have a lot going on with me. You know that."

"Yeah, I do. That's why I believe we shouldn't see each other anymore. I thought at one time you felt the same way I feel, but now . . . I guess I was wrong." Nicholas headed to the door.

"Where are you going?"

"Away from you, Sheila," he answered without looking back.

"Oh . . . now you don't want to talk to me."

"No, I don't." Nicholas still refused to look at her.

"Now who's running away?" Sheila goaded.

Nicholas paused long enough to throw back at her, "If you want to ruin your life—go ahead. I'm gone."

The loud ringing of the telephone woke Brittany up from her nap.

Tori heard Jake talking loud and sounding excited. She rushed into the room, asking, "What happened?"

"Charlene's in labor. She and Shepard are at the hospital and she's already six centimeters."

Tori clenched her fists and shouted, "YES!"

"Tori's calling Denika to see if she can watch the children, and then we'll be on our way," Jake said into the phone.

While he talked to Shepard, Tori used her cell phone to call her cousin.

"Hey . . . Charlene's in labor. Can I bring JJ and Brittany over to you?"

"Yeah. They can hang out with my kids. Just bring them on."

She and Jake hung up within seconds of each other.

"Denika said she'll watch JJ and Brittany for us. I'm ready if you are."

Jake nodded. "Let's go."

They quickly ushered their children to the SUV and climbed in. Tori could hardly wait to get to the hospital. She sent up a quick prayer for Charlene to have a safe delivery.

Jake drove to her cousin's house and dropped off the children. He and Tori headed to Charleston Memorial.

"Our little niece is going to be here soon. I can't wait to meet her."

Jake smiled. "You love babies, don't you?"

"I do. I think children are beautiful miracles. All of them." Tori released a long sigh. "I just wish we were pregnant already. I don't know why it's taking so long. We've never had any problems before."

Kate walked into the hallway just as Tori and Jake approached.

"How is she?" Tori asked her aunt.

"She doing fine. Just begged the doctor for some drugs." Kate chuckled. "I told that chile she was gonna need some. Those the pains of death . . . sho is."

They heard the shrill screaming of a young woman.

"Oh, my goodness," Tori murmured. "The poor girl." She placed a hand to her stomach.

"You sure you want to have another one?" Kate asked. "You ain't never been much for pain. And those li'l narrow hips of yours—they ain't made for childbearing."

"I'm not listening to you, Aunt Kate. I know you just trying to scare me."

Two and a half hours later, Charlene gave birth to a six-pound, three-ounce little girl.

Tears of joy spilled down Tori's cheeks. "She's so beautiful," she murmured when she held the tiny infant.

"Yes, she is," Shepard agreed. "Man, I'm a father. I'm a dad."

Kate sucked her teeth, her eyes raised upward.

"Behave," Tori whispered.

She and Jake stayed for another hour before leaving to pick up their children.

"You know what? I'm okay with it. We have two healthy and beautiful children. We are truly blessed."

Jake agreed.

"Christina is such a cutie." She glanced over at her husband. "Don't you think so?"

He shrugged. "She looked like a baby. All of them look alike."

Tori laughed. "Let someone say that about your babies."

Jake chuckled. "My children are the best-looking children in the world."

"That's what all parents say about their babies."

Before she went to bed later that evening, Tori said a prayer of thanks. Charlene had a safe delivery and was resting well at the hospital with her newborn daughter.

Jake climbed into bed with her. "Interested in a little . . ."

Laughing, Tori placed an arm around her husband. "C'mere, you . . ."

"Huccome you be so mean tuh dat man? He lobed you, chile."

"He didn't love me." A flash of wild grief ripped through her. "If he did, he wouldn't have left like that."

"You drove him away, Sheila. Dat's what you do—you drive eberyone who cares 'bout you away."

"I don't care. I don't need anybody. In fact, I think it's time for you to go back home."

"You don' want me here no more?"

"No, I don't. I just want to be alone."

"Fine. Uh don' stay where Uh'm not wanted. Uh leave as soon as uh get packed."

"Ma . . ."

Essie shook her head. "No, gal. Dis road—you got tuh travel alone. Uh not gon' let you 'buse me with dat forked tongue of yours. Nicholas iz a good man and you done run him off. Shame on you, Sheila. Uh feel sorry for you."

"Don't bother. I don't want pity from you or anyone else. I'm okay."

Sheila went to her room and stayed while her mother packed. She didn't want Essie to see her crying.

When she saw Nicholas pull up in her driveway, Sheila wasn't surprised. Her mother wouldn't have called anyone else.

She was a bit surprised when Nicholas and her mother left without saying a word to her.

She walked out of her room with her keys and purse. She needed a drink.

CHAPTER TWENTY-SEVEN

⁓

Nicholas sat in his car with the present for Charlene's daughter. Tori had left him a message a few days ago, telling him about Christina's birth.

He saw Tori's car and debated whether to go inside the store. He hadn't spoken to her since their argument. Nicholas thought it best to just let things cool down between them.

"Might as well get this over with," he muttered.

Nicholas climbed out of the car and strolled across the parking lot. One of the employees greeted him when he entered the bookstore.

He spotted Tori walking from the café and waved.

"Hey, stranger," she greeted.

"Hey, yourself." Nicholas held up the gift. "I bought a present for the new baby."

"I'll give it to Charlene," Tori responded. She accepted the gift, saying, "Thank you for being so thoughtful."

Scanning his face, she inquired, "Nicholas, what's wrong? You look like you've lost your best friend. What happened? You and Sheila have a fight?"

"Yeah. We did," he admitted. "By the way, Sheila and I are no longer together. That should make you happy."

"Nicholas, I really wish I could say I'm sorry about the breakup, but I can't—I would be lying."

He nodded but didn't say a word.

"You had to know that a relationship with her wouldn't work out. Sheila is not the woman for you. You're too good for her."

"Tori, you don't know that." Nicholas didn't bother to hide the frustration in his voice. "Look, just because you don't like Sheila—it doesn't mean that she's not the one for me."

"Well, if she was," Tori began, "don't you think the two of you would be together?"

"I don't want to discuss Sheila anymore. Let's talk about something else. You look extremely happy about something. What's going on?"

"Jake and I are going away. August twenty-fourth."

"A second honeymoon?"

"Kind of," she responded. "We really need to get away, just the two of us. It's been a while since we've done that. I'm looking forward to it. Especially the duty-free shopping."

"Where are you going?"

"Jake's taking me to Aruba."

Smiling, Nicholas said, "Nice."

"You've been there?"

He nodded. "It's been over ten years now, but I love the island."

"I'm so excited about this trip."

"I can tell." Nicholas glanced around the store. "How's Charlene and the baby?"

"They're doing great. Charlene's doing so well with Christina. It's like she's been handling babies for years."

"Give them both a hug from me."

Nicholas's thoughts traveled to Sheila and his mood shifted.

"You're thinking about her."

"I really thought Sheila and I had something special, Tori."

She nodded. "I'm sorry you're hurting. I feel bad about that."

"I'll be okay. Life goes on." Nicholas leaned down to embrace Tori. "I'ma get out of here. I have some work I need to do. Congratulations, Auntie."

*   *   *

Tori watched Nicholas walk out to his car. She hadn't seen him look so sad in a long time.

I knew Sheila would break your heart. Why didn't you listen to me?

While she felt relieved that Nicholas was no longer involved with Sheila, Tori was saddened by his heartache.

She took the gift for the baby and carried it to her office. Jake called while she was back there.

"Honey, I just booked our villa in Aruba. It's a ten-minute drive to the beach—the Tierra Del Sol Villas."

"So we were able to get one?"

"Yeah, they had a cancellation for one of the two-bedroom villas."

Tori smiled. She was very excited about her upcoming trip. In two days, she and Jake would be in Aruba.

They weren't into casino gambling, but she and Jake planned to participate in some of the beach activities, including snorkeling. Jake wanted to check out some of the rock formations and caves.

Thinking about her trip, Tori decided to stop by the mall before she went home. She wanted to purchase some new lingerie.

Sheila poured herself a glass of wine.

When she had called into the office this morning, Selma had told her that Jake and Tori were vacationing in Aruba. It was one of the islands Sheila and Jake had always talked of exploring. In Sheila's mind, it would be her and Jake as a couple. But for Jake—he'd probably been thinking of it as a business retreat.

As much as it pained her to admit, Jake never mentioned anything to her in regards to them being a couple. It had all been in her mind.

Now when Sheila fantasized about spending her honeymoon or some romantic weekend in Aruba—it was with Nicholas.

But even that fantasy had come to a crashing halt.

She gulped down her Chardonnay and poured herself another one.

Pain stabbed her heart as she thought of Nicholas. She hadn't spoken to him in a couple of weeks.

"So much for caring about me," Sheila muttered before swallowing the last of her wine.

Three glasses later, she picked up the telephone to call Nicholas. There were a few things she wanted to say to him.

"Hello . . ."

"Nicki, w-what are . . . what y-you doing?"

"Sheila?"

"Yeah, you r-remember m-me," she stuttered. Sheila took a sip of her drink.

"Are you drinking?"

A loud burp escaped Sheila's mouth. " 'Scuse me."

"I'm not going to listen to you drink yourself to death. Goodbye, Sheila."

"W-wait . . . doan . . . don't hang up . . . I n-need to talk to you . . . you."

"What?"

"You said you loved me." Shaking her head, she added, "You neber loved me."

Nicholas interrupted her. "I'm not doing this with you, Sheila."

"You doan leave someone you love, Nicki."

There was no response.

"Nicki, you there?"

Nothing but dead silence. Sheila feared he'd hung up on her.

She sat up straight in her chair. "C'mon, Nicholas. I'm trying to talk to you," she managed without tumbling the words.

"No, you're not. You're trying to make me one of those men who have lied to you, cheated on you, whatever. Sheila, I love you—only you can't accept the truth. Well, that's your problem and not mine. Goodnight, Sheila. And don't call my house drunk."

Nicholas hung up the phone, breaking her heart all over again.

"You said you'd always be here for me," she whispered before bursting into tears.

"What am I doing here?" Nicholas muttered to himself, standing outside Sheila's house.

I promised to be there for her.

Shaking his head, Nicholas rang the doorbell.

When Sheila still hadn't opened the door after he rang several times, Nicholas started to panic.

Using his fist, he beat on the front door.

"Uh coming," a sluggish voice yelled. "Jis' wait a minute."

Sheila threw open the door. "Uh thought Uh was seeing things when Uh looked through the peephole. Wha' you doing here?"

Nicholas brushed past her. "Since you won't try to save yourself—I guess I have to do it for you."

She looked like she had trouble grasping what he was saying to her. Sheila looked terrible.

He took her by the hand. "The first thing you're going to do is take a nice hot bath."

"I don't stink."

"You smell like alcohol, Sheila," Nicholas countered. "Now sit down while I run your bath."

"Why don' you join me?"

Hiding his frustration, Nicholas stalked down the hallway to the guest bathroom. He filled the tub with water and some of the bath salts Sheila had in jars around the tub.

When he walked back to the front of the house, Sheila was pouring herself another drink. Nicholas snatched the bottle from her and picked up the glass.

"Wha' you doin'?"

"Saving your life." Nicholas didn't stop walking until he reached the trash can, where he threw the bottle after pouring out the liquid.

He walked back to get Sheila and escort her to the bathroom. "C'mon . . . let's get you in your bath."

"My drink . . . I want my drink."

"No more drinks for you. Not tonight—not ever. This is not you, Sheila."

She shook her head. "You don' know me . . ."

"It's not for lack of trying on my part, Sheila."

Nicholas left her in the bathroom. "When I come back to check on you, I expect to find you in the tub."

He received a grunt in return.

While Sheila was in the bathroom, Nicholas went around the house looking for alcohol. She had everything from Jack Daniels to Parrot Bay. Apparently Sheila was planning on getting smashed.

Nicholas tossed everything into a garbage bag and took it out to the garage.

He went to check on Sheila.

"Uh jis' got out of the tub," she managed while securing the towel around her. Sheila tried to walk toward him, then stumbled.

He caught her in his arms. "I got you, sweetheart."

Nicholas picked her up and carried her into her bedroom where he deposited her on the king-sized bed. "I'm going to make some coffee."

Sheila shook her head. "Nooo . . . no coffee." She pointed to the closet. "Could you bring me my robe?"

"Sure." Nicholas did as she requested.

He turned his back on her until she made herself decent.

"You can turn around now."

Crawling into bed, Sheila whispered, "I guess you hate me."

He sat down beside her. "Sweetheart, I don't hate you. I could never hate you."

"I hurt so bad." Sheila put a hand to her face. "I hate being like this."

She closed her eyes.

Nicholas studied her. It looked like Sheila had passed out.

He made sure all the doors were locked and secured before leaving.

CHAPTER TWENTY-EIGHT

"The lighthouse was named after a ship called the *Californian*," the tour guide explained. "The *Californian*'s radio operator was off duty and asleep at the time the *Titanic* sent out distress signals as she was sinking in icy waters. This small piece of bad karma perhaps sealed the *Californian*'s fate. She went down in rough seas off the Aruba coast a few years after the *Titanic* sank . . ."

Tori snapped a couple of photographs of the lighthouse. She glanced over her shoulder at Jake and waved.

He walked over to join her. "Having a good time?"

Smiling, she nodded. "You know how much I love history."

Jake embraced her. "We've seen the old windmill, the Alto Vista Chapel and the Bushi—"

"Bushiribana Ruins," Tori finished for him.

They'd spent the last three days shopping, swimming, horseback riding and touring the island.

"What do you think about making a side trip to Venezuela? It's only about fifteen miles off the coast."

Tori dropped her camera into her tote. "I'd love to see Venezuela. I think we should do it."

Jake adjusted his sunglasses. "I don't think I've ever felt so rested. This trip was something I needed."

"We both needed it. I miss my babies, but it's been wonderful to get away for a few days." Tori felt more relaxed now that she and Jake weren't concentrating on trying to get pregnant.

She had a wonderful husband and two beautiful children. God had truly blessed her.

On Labor Day, Sheila woke up with a strange feeling in her legs. She threw back the covers to examine them. They looked and felt puffy.

She dismissed it as the result of being on her feet too long the day before. One of Madison-Moore's employees had died in a car accident, and Sheila had attended the funeral yesterday.

I stood too long at the cemetery, she surmised.

Sheila took a walk around her neighborhood a couple of hours later. When she removed her shoes, she could tell that even her feet were swollen now.

She spent the rest of the day on her sofa, keeping her legs propped up.

Her feelings turned to concern when the swelling continued for the next two days. But in addition to the swelling, she was experiencing what Sheila could only describe as inside shaking. She supposed it was probably the tremors the doctor had warned her about.

She couldn't stand it. Sheila felt like something terrible was going to happen. She considered calling Nicholas, but changed her mind.

He hadn't called her, so Sheila assumed he didn't want to be bothered with her. She would have to deal with this disease alone.

The following Friday, Nicholas surprised Sheila at her home.

"I didn't think I'd see you again."

"Why?"

"I hadn't heard from you."

"I went to Philadelphia for the Labor Day weekend." He sat down beside her. "How're you feeling?"

"I'm back on my medication," Sheila told him. "I went to the doctor on Wednesday. I've been having inside shakes."

"Inside shakes?"

"I feel like everything in my body is nervous. I just can't sit still. Dr. Daniels said I'll have them until the outside shaking starts—that's the best way I can explain it." Pointing to her legs, she added, "And my legs and feet are so swollen. They even look a little discolored. I really messed myself up, I think."

"Is there anything I can do for you?"

"Can you stay for a while? I don't want to be alone."

Nodding, Nicholas sat back against the cushions.

"This is one of the worst symptoms I've ever experienced. Can you imagine me trying to put my lipstick on and shaking all over the place?" She released a short laugh. "Or trying to put on mascara? Wow . . ."

Chuckling, Nicholas responded, "That's why you don't need to put all that stuff on. You're beautiful enough without it."

"You are so good for my dwindling ego."

"Are you still drinking?"

Sheila shook her head no. "Not since all of my alcohol mysteriously disappeared. I haven't felt much like going out to buy more."

"When did you decide to get back on your medicine?"

"After the stern lecture from my doctor," Sheila admitted. "She's right. You're right. Okay?"

"It's not about being right, sweetheart. I just don't want to see anything happen to you."

"I wasn't sure you still cared anything for me after all the things I've done."

"I'll always care about you, Sheila."

"But you don't want to be with me. Right?"

"Right now, I think you need to spend some time with Sheila. You have a lot you need to deal with. I can't help you with that—you have to help yourself. Sheila, I will always be here for you. But only as a friend."

Pain ripped through her heart. Tears filled her eyes, overflowing and rolling down her cheek.

She placed a hand to her face, trying to hide her tears from Nicholas.

The warmth of strong arms around her only made Sheila's sobs louder.

"Sssh . . . sweetheart, it's going to be okay. Don't cry."

She'd lost again. But this time, she could only blame herself.

* * *

Nicholas hated the sound of Sheila's crying. It echoed his own heart breaking.

"Sssh . . ." he whispered.

Sheila composed herself and tried to stand. Nicholas helped her up.

"I'll be right back," she said.

She washed her face, then returned to the family room where he was sitting. "Sorry for being a big baby."

Sheila sat down. "I was just thinking about something. I don't think you should come over anymore. Or call. Right now, it's too hard for me."

She wouldn't look at him, just stared down at her hands. She looked so lost and forlorn—Nicholas yearned to pull her back into his arms, but to do so would be wrong. He and Sheila were not meant to be a couple.

She had too many problems and refused to work on them.

"That's not what I want, Sheila, but I will respect your wishes. I want what's best for you."

"I can't just be your friend, Nicholas. My feelings are way too strong for that."

"I will always care for you, sweetheart. I just think you need time to get over some things. Get rid of some of that anger. Everybody is not out to hurt you, Sheila."

She didn't respond.

Nicholas stayed for another hour.

He rose to his feet. "I need to get going. Are you sure about this, Sheila? You don't want me to call or come by here?"

"It hurts too much."

"Take care of yourself. Okay?"

Sheila gave a slight nod.

"If you ever want to talk or if you need me, Sheila . . . please don't hesitate to call."

"Goodbye, Nicholas."

He resisted the urge to kiss her and walked through the house to the front door.

Nicholas didn't have to look back to know Sheila was crying. His heart broke at the sound of her sobs—the last thing he'd ever wanted to do was add to her pain.

"Lord, I need to know if I've done the right thing. I love Sheila with all my heart and I hope by leaving her—she'll become the person I know she can be."

Nicholas climbed into his car and drove away without looking back.

CHAPTER TWENTY-NINE

⟡

Two weeks passed, and Sheila heard nothing from Nicholas. He was honoring her wishes, but it didn't make her feel good. In fact, it only saddened her more.

She was shaking so badly now that she thought she would go crazy. It was a horrible experience. And her balance was so bad that she had purchased a walker, just in case.

Sheila had no choice but to call and plead with her mother to move back in with her.

Essie had been back now for a week. Sheila was grateful she didn't have to be alone in the house for now—especially on those days she could barely get out of bed or function because of the pain.

"Ma, can you help me get to my room?"

"C'mon . . ."

Essie made sure Sheila was settled before leaving to cook dinner.

"Thanks."

"You want me to give you yo' injection?"

Sheila nodded. Deep down, she felt like crying. She couldn't even give herself an injection any more. Her tremors were lasting longer and coming more frequently. She couldn't even make it to the bathroom without her quad cane. If her condition continued progressing, she would need to use that walker.

She noticed the Bible lying on her nightstand.

How did it get there?

Only Nicholas could have placed it there during his last and final visit. Or her mother. It had to be one of them, because she'd left it on her bookshelf in the den.

Funny she hadn't noticed it there until now.

Sheila sat down on the edge of the bed. As if drawn by some unseen force, she reached for the Bible.

She held it unopened in her lap.

"What am I doing?" she whispered. "I don't want to read the Bible." Looking up, she said in a louder voice, "God, you and I have nothing to discuss."

Sheila released a small sigh of resignation and opened her Bible to a random chapter. She glanced down. "Fifth chapter of Mark. Probably nothing special here . . ."

She began to read.

Sheila found herself intrigued. She was reading the story of how Jesus was on his way to heal the critically ill daughter of a local synagogue leader. Throngs of people crowded around him, anticipating the spectacle of a miracle. There was a woman in the crowd who had had a hemorrhage for twelve years.

Sheila couldn't believe it. "Twelve years," she repeated. "I don't have that kind of patience."

The most remarkable thing to Sheila was that, despite the woman's constant bleeding and social stigma, she never gave up. She had heard about Jesus and was trying to get to him. Eventually she was able to come up behind him and touch the fringe of his robe. Immediately the bleeding stopped and she could feel that she had been healed.

"Just by touching His robe? Boy, she had some radical faith," Sheila murmured.

She heard the telephone ringing, but ignored it.

Her mother came to the door a few minutes later. "It's Nicholas. He want tuh talk tuh you."

Surprised, Sheila picked up the receiver. "Hello."

"I know you didn't want me to call but I had to check on you. I hope I'm not upsetting you."

"It's okay," she murmured. She was so glad to hear from Nicholas. "I've been wanting to talk to you, too. I really miss you."

"How's your day going?" he inquired.

"As well as can be, I guess. I had to have my mama come back to live with me. Nicholas, I've been wondering about something. Did you leave my Bible on my nightstand?"

He laughed.

"I figured it was you. You don't give up, do you?"

"Not on the people I care about."

"Well, you'll be happy to know that I read it today. I read about this lady who hemorrhaged for twelve years and she was healed just by touching the hem of Jesus' robe. Now, I *need* a miracle like that."

"Did those verses speak to you?"

"Yeah. They did, actually. It was a revelation in how I need to handle my condition. That woman never gave up, Nicholas. Like her, I can't give up. I can't allow my defects to defeat me."

"This is what I like hearing, Sheila. Just because you have to accept the fact that you have MS, you don't have to let it beat you. Like the woman in the Bible, you don't have to stop seeking healing either. Jesus can heal you today the same way He healed that woman all those years ago. You have to have faith."

"I'm scared God won't listen to me. I've not listened to Him at all. I know I'm a sinner in a big way—He probably gave up on me a long time ago."

"God never gives up on us. We are always the ones to give up on Him."

She heard Nicholas's words, but she didn't really believe that they applied to her.

"Sheila, all you have to do is open your heart and let Jesus come in. But you also have to let go of your anger. You've got to forgive, Sheila."

"Even if I do forgive everyone, God probably won't forgive me, Nicholas. He doesn't want anything to do with me," she insisted.

"That's not true. Acts thirteen thirty-eight declares, *Therefore, my brothers, I want you to know that through Jesus the forgiveness of sins is proclaimed to you.* God is loving and merciful, Sheila. He is eager to forgive us of our sins.

Second Peter three nine tells us that *He is patient with you, not wanting anyone to perish, but everyone to come to repentance.* God desires to forgive us, so He provided for our forgiveness."

"So you think I need to get some religion, huh? You think that will make me feel better?"

"Sheila, I don't think getting religion will do a thing for you," Nicholas countered. "What you need is Jesus, pure and simple."

She was quiet.

"Sheila . . . you there?"

"Yeah, I'm still here. I was just thinking about what you said."

"I'd like to pray with you. Is that alright?"

"Sure," Sheila answered after a moment.

"Heavenly Father, we come to You repentant and humbled. The Scripture says that everyone who calls on the name of the Lord will be saved. Father God, we come to You asking that You please forgive and forget all the sins that we have committed against You. We offer our bodies as a living sacrifice to You, Lord. Enable us not to be conformed any longer to the pattern of this world, but to be transformed by the renewing of our minds. Father, we ask that You pour out Your Spirit upon us in an abounding measure and purge off the undesirable things in us, which are not pleasing to Your sight.

"The Living Word says that if we confess with our mouths that Jesus Christ is the Lord and believe in our hearts that God raised Him from the dead, then we will be saved. Accordingly, we rely totally on Your Word, Lord. Create in us a clean heart and restore to us the joy of Your salvation. Save and justify us by Your divine grace, because it is by Your grace that we are saved, through faith and not from ourselves, and it is a gift from You alone.

"Thank You, Lord Jesus, for redeeming us with Your most precious blood, which You shed for us on the cross of Calvary. We thank You and praise You, Lord. Amen."

Sheila ended her conversation with Nicholas, unable to describe her emotions after his heartfelt prayer. Her heart was beating rapidly and her stomach quivered. She still couldn't believe what had occurred just moments before.

There were no words to describe this newfound relationship with God. Sheila felt like a tremendous weight had been lifted. She was no longer alone.

Despite everything she'd done to him, Nicholas had cared enough to pray with her. He was truly a good man.

She suddenly felt the urge to go before the Lord in her own way. Her knees hurt, so she sat on the edge of her bed.

"Dear Lord, I don't mean to dishonor You by not falling to the floor, but you know my condition. I needed to talk to You myself, because I want You to know that I'm serious about this. This isn't to impress Nicholas. I promise it wasn't. I'm not trying to get him back or anything." Her eyes filled with tears.

"God, I need You . . . I hurt so bad and I'm so angry. I don't understand . . . I just don't understand why I had to grow up being treated so badly. What did I do to deserve all this?" Sheila wiped away a lone tear. "How do I forgive them?"

Crying harder, she closed her eyes, saying, "Okay, God . . . I'll try to forgive . . . my dad, my mother and all the people who treated me so horribly. If that's what You want . . . I'll do my best."

Sheila lay back on her bed, exhausted. Praying had taken a toll on her. The quivering in her stomach had dissipated and her heart no longer raced.

She was finally at peace.

Nicholas stood in the middle of his yard, raking up the fall leaves. October sailed in, bringing the hint of a chill in the wind.

I'm glad I called Sheila yesterday. Maybe there was hope for her after all. She'd actually read the Bible.

He threw up his hand and waved at the postman.

Nicholas made small talk while accepting the stack of mail. "Thanks, Herman."

He scanned the envelopes while walking into the house. There was an invitation of some kind from Charlene and Shepard.

Nicholas opened it.

"Christina's being christened," he read aloud.

Nicholas sat down at his desk and made a note of the date on his calendar. He didn't plan to miss the event. He considered Charlene and Tori like sisters, and they treated him like part of the family as well.

He would not miss the christening.

I'm saved . . .

Sheila kept saying the words over and over in her mind, trying to comprehend all that it meant.

Now what? What happens now?

Do I feel changed? she asked herself.

Sheila made her way over to a nearby mirror. She studied her features, trying to detect any physical changes. "This is silly," she muttered. "I don't look any different."

The phone rang and Nicholas's name popped up on the caller ID, but Sheila didn't answer. She didn't feel like talking right now.

She just wanted to keep this time between her and God. She felt almost childlike in her need to please Him. Sheila wanted to really prove to God just how serious she was. She intended to be the perfect Christian.

Although she'd told God she would forgive Jake and Tori, Sheila was having a tough time doing so. She hated them. Maybe if she was kind, generous and did everything else right—God would not hold it against her for not forgiving them.

Later that evening, when she opened her Bible to a random page, Sheila found herself scanning the third chapter in the book of Colossians. Her eyes stopped on verse thirteen. *Forbearing one another, and forgiving one another, if any man have a quarrel against any: even as Christ forgave you, so also do ye.*

"The things I've done . . . God forgave me."

One of the passages referenced was Matthew 6:15. Sheila easily located the verses and read, *But if you forgive not men their trespasses, neither will your Father forgive your trespasses.*

In startling clarity, Sheila recalled all her schemes to break up Jake and Tori. Waves of embarrassment washed over her. God had been witness to it all—yet He forgave her.

For the first time in her life, Sheila had to consider that she alone was at fault—there was no reason to blame Jake or Tori. She had been the one vying to destroy their marriage. They never set out to destroy her—just protect the love they shared.

But if you do not forgive men their sins, your Father will not forgive your sins.

Sheila suddenly felt disgusted. "How can You love me, God? I'm a horrible person. Look how I treated my own mother . . . Please forgive me . . . I want to be forgiven."

She knew what she had to do.

CHAPTER THIRTY

Christina Gwendolyn Madison was christened on October fifteenth, surrounded by her parents, Kate, Jake and Tori.

After the service, they traveled to Kate's house for a family dinner.

Kate walked over to where Nicholas was standing.

"I want to apologize, Nicholas. I should've minded my own business."

He embraced her. "It's okay. I appreciate your caring about me, Aunt Kate."

"I love you like my own son, and I want to see you happily married to a wonderful woman."

"I want that, too," Nicholas admitted.

Tori joined them. "I'm glad you could make it. Have you met Miss Christina?"

"No, I haven't."

She led him over to where Charlene sat with the baby.

Nicholas inquired, "Are we interrupting?"

"No. She just finished her bottle and now she wants to coo. Would you like to hold her?"

Smiling, he sat down on the sofa beside Charlene. She gently handed over her daughter.

"Hey, little miss. I'm your uncle Nicholas . . ."

The baby rewarded him with a lopsided grin.

"You're so good with her," Tori commented. "I can tell you love babies."

"They're so sweet and innocent. You just want to protect them . . . I can't wait to have children."

"Speaking of children . . . Jake and I have an announcement to make." She glanced over her shoulder. "Where are you, honey?"

"Right here," Jake responded.

Tori rose to her feet and moved to stand beside Jake. "We're pregnant," she announced with a laugh. "Our baby's due May twenty-fifth."

Charlene rose to her feet. "Girl, congratulations. I'm so happy for you."

Jake held up a hand. "Hey, I helped. What about me?"

Nicholas sat holding the baby while everyone congratulated Tori and Jake. He was happy for them. Tori had gotten her desire to have another child.

He thought about Sheila. She said she didn't want children, but even if she did—there was a chance she couldn't because of the MS. As much as he loved her, Nicholas didn't think he was willing to give up his desire to have children.

Having a family was too important to him.

It was Sunday.

Sheila surfed through the channels on her television, searching for something to watch. There wasn't a whole lot to choose from.

She'd had enough of Lifetime movies, and she wasn't interested in watching sports. She heard a minister named Sammy Tippit mention jealousy and flipped back to that channel.

Her mother walked into the room. "Dat Pastor Tippit. He a good li'l preacher." She sat down on the chair across from Sheila.

". . . Jealousy has its roots in insecurity—basically derived from the fear of loss," he explained. "Jealousy is rooted in fear, and fear is based in insecurity."

Sheila could feel her mother's eyes on her. She met her gaze. "What?"

Ignoring the question, Essie turned her attention back to the television.

"There's only one cure for the deep wounds of the soul—faith in Jesus. Faith is the opposite of fear and Jesus Christ is the source of security."

His words intrigued Sheila.

"It's only through our trust in Him that we find victory over the fruit of our insecurity. He is the only secure place during the storms that rage about us. It's only when we come to Him with childlike faith that we find peace in the storms of life."

Sheila continued to listen, her heart and mind opening wide.

"When God came into my life, God set me free from many things. I was no longer a slave to alcohol, sex and ego . . ."

She sat up straight, a chill traveling down her spine. It was almost as if the man was speaking directly to her.

"You have to trust in God and not in your own strength if you want victory over jealousy. Now, I have to tell you that I've had to learn it's not a one-time leap of faith. Victory is a daily walk of faith."

He ended his sermon by saying, "Jealousy and insecurity tremble in the presence of Jesus. Fear flees at the very mention of His name. He will give us His victory over jealousy if we just put our trust in Him."

"Dat a good message this mo'ning. Dat man know he can preach the Good Word."

"It was interesting," Sheila admitted. "I could relate to what he was talking about."

She wasn't the same person anymore. She sensed the changes in her. God was revealing His Word all around her—in the Bible, on television—even in a couple of magazines she'd thumbed through at the doctor's office.

Nicholas was right—you can find God everywhere. You only have to look around.

Essie's words broke through her musings. "You hongry?"

Sheila shook her head. "Not right now, Ma. Maybe in a little while."

She sat there thinking about everything the pastor had said. His words had managed to sink deep into her soul.

Amazed, Sheila read the story of Daniel and his faithfulness to God. While she tried to read several passages daily—parts of the Bible seemed foreign to her. Sheila enjoyed the parables and the stories of Hannah, Ruth, David and Samuel most.

The telephone rang.

Sheila answered, instinctively knowing that Nicholas was on the other end of the line. "Hello."

"You were on my mind, so I thought I'd check on you. Did I catch you at a bad time?"

"I was reading the Bible." Sheila held her breath, waiting for his response.

"That's great! Praise God . . ."

She laughed. "I knew you'd react this way."

"What are you reading?"

"About Daniel. He was very loyal to God. Even in danger, Daniel and his friends refused to go against the Lord. He was a brave man. I admire that."

"God looked after them because they were loyal."

"When Daniel was in the lion's den . . . I remembered hearing that story when I was a little girl. I don't know where I heard it, but I remember it. When I read about people like this—it saddens me."

"Why?"

"I can't even come close to being like them. They're just too good to be true. You know what I mean?"

"Sweetheart, the good news is that Jesus is on our side. When we give our life to Jesus, the Holy Spirit unites with Him. We become victorious over sin and death. You never have to look back at the past."

But Sheila knew that before she could totally put the past to rest, she needed to face Jake and Tori.

CHAPTER THIRTY-ONE

heila woke up the first Sunday in November and decided she
wanted to attend church. She'd been watching Pastor Henry on
television, but now she wanted to see if she could find that same
kind of preaching in a real church.

She dressed with some assistance from her mother.

"Ma, you going with me to church?"

"Uh almost ready," Essie responded.

Half an hour later, Sheila was pulling out of her driveway.

She'd bullied her mother into taking driving lessons and now Essie
had her first driver's permit. Sheila would let her drive around the neighborhood, but her mother got nervous when she found herself in unfamiliar places.

Sheila parked in the first vacant handicap parking space she found.
She and her mother got out and walked toward the church.

They slid into the last pew.

Initially, Sheila felt a little hesitant about popping up in the church
Nicholas attended, but she missed him.

"This morning I'm going to talk about how to develop a forgiving
spirit," the pastor announced.

Sheila glanced around the church, looking for Nicholas.

"The first thing we have to do is focus on God's forgiveness of us. In the fourth chapter of Ephesians, verse thirty-two, the Word says, *And be kind to one another, tenderhearted, forgiving one another, even as God in Christ forgave you.*"

Sheila opened her Bible. She almost gave up searching for the book of Ephesians until the young woman sitting beside her mother helped her locate it.

She gave the woman a tiny smile.

"The next thing we have to do is allow the Lord to help us forgive and forget. Now let me explain what it means to forget . . . I hear people all the time saying, 'Oh I forgive so and so, but I won't forget.' A person that says I will forgive but will not forget has not truly forgiven. Church, I want you to write this down. To forget means to treat with thoughtless inattention, neglect or fail to mention. We can do this if we want to. The third chapter of Philippians, verse thirteen, says *Brethren, I do not count myself to have apprehended; but one thing I do, forgetting those things which are behind and reaching forward to those things which are ahead.*"

Sheila glanced up, meeting the gaze of the pastor. Once again, she felt like this man was talking directly to her. She squirmed uneasily in her seat.

". . . Many emotions we experience are not necessarily sin," Pastor Henry explained. "Anger is not necessarily a sin, unless the object of our anger is misplaced."

Sheila considered everything Pastor Henry was saying.

Images of her parents, Jake and Tori formed in Sheila's mind.

"Don't explain it away—they came to mind for a reason," Pastor Henry stated. "The Holy Spirit of God brings them to your mind because He loves you and wants to rid you of a cancer that is eating you from inside out."

Sheila's eyes filled with unshed tears.

Pastor Henry paused before continuing. "God allows us to be hurt sometimes, as a test."

As the sermon drew to a close, the pastor stated, "Nothing is more sad than someone who needs to be forgiven, can be forgiven, and yet is not forgiven, because they won't accept it. Forgiveness is offered freely. Take it. Let's pray."

Sheila bowed her head. She had to face Jake and Tori—there was no avoiding it. This sermon was confirmation from God.

"Thank You, precious Father, for forgiving me, though I don't deserve it, and for not holding my sins against me. Lord, we thank You for giving us the power to forgive others. In Jesus' name, amen."

After the service, Nicholas walked over to where Sheila and her mother stood.

"Hello, ladies," he greeted.

"I guess you're surprised to see us here."

"I am," Nicholas confessed. "But I can't tell you just how happy this makes me. How did you enjoy the service?"

"It was good. I learned a lot." Sheila couldn't take her gaze away from Nicholas's handsome face. "You were always talking about your pastor—I figured I'd better check him out myself."

Nicholas walked Sheila and her mother to the car.

"I hope you'll come back and worship with us," Nicholas said.

Smiling, Sheila responded, "I just might do that."

A part of her wanted to ask him to join them for a light lunch, but she knew Nicholas would turn her down. He was trying to keep his distance, because that was what she'd asked of him.

Sheila turned to unlock her car.

"Would you ladies like to have dinner with me?" Nicholas inquired. "I cooked all this food yesterday, and I can't eat it all by myself."

She broke into a big grin. "We would love to join you."

He returned her smile. Nicholas was glad to see bits of the old Sheila back. She'd lost a fair amount of weight, but she still looked good.

Sheila was wearing her hair styled short, and Nicholas loved it. It made her look much younger.

He could tell that she still had episodes of trembling, but decided against mentioning it. He didn't want to embarrass her.

After the delicious dinner Nicholas had prepared, Sheila sat in the kitchen with him while he cleaned up. He gave Essie carte blanche over the remote control and put her in the family room.

He accepted the plate she'd just dried and put it away. "I'm so proud of you, Sheila."

"Don't be . . . I'm just finally getting my head on straight. And I'm working on my relationship with God. It took a while for me to get it— but I did. I can't get anywhere without Him. It's my faith in God that will get me through this battle with MS. Through everything in my life. I get it now."

"I want to make sure you're clear on one thing. Your having faith does not cause God to care, Sheila. Faith reveals God's care. Tell me something . . . what if God doesn't take away the MS? Will you still believe in Him or have faith in Him?"

"I've been reading that first chapter in James a lot lately. I know that this is a test of my faith, and even if God never heals me—I know that He can. And I will be stronger for having gone through this."

He sat down in the chair beside her. "You have really grown, Sheila."

"When I set my mind to doing something—nothing stands in my way." She broke into a big grin. "I guess you could say this witch has decided to use her powers for good. You think God has room in His kingdom for someone like me?"

Nicholas laughed. "Sweetheart, when a child of God comes home . . . I bet the angels in heaven are up there rejoicing and preparing a room for you as we speak."

Nicholas decided to stay in town to eat Thanksgiving dinner with Sheila and her mother.

Sheila struggled to fight her bouts of depression and worked hard to remain positive, despite the rapid progression of her disease.

She was a changed woman.

Essie was in the kitchen cooking when Nicholas arrived. He sat down with Sheila in the family room.

"How are your aunt and uncle doing?"

"Fine. They were a little disappointed that you and I weren't coming down to Georgia for the holiday."

"It was so sweet of them to invite me and my mother. I just didn't want your family to see me in my condition."

As if to prove her point, Sheila suddenly began to tremble.

"This is so embarrassing. You know something . . . God allowed this disease in my life for a reason—humility. I used to view my affliction as a punishment, but not anymore. I was given this handicap to keep me dependent on Him and not on my own abilities."

"I guess that's one way to look at it."

"It's the only way to look at it," Sheila insisted. "With having MS, my focus is off the superficial stuff and centered on what really matters. I've finally figured out that most of my dissatisfaction with life has come through things that don't really matter. I'm looking for victory, Nicholas. Victory over jealousy, bitterness and anger."

"Sweetheart, just trust the Lord to be your victory over all those things. When you do that, you will walk in victory. Jesus is our rock, our shield and our defender."

"It's still kind of strange for me—this newfound faith in God. I never thought I could feel so peaceful, but I do. After searching for peace all this time, I've found it in the Lord."

"We have a lot to be thankful for today," Nicholas murmured.

Sheila couldn't agree more.

Nicholas left Sheila's house feeling very happy. He thanked God for showing her true contentment after everything she'd had to endure.

That evening after Nicholas left, Sheila told her mother, "I think this is probably the best Thanksgiving I've ever had."

CHAPTER THIRTY-TWO

≈

Sheila stood outside the doorway of Jake's office, summoning up courage to do what she should have done a long time ago.

Although she'd arrived nearly half an hour ago, Sheila stayed in the car with her mother for nearly fifteen minutes, silently debating whether to go inside the building, or whether the timing was right.

With her mother's assistance, she'd made it through the lobby and up to Jake's office. Now she was standing in the hallway, feeling like an interloper.

The company Christmas party was a few days away and Sheila wanted to clear the air before the event, so she took a deep breath and exhaled slowly.

Heart pounding, she knocked softly on the door before sticking her head inside. "Jake, are you busy?"

He glanced up from his computer. "No. Not at all. Come on in."

"I wanted to talk to you." Sheila took a seat in one of the visitor chairs.

She pointed to the walker. "I'm sure you're wondering why I'm using this. Jake, I have MS. Actually my condition is called primary progressive multiple sclerosis."

Jake was stunned. "I had no idea. Sheila, why didn't you tell me?"

"I didn't want you to know," she responded. "I couldn't bear the thought of you gloating."

"Sheila, you can't possibly think I'd be happy about something like that."

"I would have been," confessed Sheila. "If it had happened to you and Tori. At least, the old me would have anyway."

"I'm not like that—you know that."

She nodded. "You were always so noble. It's one of the qualities I loved..." Sheila paused and started again. "... I liked about you. Jake, the reason I'm here is because I owe you a big apology. For everything I did to you. I know you tried to apologize to me a while back. I was so rude to you."

"Apology accepted. Sheila, I'm not going to make any excuses. I was going through a lot, but I knew what I was doing was wrong. I should've made it clear that I wanted my marriage more than anything else. You and I never should have gotten involved. I misled you, and I am very sorry."

"What exactly is going on here?" a voice demanded from behind.

Sheila glanced over her shoulder. Tori stood in the doorway with her hand resting on the small mound of her belly. She looked irate.

She's pregnant again, Sheila thought to herself.

Jake pushed away from his desk and walked over to his wife, leading her into the office. "We were having a discussion. One I think you need to hear."

Tori sat in Jake's empty chair, facing Sheila while he stood beside her, his arms folded. They were truly united.

"So what is it that I need to hear?" she inquired.

"I came here to apologize to Jake, and since you're here—to you as well, Tori."

"Really? This is new."

"Tori, I'm simply doing what has been placed on my heart." Sheila inhaled, then released a deep breath. "I'm very sorry for the things I did to you. I was wrong when I tried to break up your marriage."

Tori eyed her a moment before saying, "Thank you, Sheila. I appreciate your apologizing to me. To us. It took a lot of courage to come here." Her eyes strayed to the walker beside Sheila's chair.

"I have MS." Sheila paused a heartbeat before continuing. "I also want you both to know that I've made a decision. I want to sell my half of Madison-Moore to you."

Jake's eyebrows rose in surprise. "Are you sure about this?"

Sheila nodded. "I need to do it. I think it's the only way I'll be able to move on with my life." She pointed to the walker. "God couldn't get my attention until I was stricken with MS. This disease has forced me to take a long hard look at myself, and face some very ugly truths . . . Right now, I really need to focus on fighting this disease. I'm not going to let MS win."

"I'll keep you in my prayers, Sheila," Tori promised.

"If you'd like—we can pray with you right now," Jake suggested.

Sheila gave a small smile. "I need all the prayer I can get."

Jake and Tori came around the desk, bridging the gap between them. Tori took Sheila's right hand while Jake took her left.

He began to pray.

"Most precious Father, we come to praise You and give You the honor You so richly deserve. We thank You for being with us always and for loving us with Your eternal love. We know that You are in control of all things and we thank You for that. Father God, Your Scripture clearly tells us that without faith we can neither please You nor receive any answer for our prayer. This afternoon, we come to You on behalf of Your child, Sheila Moore. We ask that You give her the confidence that You will meet all her needs as she seeks to live according to Your Word. Lord, we thank You for helping her get over her unbelief and for removing all her fears and anxieties. Strengthen her faith, dear Lord. We love You and trust in Your awesome power. Give Sheila the peace of mind that You are with her even now to take care of all her needs. In Jesus' name we pray. Amen."

After Jake finished praying, Sheila stood up. "By the way, congratulations," she murmured. "I couldn't help but notice that you're having another baby."

"Thank you," they responded in unison.

"My lawyer will be in touch," Sheila stated before turning to leave.

Her mother was waiting for her in the reception area and escorted Sheila to the door. Sheila could feel everyone's eyes on her and hear the low murmurings. Her employees were surprised to see her using the walker.

Suddenly, she heard a hand clap followed by others. Sheila turned around. People were standing everywhere clapping their hands for her. When she looked up, Jake and Tori were standing there, clapping for her as well.

Tears rolled down her cheeks.

Selma ran over, embracing her. "We love you, Miss Moore. All of the employees want you to know that. You call me if you need anything. You hear me?"

Sheila smiled in gratitude through her tears over this small victory—that MS had not defined her as a person. She was still Sheila Moore, a respected partner in a magnificent company.

It was nice to finally hear the words she'd waited so long for Sheila to say. Then it occurred to Tori that as nice as it was to hear Sheila's apology—it no longer mattered. Her words paled in comparison to the deep peace God had given her.

"What's going through your mind right now?" Jake inquired.

"Revelation," Tori responded. "Honey, for years I have been caught up in my anger and unforgiveness when it came to Sheila. All this time, I thought I really needed to hear her admit all the things she did to me. I thought I needed her apology, but God just dropped in my spirit that the truth I'd been wanting all this time lies with Him. He is my source, my strength. God alone can minister healing. No one can hurt me as long as I am in God's hands—unless I allow them to do so."

"Sounds like Sheila may have had the same revelation."

"Wouldn't that be just like God? Every experience, no matter how painful or confusing it seems, can serve to bring you closer to Him. From the way Sheila was talking, it really sounds like she's given her life to the Lord. I'm gonna keep lifting her up in prayer."

"I still can't believe that she's leaving the company. Sheila loves Madison-Moore."

"She might change her mind, Jake," Tori reminded him.

"You're right. To tell the truth, honey, I don't know what will happen to Madison-Moore if Sheila leaves. She is behind the success of our company. I can't deny that."

"Jake, the company is a success because of the both of you—not just Sheila."

"I appreciate your saying that."

"It's true. If Sheila is serious about leaving, Madison-Moore will continue to be just as successful. Maybe now you can experience all that God has for you."

Jake broke into a smile. "Sheila's leaving is good news to you."

"I won't deny that," Tori confessed. "I forgive Sheila, but I really don't see us being friends. And I think that it's best if the partnership ends. Too much has happened."

"I agree with you," Jake said. "But I don't want to just push her out. Look at what she's going through."

"You didn't push Sheila out. She wants to leave."

Jake nodded in agreement. "You're right."

"Why don't you and Sheila both pray over this decision before either of you make a move?" Tori suggested. "Make sure this is what God wants for you both."

"I will." Jake rose to his feet and grabbed his keys. "You ready for lunch?"

Tori stood up. "Yeah. Baby and I are starved."

They walked hand in hand out of the office, down the hall to the elevators.

"I was just thinking," Tori began. "God wants to empower us, Jake. He wants us to feel good about ourselves, more excited about our future and enthusiastic about our faith. He's not gonna let you fail. Honey, just trust God and give the company back to Him."

They had a light lunch.

"I think we should have a dinner for Sheila. The employees love her," Jake said thoughtfully.

"You should," Tori agreed.

When they finished eating, Tori dropped Jake off back at Madison-Moore; then she headed back to the bookstore.

Nicholas was just getting out of his car when Tori arrived. She got out of her car and walked over to him. "What are you doing here? Checking to see how many copies of your books I have on hand?"

He threw back his head and laughed as they walked into the store together.

"I was here to pick up a few Christmas gifts," Nicholas told her.

"We have a great selection of journals, limited edition items and of course, books." Tori pointed to the next aisle. "The customers are loving the new prayer journals."

She led Nicholas over to the display. "This is my third order," Tori announced. "And we're down to five."

"I'll take all five," Nicholas said. He flipped through one. "I'm going to keep one for myself."

"Jake and I each have them. I love mine." Tori waved at a customer. "Hey, do you have a few minutes to talk?"

Nicholas glanced at his watch. "Yeah, I have about an hour to kill."

They found an empty table in the café and sat down.

"Nicholas, I saw Sheila when I went by Jake's office earlier. She told us about the MS."

"I'm glad she did. I hope you understand that this was not something I could talk about. I'd made Sheila a promise and—"

Tori interrupted him. "I totally understand, Nicholas. I can even understand why she didn't want us to know. Having MS has changed her."

He agreed. "She just got saved a few months ago, too. That's had the biggest effect on her."

"I'll say . . . Sheila also said that she wants out of Madison-Moore."

"Really?"

"Sheila never mentioned this to you?"

Nicholas shook his head no. "I never thought she'd leave her company. This is a surprise."

"I suggested to Jake that they pray about it some more before they do anything."

"She wouldn't have mentioned it if she had no intentions to follow through."

"She's not the same person," Tori said. "I can see how much she's changed."

"I think she's really trying. I'm very proud of the strides she's made."

"You still love her?"

Nicholas nodded. "Sheila's a special woman."

"Do you think you two will get back together?"

"I don't know."

"Well, you were good for her."

He shrugged. "The way I see it—I was just a way to introduce Sheila to the Lord."

Tori frowned. "Come again?"

"I think God used me to help Sheila open her heart not just to being loved, but also to Him."

"But can you just walk away?" Tori asked.

"I really don't have a choice. I want children. Sheila's not interested in being a mother. Even if she was, her MS is progressing pretty rapidly. Children for her may not be possible."

"I understand."

"Maybe our relationship wasn't meant to be a lifetime. It's possible that it's served its purpose and now we're back to just being friends."

"And if she changes her mind? About having children or adopting. What then?"

"I don't know. I guess we'd have something to discuss."

"You must really love her."

"I do," Nicholas admitted. "And if there's a chance to spend the rest of my life with her—I'm open. But she has to be the woman God has chosen for me."

The heavy cloak of despair that had held Sheila in bondage for most of her life was gone.

She wasn't sure how she'd feel after facing Tori and Jake. It took her completely by surprise when they offered to pray for her.

Sheila's first thought had been that Tori was truly a saint. Forgiveness had come so easily for her—Sheila couldn't deny she still felt remnants of bitterness toward them, but she knew it would take time.

She'd considered calling Nicholas to tell him what happened, then changed her mind. She needed time to let everything sink in. She was no longer a part of Madison-Moore.

If she were to be truthful, Sheila had to admit her feelings for the company had changed a long time ago—when she relocated to New York. Madison-Moore just wasn't the same without the closeness she once shared with Jake.

It was time to move on. Sheila vowed not to look back.

CHAPTER THIRTY-THREE

"Merry Christmas, Ma," Sheila greeted.

"Hey. How you feelin' tadey?"

"Okay. I haven't had much pain today." She pointed to the presents underneath the Christmas tree. "C'mon . . . here. I want you to open your gifts."

Sheila followed her mother over to the sofa, careful to lean against the furniture for support.

Essie helped her sit down near the tree so that she could reach most of the presents with ease.

"I want you to open this one first," Sheila directed.

While Essie unwrapped her gift, Sheila said, "There's something I've been meaning to discuss with you."

Her mother's hands stopped moving.

"I need to apologize to you, Ma. I've been so mean to you, and I'm truly sorry for being such a terrible daughter. I know I don't deserve it, but I hope you'll please forgive me."

Her mother's eyes became tear bright.

"I love you so much, but there were so many times I also hated you. I was so angry because of the way I grew up—the way I looked—the way

I dressed . . . I blamed you. I blamed you for everything, and it was wrong." Sheila wiped away a hot tear. "I actually looked down on you."

"Uh know'um you blamed me for yo' deddy leavin'. Uh was so hartsick when he left. Uh sorry Uh weren't dar for you."

"Ma, you panicked back then. And you had nowhere to turn. I think I understand that now. I definitely understand how much it hurts to love someone and not have the love returned. I don't think I ever really understood until this minute what you must have gone through. I certainly didn't make things easy for you. I became so focused on what I wanted that I didn't care what I did to get it," Sheila said.

Essie seemed surprised by her daughter's admission.

"Ma, I haven't been a real nice person. I know that. Lately, I've been doing a lot of praying. I was finally able to forgive my dad. God laid it on my heart that I needed to ask for forgiveness as well. I had to forgive you, Ma—not just for bailing out mentally on me, but for everything, and I need you to forgive me."

"What did uh do tuh you, Sheila?"

"You embarrassed me," she responded. "Kids at school always made fun of me. You made my clothes, Ma. And they looked handmade. They laughed at the way I talked. I was ugly." Sheila's voice broke. "I hated you because we lived in Frogmore. We were different from the other kids in school. They picked on all of us from Frogmore. They were so cruel."

"W'y you neber tell me dis?"

"You wouldn't have moved. I wanted to live in Charleston, in a new house, and wear store-bought clothes."

"We neber hab much money, Sheila. When yo' deddy left us, Uh did what Uh could—the best Uh could for you."

"I realize that now. Ma, I've been so foolish."

"Uh wish you'd come talk tuh me. Uh didn't know you hurt so much ober all dis."

"Ma, please forgive me."

Essie crossed the room and sat down beside her. She suddenly embraced Sheila. "Gal, Uh luv you so much. Uh die for you."

Her mother burst into tears, sobbing hard.

Sheila tried to comfort her. "It's not all you, Ma. I was an angry person. That's all I can say. I feel like the weight of the world is off my shoulders, finally. My anger and resentment controlled my life. Anger had become my entire being, and I don't want to live that way anymore."

Wiping away her own tears, Sheila vowed, "I'm not going to live that way."

"Uh so proud of you, Sheila. Uh so full right now—just so proud. Always bin proud of you."

They sat there holding each other, crying and wiping away tears.

Sheila pulled away slowly. "C'mon, there's a lot more presents to open."

Essie wiped her eyes with the back of her hand. "Uh full right now. I ha' my baby back. Oooh, t'engk Gawd." She burst into another bout of crying.

Smiling, Sheila handed her mother a tissue. "If you keep this up, you're going to make me cry again. Now I really want you to open this one gift. We can cry some more later. The others can wait."

Her mother dried her tears and opened the box. She held up a check. "What dis for?"

"Ma, I know how much you love your house, so I was thinking— actually, it was Nicholas who gave me the idea. I'd like to refurbish the house. Have everything restored for you. You stay here with me but you can visit home when you want to. We can go there on the weekend and fish. Nicholas taught me how."

Essie's mouth dropped open. "You fish?"

"A little," Sheila responded with a laugh. "He's taught me a lot. Nicholas is a good man. I just wish I'd treated him better."

EPILOGUE

One year later

"My symptoms have ranged from fatigue, dizziness, tremors and numbness," Sheila told the people attending the monthly support group. "I also experience an imbalance when I walk and have to use a walker. Symptoms come and go suddenly . . . they can be mild or severe. It's a very unpredictable disease. My doctor kept telling me in the beginning to go ahead with my normal life. She told me to work around my problems . . ."

Sheila paused when her eyes landed on Nicholas, who was standing in the back of the room.

They still talked from time to time. Nicholas was a man of his word—he'd promised he would not let her deal with her MS alone, and he was keeping his word.

When she spoke to him earlier, he never mentioned anything about coming tonight.

She quickly pulled her attention away from him and continued. "I desperately wanted my life to be normal again . . ." She lapsed into her testimony and how her life changed because of her faith.

"I didn't expect to look out into the audience and see you," Sheila stated as she approached Nicholas after the meeting. "You didn't tell me you were coming to the meeting."

"I wanted to surprise you."

"It was a nice surprise."

"I spoke to Jake earlier," Nicholas told her. "He and Tori just had a little boy. They named him Jacob."

Sheila smiled. "I'm real happy for them."

Nicholas studied her face. "I believe you are," he said finally.

"I am. They seem to be wonderful parents."

"You ever change your mind about becoming a mother?" Nicholas asked.

Sheila met his gaze.

"I think it may be too late for me. My condition is worsening. I'm not sure I'd be able to even adopt now."

"Just so you know, I believe you would've made a great mother, Sheila."

She gave him a sidelong glance. "I may never know. I know you really want children, so what in the world are you waiting on? You need to get yourself a wife. You're not getting any younger, you know."

Nicholas laughed.

"I could kick myself for letting you go," Sheila blurted.

He wrapped an arm around her. "Maybe next time you'll be more careful."

Sheila elbowed him playfully. "Don't be mean, Nicholas."

"I'm not. I'm just being truthful."

"I'm really sorry for the way I treated you."

His arms encircled her, one hand at the small of her back. "It's okay."

"Life is crazy, you know? I chased a man who didn't love me for years, and then finally—I find a man who's free to love me . . ." Sheila shook her head sadly. "I go and mess everything up."

Looking into his eyes, she murmured, "Thank you so much for opening up my heart. I think you were brought into my life to show me that I could be loved."

"Sheila, I want nothing but good things for you. You know that, right?"

She nodded. "And I want the same for you. Nicholas, I really do love you, and while I don't know what is going to happen in the future, I will make this promise. If we end up getting back together—I will never, ever, take you for granted."

"I believe you, sweetheart."

"I guess I'd better get home. I'm feeling tired."

"Did you drive tonight?"

Sheila nodded.

"I'll follow you home."

"Nicholas, you can't be my savior forever. I've got to travel down this road on my own."

He nodded in understanding.

After a moment, Sheila said, "I've been thinking about hiring a driver. I . . ." Her voice died.

"Hey, you zoned out on me," Nicholas commented. "What are you thinking about?"

"The defining moments in my life." Meeting his gaze, she added, "I think the secret to a great life is being able to live life to the fullest by embracing the defining moments in our lives."

"What do you think is your defining moment?"

"I've had several. One was when I realized that God truly loves me—no matter how I look or how I've behaved. I realized that with Him—He doesn't care about skin color, outward beauty or a spectacular body—none of it really matters. I think my most important defining moment was when you guided me toward the path leading to eternal salvation. I'd been on the wrong road for a long time, but, praise God, I'm here . . ."

She smiled.

"I'm forty-two years old, never been married and I have multiple sclerosis . . . Nicholas, I can truthfully say that I've never been happier."

AUTHOR'S NOTE

In writing *Defining Moments*, I have taken liberties with the Gullah dialect of Low Country South Carolina. My intention was to convey the richness of this beautiful language while retaining its accessibility for readers unfamiliar with its patterns.

DEFINING MOMENTS

JACQUELIN THOMAS

QUESTIONS
FOR DISCUSSION

1) Many of you met Sheila Moore in *The Prodigal Husband*. As you read *Defining Moments*, did this story give you more insight into who she really was? How many of you can relate to her, or have been in that same dark place? How did you overcome?

2) Jake and Tori Madison were also introduced in *The Prodigal Husband*. Although Tori had willingly forgiven Jake for his affair with Sheila, why do you think it was much harder for her to forgive Sheila?

3) Sheila loved Nicholas—yet she pushed him away. Why do we allow hurts from our past to drive a wedge between us and the people we care most about? How can you have victory over rejection? Read Ephesians 1:6-11, 3:16, I John 5:4 and I Peter 2:24 and discuss.

4) Discuss Sheila's relationship with her mother—do you believe that she truly loved Essie? Why or why not? What was at the root of their relationship?

5) At what point did Sheila seem to give up her fight with MS? Why?

6) For both Tori and Sheila, forgiveness did not come easily. What was the defining moment for Tori that prompted her to forgive Sheila and finally lay the past to rest? And for Sheila?

7) John 15:11 says, *These things have I spoken unto you, that my joy might remain in you, and that your joy might be full.* By the end of the story, Sheila's MS has worsened but her attitude is one of joy. How many of you can choose joy in the midst of a storm or while dealing with an illness?

8) In what way did Nicholas impact Sheila's life? Do you believe she was a better person because of him? Why or why not?

9) Throughout the story, Nicholas continued to stand by Sheila, despite the fact that she'd hurt him. At the end of the story, it was clear that they were still friends, but do you think that friendship will progress into something more?

10) In order for Sheila to completely move forward with her life, she needed to release the anger and bitterness she felt for Jake and Tori. What was the one final act that freed her from the past?